OffSet

OffSet

Anna Trompetas

Chapter 1

Sam

December 2041, BBC World News.

"40 years after the terror attacks that saw the deaths of nearly 3,000 innocent US citizens in New York and Washington DC, a winter storm caused by a bomb cyclone - an extreme drop in atmospheric pressure - is battering the cities, part of a cold wave that is sweeping the entire country from East to West Coast, with the number of casualties predicted to be one thousand times that of 9/11. But where should the United States government turn to seek justice this time?"

-42F. We sit in the living room, the only room of the house with carpet. The power has been out for over 36 hours. Phone Lines and internet too. You can see the useless cables striping the whiteness outside through the window. Occasionally one of the birds, frozen solid to the line, becomes detached and tumbles into the oblivion below it. Frozen people, too - some still standing upright, like a macabre nativity scene - are discernible when a gust of wind redirects the curtain of weather for a moment. She had seen a small dog there too, at first. A terrier, maybe. Not anymore though. He - and his little tartan coat - were invisible after the first fifteen minutes of sweeping snow, which followed the arrival of the cold, cementing it in. But Lottie hasn't forgotten he is there. She pulls herself up on the sofa at intervals - like a beetle trying to right itself, bundled limbs ineffective - to peer out of the window, looking for him.

Sometimes one of the blankets slips down from her shoulder like a loose bandage, and Ethan calls to her to sit back down between us. His voice croaks. The end of his nose is blackened, dead looking, like a moulding potato. I wonder if mine looks the same. It is cold. The kind of cold where your bones feel heavy and ache, where you feel more aware of your own anatomy; the cold is not just in your bones but in their marrow. You feel sluggish, and it's almost as if you can feel the viscosity of the blood in your veins, sludging through your arteries, struggling. Listless. We have a thermos flask of water, but the water is already cool. Not fridge-temperature, not yet, but losing heat quickly, and more so when we open it to drink. It is a toss-up between drinking it before it freezes, and keeping the lid on to try and stop it doing so. When someone wants a drink, they have to go under the pile of blankets and wait for a pocket of air to warm from their breath, and drink it there, or it will freeze on their lips. I learnt this the hard way. A sheet of ice formed over my bottom lip and cracked, splitting the skin. It is dry and sore now, hard to differentiate between scab and ice. Lottie doesn't stand up as regularly now. She has burrowed under my innermost layer of blanket and I can feel the pressure of her chin against my abdomen, but can't make out the feeling of her skin on mine. Just numbness. I slide sideways so that I am resting on my elbow, half-reclined, leaning against Ethan's thigh. I close my eyes, and in my mind I zoom out from the scene. Up above the roof of our house, our street, obscured by white. Javelins of ice slant from gutters and lampposts, up to a metre long, water and snow frozen solid in a matter of seconds, like a sped-up timelapse. I rise higher, see further. White, nothing but white. Spears of ice decorate the Washington monument, the White House perfectly camouflaged, invisible but for the battered frozen flag, immobile in the ripping wind, the contradiction of the storm. There is little movement now, in the scene of my mind's eye. Anything that could be wrenched from its place has been re-deposited and buried elsewhere, locked in place by a cage of ice. Lines of cars, hundreds of miles of them, on motorways and slip roads and highstreets, images we saw on the news before the power went out, have been absorbed now by the storm, their passengers long-dead. Six hundred thousand; that was the last estimate, before the cold seemed to penetrate the walls and wires of the house and strangle the life out of it. The freeze had been heading straight across the country for Los Angeles, the land of air-conditioning and sports bras, surfing and chihuahuas. Not prepared for this. But no one was. This is America, for God's sake. This doesn't happen here. Not to us. A shattering noise pulls me from my wandering, back to the room, as the wind screams through the gaping frame, ice or glass shredding into our scalps. I can no longer feel Lottie's breath on my stomach. I shake her, perhaps too aggressively, perhaps not moving her at all, unable to feel. She slumps against me, and with a great effort I heave her to an upright position. Her lips are blue-grey, and her mouth hangs slack. Ethan, too, is still, lying on his side now, curled half around us. I tug at the blankets that suffocate me, and throw them to the side, and lie down next to the bodies of my husband and daughter. The family next door is already dead. The whole street is still. The whole city…-

Sam slammed the laptop shut: things would be getting tighter. She couldn't read to the end, to see how or if the mother had survived. She felt attached to the writer of the article in the way that people become to an individual, a protagonist, humanised by their story in the way that statistics never are. But she was more attached to herself, to what this latest disaster would mean for her own life; she didn't need her misery compounded by someone else's. She looked around her small South London flat. The room smelled slightly musty. Only when you inhaled deeply, as if the smell were contained only in the final ten percent of air you breathed in, only if you really tried to smell it. Which she really tried not to do: but there was something compulsive about chasing that elusive odour, the one that hung on the edges of your aromatic vision, checking it was still there, or as if by sniffing hard enough you could hoover it all up and remove it altogether. The spores on the plaster around the window frames were less disembodied. Each epicentre radiated perfectly circular patches of mould, like a ripple expanding across liquid. Every surface in the room held drying laundry. A bra hung from each of the white plastic light fittings on the wall to the left of the door, which provided the only artificial light to the room, and two damp pairs of jeans were slung over the door, parent and child. Sam sat against the wall under the pockmarked window frame, laptop propped on her knees. The smell of barbequed meat drifted through the window, masking the funk. She missed chicken. She opened the laptop back up and licked her fingertip to scrub at a smear on the top right corner. She flicked onto her online banking. She wasn't used to having money in her account, even with the loan repayments going out; enough for the heating, though she had no allowance left anyway. The positive figure on her account balance gave her a little rush of endorphins, a slight warm tickle in the pit of her stomach. She scratched at her neck absent-mindedly and flinched when she caught it, like scratching a mosquito bite or a mole when you've forgotten it's there; the source of the itch, begging to be scratched and rewarding you with a sharp stab of pain when you obey. She scratched more gently, in a circular movement around it, and that seemed to relieve the itching sensation. At the clinic they'd told her she would get used to it after a week or so, and it had only been five days. She put the laptop on the floor next to her and stood up, stretching and yawning.

"Mum! What's for dinner?"

Lucas was in the bedroom, slumped backwards over an orange beanbag on the floor, feet higher than his head, watching television upside down.

"How about we get pizza?"

He flung his legs sideways onto the floor, wriggling his torso into an upright position worthy of engaging with such an unprecedented suggestion.

"Watch your neck! I'm always having to tell you not to sit like that."

"Really? Pizza? A takeaway?"

"If you've done all your homework."

"I have!" He scrambled to his feet and raced over to his bookbag, dumped unceremoniously behind the door.

"We only had reading, and I've done it all!"

"And put it neatly back in your bag behind the door?" She raised her eyebrows.

"I did it in after-school club with Miss Brockley. And I have a worksheet. But… Miss said I'm not allowed to print it. Is that right?"

"You can do it on the laptop, if you're quick." She looked at the small monitor on the wall above the light switch. "Actually, you can do it tomorrow. Come on. Get your coat."

"We walking?" Lucas looked out of the window dubiously. "It's all soggy outside."

"It's fine. Nice hot pizza at the end of it!"

"Can I get cheese?"

"Yes of course. Special cheese."
"Cheeeeese!" Lucas started running in figures of eight around the small room, arms out like an aeroplane, his coat flying behind him like a cape. "I love cheese."

"It's not letting me put the packaging through on the system." The man tapped at the screen in front of him, at a loss. "It says you have no disposables left."
"Not even if you put them both in the same box?"
He spun the screen round to face her, where an error message was showing.
"Nada. Zilch. Sorry love."
"So what should I do?"
He shrugged, placing his palms face-down on the counter, emphasising finality.
"That man has boxes." Lucas pointed through the window at the man loading pizza boxes and bottles of coke into the boot of a navy BMW, and chatting to a smiling checker.
"Don't point, Lu. It's fine." She turned to the man behind the counter. "It's fine." She said again, with more conviction.
The man shifted uncomfortably. Sam glanced up at the Checker drone hovering outside, its whirring muted by the glass, and thrust her chin forwards and to the left so that her hair fell forwards to cover her neck.
"Right, well we'll just come back with tupperware then."
"Right you are love."
The man looked relieved and turned to busy himself rearranging the soft drinks in the fridge.

By the time they had walked home to pick up the containers, Lucas was hungry and exhausted and refused to leave the house again. The jam sandwiches they ate tucked up on the sofa felt symbolic. *No matter what you do, you'll never change anything.* The following morning, the familiar sick-feeling jolted through her, a wave of shock as the alarm snatched her from elsewhere. She reached onto the floor groggily, feeling around for her leggings and a jumper on the floor, slipping them under the covers and squirming into them without letting the duvet expose her shoulders.

"We have to walk *again*?"

"Look on the bright side Lu." She mashed a banana with the back of a fork, scooped granola from the jar and placed it in front of him with a flourish designed to head off the inevitable scepticism of a five-year-old presented with suspicious new breakfast food. "Look at all the car windscreens. All the ice. Not going to take us long to de-ice the windscreen with no car!"

Lucas looked at her as if she was a bit dim. "That's a silly thing to say Mumma. If you don't have a car you don't have any windscreen, so how can you dice it at all?"

"*De-ice.*"

"You couldn't do that either." He looked confused, gave a little shake of his head, and began to sing *Always look on the bright side of life,* just those lyrics, tunelessly, over and over, as he thrust his little arms into coat sleeves, as he swung on her arm, jumping over cracks in the paving stones and dodging drains.

"Do do, dodododododo. *Always look on the briiiiight side of life.*"

"Hurry up Lu. Stop doing that. I'm going to be late for work."

"I thought you didn't have a job anymore mummy. I thought that *horrible woman* told you not to come any more."

"She just reduced my hours Lu. And don't call her that. You mustn't repeat everything mummy says."

"Mummy's boss is a hooo-rrrible wo-man. Do do dododododododo," he sang in the same tune.

By the time she was hurrying up the driveway of Greenfields Manor, her neck and armpits were damp. She tugged at her collar, trying to allow air to circulate through her clothing, and slowed her pace to a brisk walk, glancing up at the cameras as she approached the house. The garage doors were closed, so she couldn't see if the cars were here, but she hoped her employers had already left for the day. She pressed her finger to the keypad, wriggling her other arm out of her coat sleeve as she waited for it to scan. The door clicked open, and she stepped into the entrance hall, holding her breath to listen for signs of life. Nothing.

"Hello! Just me!" She called out.

Nothing.

"Music: on. Whole house."

"Unauthorised request."

Sam pursed her lips and channelled the monarchy.

"Music: on. Whole house."

Abba began to play from hidden speakers situated in the corners of each room.

"The winner takesss it allllllll!" she sang as she got the mop and bucket from another cupboard in the hallway. *Living the life.*

Chapter 2

Alice

Why did rooms always get messier before they looked any better? Alice sat back on her haunches and surveyed the floor of her son's bedroom, a huge pile of Lego painstakingly sorted from the other debris that had been hidden amongst it; crayons with the paper sleeves peeling off, a couple of bouncy balls laced with dog fur, some batteries, coins, Ikea pencils, a colander that had once been used in the sandpit and ever since repurposed as a toy, far more desirable to him than anything actually intended for children, and somehow, inexplicably, one of her red-soled Louboutins. Tidying was not for quitters. But sadly, a quitter she was. Not in everything: she had been known to last for eighteen hours straight at the all-night parties she would go to before becoming a mother, and subsequently to sit for another twelve hours in front of a series of *The Lubrinos.* Nor would she quit when making her way through an extra-large pizza, and definitely, definitely not when having an argument with her mother. But in boring, quittable things like swimming lengths, or doing her physio exercises, or decanting pantry items into the expensive jars that Andrew had bought so that little threads of flour no longer stencilled the shelf in the cupboard and the spices lined up in uniform, she definitely considered herself a quitter. And tidying fell firmly into that category. She imagined Andrew's face if he came home to see the entire contents of their four-year-old's toy dinosaur collection strewn across the floor, the Triassic and Jurassic and Cretaceous periods defying all laws of chronology as they gallivanted together on the thick beige pile of the carpet, a drought-ravaged landscape of wild grass. She wondered if she could stop him going into Tommy's bedroom until the following day, when the house-keeper would be in, and she could finish what Alice had started. *Yes, she would leave the rest for her.* She had made a valiant effort, and though the mess was more *visible* now than it had been in the hidden chaos of the three large laundry baskets moonlighting as toy storage, she had at least set the wheels in motion for the tidying process, and that was the critical part. She looked at her watch. *Two thirty-five.* She needed to go in just under an hour. She stood up and stretched before padding along the corridor to their own room, closing the door to Tommy's firmly behind her. Andrew never went in there anyway, save for the rare occasion when she managed to convince him (usually with the promise of sex) to go and read Tommy a quick bed-time story. She wondered, sometimes, whether Tommy would even notice if they split up. "*I* wonder if *Andrew* would even notice." Sophie had said at spin class last week when Alice had voiced this musing over a carrot and clementine smoothie in the cafeteria of the leisure centre. But he would, of course. Who would take care of paying the house-keeper, or sorting out Maisie's grooming appointments, or schmoozing the other parents so that Tommy was always kept well-supplied with playdates and birthday parties. Who would buy the presents for those parties, £30 a pop on a plastic fire engine or a book about Gerard the gender-neutral giraffe? Andrew would notice her absence, she was sure about that, though he probably didn't think so.

Not because them separating hadn't crossed his mind, because she knew it would have, on one of those summer evenings, when the balmy August sun could not thaw their frost. That was the thing about men, she thought; they had no imagination. No willingness to engage with the hypothetical. She remembered once, in the early years of their relationship, when things had been good - great even - and she had asked him 'would you cry if I died?'. She had never seen him cry. And he had answered 'I know I would be sad, because obviously everyone is when someone they love dies. But it's just hard to picture it? Like I can't imagine being sad about something that hasn't happened, you know?' So of course he didn't *worry* about her leaving him, because you can only worry about something that you are already living in your mind, suffering through that worst-case scenario in your imagination so that it might as well already be happening, and, indeed, it would be better if it were, because at least then you wouldn't have to worry about the *what if* anymore, and it would be closer to being over and done with. But Tommy. *What would he make of it all?* She had read enough and heard enough and seen enough - online, at the school gates, the hushed gossip about Arabella in Year 6, whose pilot father had run off with an airhostess (a '*trolley dolly*', they had called her, righteous noses wrinkling), failing her eleven-plus. *The daughter, not the trolley dolly,* they had clarified, with added superciliousness. Yes, she knew a *broken home* could spell disaster for a child's development. Plenty survived it, of course; but she wanted better for Tommy. *Tommy.* Freckled nose, anarchic brown hair, fleeing the orders of the comb, one white sock perennially bunched around a stocky ankle. Draped around Maisie's neck was where she pictured him, like a second lead. Maisie, their long-suffering Golden Retriever panting, smiling, looking up at her as if to say, *What the hell is this?*.

She surveyed herself critically, turning on tiptoes to check the profile of each leg in the mirror, assessing for change. She flung her head forwards, then immediately back again, catching her long dark hair and scooping it into a ponytail ready for her class. This explosive hair-styling technique used to take Andrew by surprise at the start of their relationship. He would jump back in mock horror and shout *Attack! It's the attack of the hair! The abominable hairman is after me again!* Nowadays he would huff and take a theatrical step backwards, or around her if he happened to be passing within the radius of her hair length and say *you nearly hit me in the eye again.*
She had read once, in a women's magazine in the waiting room at the clinic, some statistic about men and women in relationships. Apparently, women entered relationships hoping to change their partner, to mould them into the image they had of a perfect spouse, whilst men just wanted theirs to remain as they were. *I've held up my end of the bargain* she thought, examining her bum in her gym leggings. And he, sadly, had upheld his. She'd never wanted him to change; not consciously, or at least not now, as she looked back with the wisdom of hindsight. And if she had wanted him to change it would have been small things; putting the toilet seat down, buying her flowers on their anniversary, being less fastidious about organisation. But not this. The distance, the coldness. She wasn't sure that it was that though. Wasn't sure that it was all of him that had changed, but rather the "him" that existed within their relationship.

She had seen him, one Thursday, saying goodbye to his work friends outside the pub. She'd offered to pick him up on her way from the gym (work drinks usually ran their course at a reasonable hour when you left the office at 2pm, as they always did when they closed a big deal. Skew-whiff ties and their skew-whiff bearers stumbling towards the nearest kebab shop, gremlin versions of the impeccably-dressed-and-mannered men who had signed on the dotted lines mere hours before). She had pulled up on the other side of the road and turned off the engine, waiting for him to come out of the Rose & Anchor, when she had spotted him standing with a small group on the curb. He was bent double with laughter, batting at the air as if to signal that he had more to add, except he couldn't catch his breath. She'd opened the window a crack, and leaned the side of head against the glass, and the sound of laughter had trickled through the small gap in the glass, narcotic, transporting her. Except in the memory she wasn't sitting in a car across the road, head against a window in mourning; she was standing beside him outside the pub, cold fingers soaked in beer where it had sloshed over the rim of the glass, laughing with him, each of them adding addendum after addendum to the joke until it fell flat, and they laughed about that instead. No, it was the version of himself which he presented to her that had changed, which meant the old him was still there, but only available to other people.

She grabbed her gym bag from the bottom of the wardrobe and headed down the stairs, stopping to take a pair of steaks from the freezer and toss them onto the counter to defrost for supper, and to give the avocados a gentle squeeze in the fruit bowl. Mulch.

"Home."

A soft buzz, and pale pink light from each corner of the ceiling acknowledged the address.

"Dim internal lights, turn on front and back security, lock back door, set pool cover to open at-" She looked at her watch "four thirty-five pm, and water temperature to thirty degrees." She ran through the checklist in her head, mapping the commands on her fingers. "Order two avocados for seven pm. Oh; and warm the car."

"Please confirm which vehicle requires temperature control to be activated."

"Land Rover."

"Land Rover temperature control activated."

The lights in the cafe at the leisure centre were always a couple of degrees too muted, so that they had to hold the menu cards close to their faces to make their selections. Her best friend, Sophie, sat back in her chair and rolled her foot in a slow circle, stretching her ankle, luxuriating in the ache of lactic acid after the class.

"I can't believe you're getting her to come less often. Mine struggles to keep on top of things with her full five days!"

She and Alice had been friends since Freshers' week at Durham, and now had children the same age. Partly coincidence, primarily careful engineering of their husbands' psyche, guiding them into thinking that it was the perfect time to reproduce at precisely the same time. Same evening, even, it had ended up being, that they'd agreed to finish inside their wives without a condom.

Like jumping out of a plane and then realising you forgot your parachute, and then remembering you intentionally didn't bring a parachute. Just goes against everything you've ever trained yourself to do. Mental. Andrew had said in awe, as he scrolled aimlessly through his phone in post-coital contentment.

"I just don't feel like we need her to come that often. Plus Andrew is so tidy."

Sophie pulled a face. *Tidy,* like *nice,* and *predictable,* was a turn-coat word: a descriptor neutral enough that it could be repurposed by either side depending on the context. For Sophie, it compounded her disdain. "How are things with you two anyway?"

"Oh, you know." She took a sip of juice and chewed on the plastic straw to buy herself time. "They're…" She cast around for a word neutral enough to extinguish the conversation. "Fine." *Another example.* "They're fine."

"You sound like Sienna when I pick her up from school." She put on an excitable voice and flapped her hands theatrically. *"Did you have a good day at school Sienna? What did you have for lunch? How was PE?"* She hunched and her voice turned sullen as she played the part of her daughter. *"Fine."* She sat up in her seat and rolled her eyes. "Honestly, £30k a year and for what? Not even a rundown of the shitting dinner menu."

"You have way too much energy. Get yourself back on the treadmill - and as if you care whether the dinner ladies are serving up peas or sweetcorn."

"Kale, actually, last time I gave up trying to get it out of her and had a look online."

"Kale?! Ludicrous. These kids eat better than us."

"Ha. No way did she touch any of it. Anyway, I see what you're trying to do. Changing the subject on me."

"That was you actually."

"Well, whatever. Andrew? You've got to make a decision at some point."

"Do I? Can't I just bury my head in the sand?" She stuck out her bottom lip.

"There you go again with the Sienna impression. Uncanny. No you cannot! You've been feeling crappy about all of this for months now."

"I just keep changing my mind about how I feel. Like sometimes it feels terrible, like the end of the world, like I can't spend another second like this. And then I wake up the next day and feel like I was completely overreacting. Like I can barely remember what I was even upset about."

"It's called being a woman. Hormones everywhere. I cried because Marta bought the wrong type of toilet paper yesterday."

"Yes, that's basically the same. Thanks Sophie."

"No problem, any time. But seriously-" She drained the last of her juice so it rattled up the straw, and cleared her throat. "You need to pull your finger out."

Alice looked at her stone-faced, indicating that she had nothing more to say on the matter. Sophie held up her hands in defeat.

"Alright, I've said my piece. I'll get off your case. But while we're on the topic of you being useless and indecisive-"

"- are we?"

"Yes, we are. So on that topic, I also wanted to ask, what about that *other thing*?" She tapped a meaningful index finger on the screen of Alice's phone.

Alice pulled a face. "It's just not my thing."

"You know the next cap tightening is on the 14th? And it's only going to get worse from here, after this storm business in the States." She waggled her empty cup. "No more of these. And why wouldn't you? It's win-win."

16

"Win-win for who?!"

"*Whom.* Win-win for *whom.* And it's win-win for everyone."

"Who even says *whom* in real life? You just sound like a twat."

"We'll have to agree to disagree. But honestly, it benefits you both. You *and* the counter. Honestly, a lot of the changes are good for them. Lifestyle improvements. Or are things they couldn't have afforded to do anyway."

"I just don't like it. It all feels a bit backwards."

"Suit yourself." Sophie jumped to her feet. "I'm getting a flapjack. Want one?"

In the car on the way home, the radio droned, depressing; "*... meanwhile across Australia there are more than 400 fires burning, with an area the size of France currently on fire. It is estimated that more than 2 billion animals have lost their lives, and 5 million people have been-".* She hit the arrow on the screen so that the hourly environmental update was replaced by soothing jazz. She tapped her fingers on the steering wheel, tracing the melody. She pulled into the garage, clicked off the engine, and headed through the pool room. She stripped off her gym kit, depositing it in a heap on the floor. She didn't bother putting on a swimming costume. It was one of her favourite things about having her own pool - the feeling of swimming naked. She wasn't sure why it felt so different to swimming with a bikini or costume; it wasn't like the water couldn't get through them onto her skin, or like they were restrictive or uncomfortable. Maybe the pleasure was psychosomatic. Either way, she shivered in anticipation of the water on her scalp, her neck, her waist. She swung her arms backwards and dived into the water.

"Fuck!" She shouted the word with her mouth half-submerged, so that it might have looked to an outsider as though she were drowning rather than just cold. She lunged for the side and pulled herself up and onto the side in one movement.

"House: What temperature is the pool?"

"The pool is eighteen degrees."

"What the-..?" She looked over at the control panel above the light switch. It was only then that she noticed the small red light flashing. "Fuck!" She said again. She pulled two towels from the pyramid of clean rolled pool towels, wrapping one around her waist and draping the other over her head, drying her hand on one corner so she could use her phone.

She opened her *Output* tracker. One alert:

Monthly energy limit for outbuilding reached. Renewal date: 20th December.

And below it four notifications:

Monthly mileage limit 97% used. Renewal date: 20th December.

Monthly plastic limit 82% used. Renewal date: 20th December.

Monthly meat and dairy limit: 94% used. Renewal date: 20th December.

And below it, the link: *Find out more about extending your limits.*

It was December the 2nd.

Fuck, fuck, fuck.

Chapter 3

Sam

"Final kilometre" a speaker blared as the runners rounded the bend and emerged from the wooded area onto a slight downward incline. Sam felt her pace increase naturally with the help of gravity, her feet thudding into the packed ground, hundreds of other feet pounding beside her, a sea of pink, contorted faces of friends and relatives bobbing on t-shirts. As she approached the *Race for Heroes* finishing-line she felt elated. It felt like such an indulgence, paying the £10 registration fee, paying a bus fare to get here, calling in a babysitting favour for Lucas, all for something so… unnecessary. So wonderfully pointless. She had loved cross-country at school but it, like so many other things that scored highly for enjoyment and nothing much for purpose, had dropped off the radar. She slowed to a walk, looking around at the other runners chatting and stretching. She walked towards a sign advertising free energy drinks and protein bars, sponsored by a big corporation. She was starving, still acclimatising to the change in diet. "Hello! Well done - great time!" She smiled back at the young girl with short, bleached hair, who bobbed on the balls on her feet behind the table. "Help yourself, they're all free. And I'm not looking if you take a couple of extra for the road. The chocolate and coconut ones are the best." She inverted the pockets of her tracksuit bottoms conspiratorially so that Sam could see four or five crinkle-cut wrapper ends poking out. Sam walked to the other end of the tables to have a look at the options, feigning indifference. "Do you have any... plant-based options?"

"Oh, sure!" The girl pointed to a box on the far-right of the table. Then she glanced at Sam's neck. "Oh. Oh, sorry. None of these are Counter-friendly really. Sorry."

"No no, it's okay. I'm not really hungry anyway."

"We have bananas? And oranges." She pointed to a fruit bowl at the other end of the stall.

"Yeah, great. Thanks."

She stuck the banana under her arm whilst she untied the sweatshirt from her waist, and shivered as she walked back towards the bus-stop, rapidly-drying sweat doing its job a little too effectively. She snapped the stalk of the banana downwards and crammed the top into her mouth as she stepped onto the bus and tapped her phone against the reader. It beeped at her. She tapped it again.

Transaction failed.

Irritated, she flicked the banana so that the strands of peel covered the exposed top, and shoved it into her pocket, rummaging in the other one for her card.

The driver held out his hand, blocking the reader. "Insufficient allowance. You can't use your card unfortunately."

"What? I have plenty in my account."

"Not money, fuel allowance."

She felt colour rising in her cheeks. "I still have public transport."

"Not what it says here."

"Hurry up!" Someone a few places behind her in the queue called. "It's cold!"

"I'm afraid you won't be able to travel today." The man looked over her shoulder to indicate that their interaction was complete.

"Are you okay? Do you need to borrow some money? I'll pay for her."

A sympathetic lady with a thin grey bun and a wheeled shopping bag tapped her on the shoulder, addressing the driver. A tall, stern looking Checker peered around the woman's head, assessing the situation.

"No can do I'm afraid." The driver finalised. "It's not money. It's-"

"Don't worry, I'm getting off." She turned back to the lady. "Thank you so much. I'll walk. It'll do me good to stretch my legs after the run."

"Are you sure? Rain is coming." The lady looked up at the sky dubiously.

"Yes, positive." She stepped over the lady's shopping bag, around the nosy Checker, his green boiler suit streaked with rain now, and onto the pavement. A drop of rain landed on her shoulder and slid down her back. She didn't understand - she had unlimited travel on public transport in her package. No cars, fine - but she had got the bus here with no issues. She ducked under a tree as another drop of rain landed on her ankle, just above her sock.

An email notification caught her eye. The subject read: *"Congratulations! You have been upgraded to the gold package."*

She picked up her phone to call her mother, who was minding Lucas.

"Mum, hi."

"Alright love? How was the running thing?"

"It was…" She swallowed. "The running was fun."

"Good! Lucas and I have been playing lightsabers, with a couple of those cardboard tubes that you get wrapping paper on. Like we used to when you were little, remember?"

"Mum I'm going to be a bit later than I said, sorry."

Her mother's tone turned to one of concern.

"Everything okay love?"

"Yes I just… I missed the bus."

"Oooh no, we can't be having that. It's starting to rain."

"I'll be back soon, it's only forty minutes to walk it."

"What about the next bus?"

"It'll be quicker to walk. Give Lucas a kiss for me."

"Will do love. See you soon."

She put the phone back into her pocket and pulled out the rest of the banana. She took a bite, but it stuck in her throat and she gave a small cough which came out as a pitiful whimper. She swallowed and tossed the rest in a bin as she walked past, and then folded her arms across her chest and hugged herself, pulling the cuffs of her jumper over her fingers. She didn't realise the terms could be changed without her approval. She pulled her phone out of her pocket again and opened the email. A bullet-point summary of the changes were outlined in the body of the email, and in fine print at the bottom a small message read:

To give notice, please click <u>here</u>. Your notice period is 6 months. To see your terms and conditions, click <u>here.</u>

It had been a Saturday in November when she had signed up. She'd been sitting on the bench at the playground. Lucas was in his slide-phase. Up and down he would go, careering off to the side as he landed to shave a critical second or two off the time it took him to get to the bottom of the stairs to clamber up again. He came over, cheeks red, smelling faintly of sweat and grass. "Ice cream!" He had cried, beseechingly, pointing at the van that had pulled up on the scrubby patch of concrete near the gate. "Please Mumma, pleaaaaase." *What was an ice cream van doing here in November?* She hadn't budgeted for it, had thought that this late in the year, she'd be safe. *Safe from ice-cream.* She wondered how many other mothers' hearts skipped a beat at the sound of the van, for how many others it meant being forced to choose between not paying your bills, and disappointing your child. She had gone through the contents of her pockets, in her head at first, till she was reasonably sure she had some coins in there and could risk checking with her hand, a tell of capitulation that Lucas would never miss. Sure enough as her hand went to her pocket his mouth opened and his eyebrows shot up, and he'd hopped from one foot to the other. Her fingers closed on the money and she handed it to him. "There you go. Make sure you check you have enough before you order. The big coin is two pounds and the smaller silver one is twenty pence."

"Am I going on my own?"

"Yes, go on. I'll watch you."

"What one do you want? *Choc-lit*?"

"No, none for Mumma. I'll steal some of yours!"

"You won't be able to catch me!"

She kept one eye on him as he skipped over to the van, the other glancing at her phone which had vibrated a message alert in her lap.

"Hey Sam, hope you're well? Just to say that we are going to cut down on cleaning a bit for a while. Could we change to two days a week? You can pick the days! Just let me know :)"

She swiped the message away, and dropped her phone back into her lap, squinting through the sunlight to where Lucas was on tiptoes at the window of the van. He turned to her and grinned, giving her a double thumbs-up. She picked her phone up again, willing the message to have changed. *Two days.* And she could pick the days. *How generous.* What was she supposed to do with her income halving overnight? The MOT was due on the car. Lucas's school trousers had a hole in one knee and the screen of her phone was cracked. She rubbed the pad of her thumb over the little spidery lines above the message. One of them snagged at her so that blood beaded on her skin, and she transferred it to her mouth while she considered her response. She'd opened her banking app and an advert had caught her eye. She had seen it before, but not really paid it much attention.

OffSet - Sign up now for immediate pay outs. Cash in your account in under an hour!

She'd sucked at her thumb, then clicked on the link. A bright green-and-white logo, and photographs of smiling people - ticking all the diversity quotas - accompanied the slogan in neat italics. *OffSet: funding and balancing the world we live in.* The signing bonus had been in her account within forty-five minutes. Enough for the MOT, for a new phone, and to buy uniform for Lucas. Except that the MOT was no longer necessary.

Her mum lived in one of the high-rise blocks near the Oval cricket ground. Posters peeled off chewing-gum-spotted walls warning against dealing and knife-crime, as if the option not to sell drugs simply hadn't occurred to people, or they just hadn't realised it was illegal. By the time she reached the sixth floor she had warmed up, though the rain had only got harder. She knocked, then quickly pulled the jumper over her head and slung it around her neck. Lucas greeted her at the door and bashed her with the cardboard tube. "Pow, pow. You're all wet Mumma."

"Am I? I hadn't noticed."

"Really? But look! He tugged at her shorts, and a cascade of drips rained onto the welcome mat.

"It's called sarcasm Lu." It always amazed her, the reminder that sarcasm was learned, that something so second-nature was not inherent. It was one of the beautiful naivieties that made her want to squeeze him to her and never let him go, never let him grow. She felt a bit better.

"Is there a spare sword for Mumma?"

She lay in bed that night worrying, as she often did, about how she would provide for her son. *No more public transport.* It isolated them, narrowed the walls of their world to just a couple of kilometres in any direction. Lucas had never even seen the sea. She had been hoping to take him next summer. She shivered under the covers, unable to get warm. She looked over at Lucas's bed in the other corner of the small room, the top of his head the only thing visible under the bunched duvet. He deserved so much more than this.

For the first time, she felt relief, not sadness, when the doorbell rang to announce Caleb's arrival to collect his son. Relief at the prospect of a few hours not feeling guilty about all that she could not provide for him. And then, of course, guilt at feeling relief. A checker drone circled lazily in the street outside, indifferent to the banalities of human emotion.

"Dad!" Lucas came rushing down the hallway, only one arm and his head in his t-shirt.

"Hello son. Bit cold in here to be running around half-naked isn't it?"

Sam caught him round the waist and reached through the other sleeve of his top, catching his flailing hand and tugging it back through for the third time that morning.

"It's like a fridge in here." Caleb added when she didn't nibble.

"Yes, thanks Caleb. I had noticed."

"Just showing concern, that's all."

"Concern doesn't put food on the table or keep the carbon meter topped up I'm afraid." She lifted Lucas off the floor and pushed his feet out from under him with one leg, lowering him to sit on her lap in one deft movement, reaching for his shoes. Caleb raised an eyebrow.

"It's the eleventh of the month. You should have loads left. How come you're short for heating already?"

"Pass me that other shoe would you?"

He handed her the tiny trainer with one hand, and with the other he tugged at the scarf draped around her neck. She made a grab for it but he was too fast.

"Sam!"

"What?" She said, grabbing and wrapping and glaring.

"Why didn't you ask? I could have upped my payments."

She took the small red backpack from the hook, unzipped it, and passed it to Lucas. "Lu, go and grab three toys from your room that you want to take to dad's."

"My Lego?"

"Whatever you want, go on, run."

She stood up, and Caleb put a hand out to her, hovering a few centimetres above her shoulder, cupping space. The gap was small, but the air in between pulsated with everything it represented.

"Why didn't you ask me for the money? He's my son, I'd never let him go without."

"We're fine, Cal."

She could see the hurt in his eyes, hear the argument sucked back as he inhaled and sighed. His arm fell back to his side.

"You know I'm sorry Sam." He said, for what felt like the twentieth time. "I would never do something like that. Not when I'm me."

It was true that it hadn't been him. The version of him that existed when he drank. When she remembered those times it was how she imagined a werewolf transforming in a children's cartoon, the eighth, ninth, tenth pints of beer a full moon and the aggression sprouting like bristles from every pore, no way of reasoning with him until the effects wore off. Him, but not him. That had been enough for her to forgive him the first time, her willpower fading even before the bruises on her sternum and the lump on the back of her head. It hadn't been him, he wasn't in control. But it had been him who had chosen to drink the next time, who had willingly gone out into the full moon and fuck the consequences. She had held out longer that time, the skin on her cheekbone turning from purple, to green, and even to pale yellow, before she fell to her knees beside him in this same hallway and hugged his head to her chest, squeezing it gently until the sobs grew infrequent and he felt reassured enough in her forgiveness to plan his next trip to the pub. They say it takes an average of seven incidents for someone to leave, and Sam had changed the locks after the fifth. Better than average. She was proud of that.

Lucas came back with the backpack gaping, trailing a Hansel and Gretel of Lego bricks through the hallway. "Why's Grandma here again?" He asked, looking past Caleb to the car where his grandmother sat, filing her nails. She waved at Sam when she saw them looking.

"Grandma likes seeing you Lu."

"But I want to play football with dad."

"We can still play football Lucas, Grandma can keep score, like last time."

"But why does she always have to come?"

"Your mum prefers it that way Lucas. You don't trust me, isn't that right Sam She thinks we need a grown-up or we'd get up to no good, isn't that right?"

Lucas giggled and ran past him to the car.

"Don't put this on me. You agreed to it being this way. You're lucky I'm letting you see him at all."

"*Letting* me?" His face clouded and he tapped his teeth together, considering. "He's my child."

"And I was your girlfriend. That didn't mean much did it." She hissed at him, anger and shame rising. "We've been through this. It was your idea!"

The drone hovered closer, witness to their humiliation.

"Only when you were stopping me seeing him altogether. We can't keep this up forever. My mum has a life you know. And it's embarrassing."

"There's worse things in life than being embarrassed Cal." She said, and those things hung in the air between them, heavy, sad.

"I'll drop him back at four."

She was folding laundry when her phone buzzed a notification. *You have received 40 house carbon-points from: Caleb.*

And not long after a text: *I miss you.*

Chapter 4

Alice

"Bag?"
The checkout assistant thrust one towards a man next to her.
"No, thanks."
She glanced at his neck.
"Oh. Sorry."
The man was balancing an armful of onions and potatoes, like an overly-ambitious juggler, one wedged in each pocket of his tracksuit, small flakes of onion-skin dandruff clinging to the bobbled material. The check-out assistant turned towards Alice. "Can I help you with your packing ma'am?"
She retraced the assistant's gaze to the man with the onions. A mixture of curiosity and mild repulsion dragged at her eyes so that the man noticed. He used his chin to stabilise the armful of vegetables, freeing up his right hand to flick his collar up with a well-practised movement, concealing the small green disc set into the skin on his neck.
"Sorry, no, thank you. I can manage." The man imitated an air of control to the onlookers who knew he had none. Alice accepted a plastic bag and turned to her shopping, adding up the pigs in blankets one more time and mentally allocating them - five for Andrew, two each for her in-laws, three for Tommy, plus the extra one that she would hide in amongst the Brussels sprouts, digging it out for him when he thought his favourite part of the

meal was over - something she used to do for Andrew in the early days of their relationship, his delight now only replicable in miniature, only half his, on the gravy-streaked face of their son. By the time she had packed her shopping neatly into categorised bags; freezer, fridge, larder one, larder two, back pantry, upstairs bathrooms, cleaning products, plus a few bits of makeup directly into her pockets, the green disc and the onions and the man had gone.

"I thought we were going to get the cleaner to go. Here, give me those."
He stepped forwards, sliding off the bar stool to relieve her of the bags whose handles were cutting into her fingers.
"Thanks." She said, surprised at his forwardness, releasing the breath that she didn't know she had been holding to help carry the weight of the bags, supporting her torso from the inside.
"You sit. I'll get the rest."
She felt a twinge of sadness, or nostalgia, or remorse; she wasn't sure what it was. A sort of emptiness expanding in her chest which her mind rushed to define. It was all mixed up. Now, in this moment, when an exchange between them was pleasant, she felt a sense of loss, not pleasure. It was when things were acidic between them that this new phase of their relationship felt bearable. Contempt was more tolerable than doubt or regret. She perched on the stool next to his, noting, then taking, the large glass of red from its position next to his laptop.

"The pool is cold, by the way. In case you were planning on using it."

He stacked the last of the meat in the freezer, removing the cardboard packaging to minimise the space they took up. Sausages on the left, chicken thighs on the right. Seafood in the bottom drawer; shellfish at the bottom, fillets on top. The same as always. *Tidy.* Today, *tidy* filled her with affection.

"I know." He sat down. "I was thinking, about the pool. It's a bit… excessive, maybe. Given what's going on. It uses about half of the energy quota, and it's just for us." She bristled; in her jaw, across the back of her shoulders, her nervous system mirrored her defensiveness. It was all very well making *sacrifices* when it involved something important to her. Where was this ethical magnanimity when it came to his golf weekends abroad, his big car, his insistence on eating *real* steak, even after failing to differentiate it from the lab-grown version in a blind taste test at a friend's BBQ last summer. She was determined not to be the one to sour things tonight - partly because things being soured wasn't good for either of them, and partly to prove that it was he that always turned things sour, not her. That it would happen whether she made a comment or not.

"The caps are tightening again in two weeks, did you see." He continued, oblivious to her irritation.

"Yes I saw. You'll need to get the train to the office."

"I'll work from home. That's what everyone is saying on our desk."

"Mmmm." She sipped at his wine. "Oh, did you want a glass?"

He looked around for his glass, then back to the one in her hand. "Oi!" There was a pause where the energy between them teetered, dancing on the edge of a knife.

Then the corners of his mouth twitched. "Nothing nice is safe around you."

"Well it was evaporating. It would have been a waste to leave it there."

He grabbed the bottle from the counter, and glass from the cupboard, and poured himself a generous serving. "Top up?"

She considered. A glint of old Andrew, or old *them*, whichever it was, was perceptible in the way he waggled the bottle at her enticingly. She had been planning to go upstairs and work on her painting, but she couldn't snub him.

"Sure. Thanks."

"So, how was your day?"

"Oh you know, same old. I saw Sophie, she was moaning about Sienna again. Apparently she isn't giving her a thorough enough run-down of her day at school."

Andrew gave a faint snort of laughter. She felt warmed by the relic of a time when she could make him laugh about anything. She remembered once, at his uncle's funeral, muttering some joke to Andrew under her breath, trying to lighten the mood, and both of them had ended up shaking with suppressed laughter in the pew, digging their fingernails into their palms, reciting *dead puppies dead puppies,* over and over, to try and counteract the giggling, but then Andrew had said *I can't believe dead puppies make you more sad than dead Uncle Henry,* and this had just made them laugh harder, so that Andrew's great-aunt Susan had looked over at them with disgust. Emboldened, she continued, "And then she was rabbiting on about how this ridiculous school they are sending her to is serving the kids kale. Kale! And Sienna doesn't eat it-"

She trailed off as he reached across the counter for his iPad. She waited a few more seconds, testing him, waiting, counting five seconds of silence, ready to jump on him with proof that he wasn't listening to her, again. "I know what you're doing. I noticed you stopped speaking. I was listening. I was just getting my iPad to show you an article that I saw today."

His voice had deadened, his syllables clipped.

"I wasn't doing-"

"Yes you were. Setting little tests for me, traps. And the worst part is I think you *hope* I'll fall into them, *hope* I'll fail, just to give you ammunition."

She was outraged, but later that night as she lay in bed beside him, she thought *maybe he's right.* The constant underlying tension was more difficult to navigate than outright confrontation. At that moment, he rolled over, expelling a big sigh of breath.

"Sorry" she whispered in the darkness. "I'm sorry." She tried again, louder this time. "About earlier." Her heartrate quickened at the admission. So often she had tried to apologise for her part in escalating something, and found herself unable to form the words, adrenaline surging with each failed attempt as though she were summoning the courage to jump off something high, losing courage at the last moment, toes over the edge, the vertigo of *almost* worse than the fall itself. Andrew gave a faint snore. Alice got out of bed, giving up on sleep, and went down to the kitchen to get a glass of water.

When she was awoken at seven thirty, it was by Tommy, prodding the soft area in front of her shoulder, below her collarbone. He always knew where the weak spots were, where he could get her attention with minimal effort, little fingers burrowing.

"Mummy wake up."

She gulped down the glass of water on her bedside table, washing away the fog.

"Sorry Tommo. I must have overslept." She sat up and pulled him onto her lap for a hug. "How did you sleep? We better get you ready for school."

"No school. Saturday."

"It's not Saturday, silly. It's Thursday. Come on, we're going to be late."

"No school." He said again. "Daddy home."

"What? Daddy's at work Tom. Come on, up you get."

Just then she heard a cough downstairs, followed by the scrape of a chair and the sound of the kitchen tap running. Then the smell of coffee.

"What are you doing home? Are you ill?"

"I told you - working from home."

"Already? I didn't think that would be for a while."

"Coffee?"

"I'm late taking Tommy. You should have woken me."

"I didn't want to disturb you. You seemed like you needed the rest."

She surveyed him, looking for signs that he had heard her midnight apology. She couldn't read him.

"Well, we've got to rush now. Come on Tommy, shoes on."

"No school!" He slid onto his knees, fastening his arms firmly around Maisie's neck. The two of them looked up at her beseechingly.

"Behave yourself young man. Listen to your mother."
Andrew peeled Tommy's fingers apart, scooped him up,
and gave him a kiss on the forehead.
"I can manage." She snapped.

Rebecca and Bel, two of the *gate mums* as she thought of
them, were chatting in the carpark as Alice emerged from
the school gate, the bell reverberating her exit.
"Oh, Alice! Hi! Rebecca and I were about to grab a coffee.
Want to join us?"
She scanned through the usual list of options for excuses
to hurry off, before remembering Andrew was at home.
"Yeah, sure. Why not."
Bel looked taken aback. "Oh! I thought you'd be off to the
gym, or the garden centre. And how is the leaking
shower?"
Alice searched the woman's tone for passive-aggression,
but found none. She seemed genuinely pleased. Maybe
this was actually how nice people interacted. *Now what
had she told them about a leaking shower?*
"Yes, fine, fine. Andrew sorted it."
"Oooo, he's a keeper, your Andrew." Rebecca nudged
her way into the conversation.
"Yes, I suppose he is. So where is this cafe?" She smiled
enthusiastically at the women, compensating for her
social rust. "Lead the way!"

Alice bought the coffee, in a surge of affection for the
women who welcomed her unconditionally, unaware
that she had pigeon-holed them as vacuous and frivolous.
She waved their readers away when she returned to the
table with the tray. "Points are on me." She said when
Rebecca protested, and she felt pleasure at the small act of

generosity. "They only serve oat milk here anyway, so it was nothing."

"Well, next week it's on me." Rebecca announced grandly, and sucked in a breath to indicate she had more to say, looking between the other two women to build suspense. "I've gone for it!"

"You haven't! Ooo Becky, I can't believe you caved!" Bel chided her with mock horror, in the way Alice's mother might chastise her father for having a second slice of cake, almost imperceptible wisps of smugness hiding in amongst the playfulness.

"Only the most basic package. With the flight travel add on. Greg is desperate to visit his parents in Australia."

"Yes, we've been thinking about buying travel allowance. Egypt pretty much wiped ours out."

"Sorry, the basic package..." Alice felt her neck warm, immediately regretting exposing her naivety. "I mean, I know about the flights, that's simple. You are just buying someone else's flight allowance, right" She paused long enough for them to correct her, but not long enough to indicate she was unsure on this, the most straightforward of off-set transactions. "So, the basic package, remind me…" She faltered, offering the start of the sentence to the group to pick up.

"It's not much, really. You get an extra 500 NC points, and-"

"NC is nutri-carbon. Food and drink, mainly for extra meat and dairy and stuff."

"She knows that, we all have to track those even if we don't off-set."

"Just saying, it's pretty key for even a low-level cheese addiction."

Bel and Rebecca laughed. Alice laughed too.

"And how does it work, with the package for those? What do you pay the counter to do?"

"Vegan. Although they can still eat honey apparently, according to Tim, the barman at the pub on the green. So not properly vegan."

"With bronze you also get 500 travel points, and 100 disposables. That's why I originally upgraded to be honest. Those are a lifesaver with a toddler." Bel sipped at her coffee and set it back on the saucer before continuing. "Nappies burn through disposable points like there's no tomorrow. But once you get used to a bigger allowance it's pretty tough to go back."

"Plus you'd be screwing your counter over, surely. Taking the income away again." Alice turned the moral question over in her mouth even as the words came out of it.

"That's a better way of looking at it, thanks Alice. You can come again." Bel patted her on the knee.

"That courgette and gorgonzola pasta good for dinner Al?"

From coffee, she'd gone straight to the art studio where she and Sophie rented spaces. After two hours Sophie had left but she had stayed, canvases and clay revolving around her as their artists came and went, putting off her return to the house.

"Oh yum, yes, do we have walnuts?"

"Of course." He produced the bag with a flourish.

"You're in a good mood, what's up?"

"Nothing. I don't know, I suppose I am. It's been nice being at home today. Tommy and I played three games of Racing Frogs when I finished. I lost, but it beat crawling along the M25 in rush hour."

"Yes, thanks for picking him up. It was nice for me too. I went to the studio with Sophie."

"I'm pleased you went. What are you working on?"

"Plant pots. Like those ones we saw in Milan, by that cafe. But smaller. And I went for coffee with the school mums this morning."

"Oh yeah? Such a lady of leisure."

Alice pulled a face but let it slide. "It was nice actually. They're alright." She pulled the big saucepan from the cupboard under the counter and set it on the induction hob. "Bel is actually training to climb Everest with her brother. To the summit."

Andrew raised his eyebrows. "Not bad for a - what did you call them? - vapid busybodies?"

"Oh god, I'm awful. I don't even know why I said that. It was easier to accept not being in the gang if the gang was one I didn't want to be a part of, I suppose." This admission made her feel vulnerable, and she took a bottle of white wine from the fridge to re-armour herself.

Andrew looked at her as he added salt to the water. He saw it all - the self-awareness, the vulnerability, the admission of hypocrisy. He had always been able to read her. That was what had made their relationship fullest at the start, and what she found most uncomfortable now that the closeness had lessened.

"How much salt do you need!" She deflected his gaze with criticism, as she often did these days.

"You do it then." He thrust the packet of spaghetti into her hands.

"I thought you were making dinner?"

"I was doing it wrong apparently. I've got emails to reply to anyway. A bunch came in while we were playing Racing Frogs."

"Right." She tore open the packet and felt sadness. She had been looking forward to dissecting the OffSet question with Andrew. They would always settle naturally into opposite sides of the debate, regardless of their true stance on the matter, in an unspoken strategy to cover all bases between them and properly tease it out. It was a safe space for difficult political issues, to think aloud and be allowed to take words back, or to edit them or qualify them retroactively when more insight rendered them obtuse. But she had spoiled things, again, niggling at him. Or had he overreacted? Or was it both? She couldn't be sure.

"Mum! Muuuuum!"
Tommy's voice reached into her misery and confusion.
"What is it Tom? Come in here if you want to talk to me."
Tommy came into the kitchen by skating across the tiles in his sock, pulling himself along the edge of the counter.
"Maisie's sick." He wrinkled his nose. "Not that stinky cheese pasta again?"
"I'm making yours with cheddar, don't worry. What's the matter with Maisie?"
"Can I pick out the green things too? And she's being all funny on the sofa. Dad said she could go on the sofa by the way." He added quickly. "We put the purple blanket on it first."
"What do you mean, funny? What's wrong with her?"
She turned off the stove and drained the pasta, resting the colander on top of the pan.
"Come and see." He clutched her hand. "Pull me along the floor, I'm playing the game where you can't lift up your feet."

Maisie was lying on the sofa where Alice never usually let her sit. Her tail flopped feebly when they came into the room, and she whined.

"What is it, Maisie-moo?" She perched on the edge of the sofa next to her and stroked her warm side. Her tail wagged a bit more.

"She's okay Tom. Maybe feeling a bit sick. We'll take her to the vet's tomorrow. Don't worry. Go and get dad for dinner."

"Iron deficiency." The vet proclaimed without examining her, as soon as the door to the consultation room had clicked shut and his fee was sealed. "Seeing more and more of it at the moment. You feeding her vegan?"

"Yes, but the proper vet-approved stuff. V-Nine."

"Not a failsafe for all dogs unfortunately. Especially big girls like Maisie."

"Non-plant-based dog food is about 300 NC points a month though isn't it."

"450, for a dog her size. Even if you go hybrid it'll be at least 375."

"Right."

"I can prescribe her some supplements for now, but long term there is no substitute I'm afraid."

Maisie licked his hand, and he offered her a bone-shaped biscuit which she took gently from his hand, before snuffling around his pocket for another.

"Come on Maisie-moo. Thanks for your help. Shall I get the supplements from reception?"

"Yes. I'll send it through to them now."

"But they won't work long-term?" Andrew tugged at tiny weeds in between the cracks on the patio while she relayed the vet's prognosis to him.

"That's what he said."

"So now what are we supposed to do? There's no way we can switch her to meat without cutting it out ourselves. Which I am not willing to do for a dog, even for Maisie."

"No, I know. Of course not."

"Well what did the vet suggest? There must be other options, there's no way everyone with a dog is going vegan. That's ridiculous." He yanked at a particularly stubborn weed, and a clump of earth burst out with the roots and scattered over his suede loafers. She watched him work for a while, hoping that the suggestion might occur to him first so that it didn't have to come from her. But when he didn't speak, she said: "Well, there is one option. I don't know." She scraped some of the discarded weeds into a pile with the edge of her shoe. "Maybe we should think about signing up. Just for this…"

"I thought you hated the idea."

Yes, thank you Andrew. She thought, familiar bitterness rising. *I think that is implied with my reluctance to do it, even now. I don't need an 'I told you so'.*

"Well, I think it's our only option."

"Work would probably cover the bronze option, to give me the mileage to come into the office once a week. So we wouldn't even have to pay for it. Plus I would like to have the pool heated again."

She noted his generosity in shouldering some of the need, absolving her of the guilt of the suggestion. He never really used the pool.

"I love you Andrew."

He looked up at her, weeds dangling in surprise.

42

"You too."

Chapter 5

Sam

Sometimes, when she looked at Lucas, she couldn't believe that he was hers. The disbelief had morphed through various stages over the short course of his life. She hadn't been able to believe that she could tolerate the screaming and the sleepless nights, even (just about) when he had suffered relentlessly with croup at three months old. Then, she couldn't believe that she wasn't repulsed by his runny noses as a toddler. Not the yellow crusty phase, nor the transparent stringy goop phase, nor the phase where a fluorescent green film stretched across the entrance to each nostril, sometimes popping and reforming as he snuffled. And then there was the screaming stage, where a cloud of fury could drift in from nowhere, attracted by a wrongly-shaped raisin, or because he only had ten toes, or because he wanted the yellow cup, and then again because he was given the yellow cup. At least, she'd thought it was a stage. Hoped it was. Some part of her still hoped so, although at five his reactions were still incandescent, illogical (to her), and inconsolable. And the internet forums were no longer all *Hang in there momma, It's normal, Part of development, The terrible twos,* but instead all *Oh dear, Still?, I couldn't imagine!* Acronyms bandied and keyboard psychiatrists activated. "The ferocious fives" yielded far fewer results on google search. Miss Brockley, Lucas's form tutor, had begun asking to speak to her after school.

In the carousel of fixations, football was the flavour of the week. This was convenient as he was invited to his third football-themed birthday party in as many months. The red t-shirt that she had dug out of the back of his chest of drawers, ever so slightly too small, was also now covered in mud. Little legs scuffed at shins and the ball zigzagged and rolled almost as if completely at random, shrill voices chasing the win. It was about eighteen goals to sixteen by the time the whistle blew, coordination on both an individual and team level all-but non-existent.
"Mumma! Did you see me! Did you see me kicking it!"
"Yes, I saw you. Great kicking Lu. Go on, run over there with your pals. There'll be snacks!"

She wandered over to the striped parasols and long tables of party food. A table at the end held a stack of colourfully-wrapped presents. It had been a relief to realise she had the money to buy a present for the child for the first time. She had sifted through Amazon, reeling not at the prices of the items, but at the carbon points, some as high as 10% of her new monthly allowance. The new green *counter-friendly* tab had been a saviour, and after trawling through a range of 'plant them a tree' or 'sponsor a wind farm' e-giftcard options, had settled on a hemp t-shirt with a picture of a dinosaur wearing sunglasses on, which she could collect from a nearby depot without packaging for a further 20% reduction on disposable points. She slid the paper-wrapped package in amongst the others and stepped back as if completing a covert mission. She had learnt that poverty and shame came in many forms.

At the food table, Lucas was hanging back, one finger hanging from his lower teeth as he considered.

"Just let me know what you want poppet, and I'll help you key in your points." The birthday boy's mother waved a serving spoon over the spread.

Sam flinched inwardly at the realisation that the child's parents had not absorbed the points for the party food themselves, that they would be passing them on to the kids. She had hoped to trade in some of Lucas's spare NC points for house points for heating again this month, and by eating the same diet as her, he should have had some spare. He gnawed on his finger with his top teeth agitatedly.

"That's right Lu, go on." She stepped forward and nudged him in the small of the back. He looked up in confusion. "But it's chicken nuggets Mumma. *Chicken* nuggets."

"Don't you like chicken pet? Everyone loves chicken nuggets."

The child's mother was hovering. "All needs eating up, don't be shy."

"It's okay Lu." She said more firmly. "You have whatever you want. Go on."

"Rude, isn't it?"

Sam jumped, as if caught in the act of doing something shameful. A short, olive-skinned woman with close-cropped dark hair and navy overalls was standing behind her, leaning in over her shoulder, mouth close to her ear. Sam turned to face her, taking a backwards step to re-establish her personal space.

"Am I that readable?"

"Like a book. Probably only because I'm thinking it too though. Don't worry, I don't think *they-*" she nodded a head towards the parents serving food and programming points into the kids' devices, plates held just out of reach until the transaction was complete, "- even think about the fact that this might be a real unexpected shitter for some people. Not exactly hosts with the most, eh?"

"I mean, I wouldn't expect someone else to cover us." The woman raised a sceptical eyebrow.

"Okay, well I guess I'd assumed they would. It would be like asking us for money for their party food, you know, *before.*"

"And it's not exactly a secret that some people here will be tight. Even though yours is pretty hidden."

"It's meant to be completely hidden, to be honest. I'm not used to people seeing it just yet. Not that you shouldn't, well. You know." Sam shrugged apologetically.

"The green compliments my eyes." The woman winked at her. "I'm Maya by the way. I'm groundswoman here."

"Sam."

"Got many friends who are Counters, Sam?"

"Not really. Since me and my boyfriend split up, money's been pretty tight. And I need to get Lucas - that's my son - some tests. He's having a hard time at school. And at home, to be honest. Sorry, I don't know why I'm telling you my life story."

"You're all good. I remember when I signed up. Felt like an absolute piece of turd."

Sam laughed at the choice of words. "Well, yes. Basically. And then I feel stupid because I chose it!"

"Not really a choice though, is it. Some fucked up world where you'd go ahead and choose this."

"I guess."

"Here, let me give you my number. Counter friends! All turds together."

Sam laughed again, and took Maya's number. She wouldn't use it though. That would be yet another admission of defeat, yet another way in which she would be accepting that this was more than transactional; it was an identity.

A single shriek from the food queue. Commotion. Parents turned towards the noise, uniform in their desperation for it to be caused by someone else's child. Sam's prayer, as usual, unanswered.

"What happened Lu?"

He couldn't speak. Distress distorted his features, balled his fists.

"Lily's skipping rope knocked his plate. Just an accident." The mother of the birthday boy pointed towards the nuggets scattered in the grass. "There's no need to be upset." She picked up the empty plate and tried to pass it back to Lucas. His face was scarlett with the exertion of the game and the subsequent chain of events. The shame of preparing to say no, the confusion of being told to say yes, the shock of dropping the cargo that he had been conditioned to view as so precious. Right back round to shame at all the attention on his mistake. The circle of emotions had short-circuited him, trapping him in a loop. Overloaded already as he was, self-preservation dulled his senses so that he couldn't even process the plate being offered back to him. His arm jerked, and bashed the plate in her hand.

"There's no need for that behaviour. No need for violence. None at all." The mother huffed.

"He wasn't being violent. Come on, you're being ridiculous." Maya stepped forwards, taking the plate and the control. "He's just upset, give the kid a break."
Sam was flooded with gratitude at not having to deal with the woman as well as her son. The novelty of sharing the load, the space it afforded her to present her child with the entirety of her mental capacity. "I'm going to help you move away from here, Lucas." She said to him quietly, so that the others wouldn't hear her. "Mumma's going to need to touch you now, ok?"
She put a tentative hand on his arm, and when he didn't react, gripped his upper arm more firmly and steered him away from the tables of food, the air static with the implication of rolling eyes and tutting mouths that the other parents were too polite to express, but not too kind to feel. His chest was heaving, but his lips were pressed tightly together, sealing in the sound and breath of his emotion. She crouched down in front of him. "Lucas? Look at me." His eyes darted around, anywhere but at her face, like a caged animal. "Lucas. It's okay to be upset. Breathe." After a few moments he opened his mouth and gasped for air, and his tears came in great shuddering gulps, wracking through his little body. He fell against her, and she put her arms around him like a barrier, wishing she could protect him from everything, but feeling like instead she was destroying him.

She took a rushed cold shower that night, turning off the flow of water whenever she paused to use soap. The contrast of warm tears and frigid shower water made her shiver in misery. She cried about the reaction of the birthday boy when he opened his t-shirt. "Scratchy!" He had said, rubbing the material between his fingers;

"stiff!". She cried for Lucas, slipping his small hand into hers on the way home, and telling her he was sorry. And she cried for herself, unsure how she was going to keep the lights on, how she could continue to restrict their world without crushing her son, like carving out a small pocket of air in an avalanche.

Chapter 6

Alice

Alice remembered exactly where she was when they made the announcement. It was a cold day, the kind of day that prompted climate-deniers and middle-aged white men to make rubbish jokes - *I wouldn't mind a bit of global warming to be honest* - and the 42nd 'Conference of the Parties'. COP42, the first UN Climate Change conference after the 2036 famine in Sub-Saharan Africa responsible for the deaths of two hundred million people. The developed nations had offered reparations - substantial ones - but a coalition of governments from the Indian subcontinent had put their foot down. Indian Prime Minister Chandra Desai Singh had given his famous ultimatum. *We have nothing left to lose*, read his powerful conclusion, *it is not possible for our demands to be too great.* The discussions had been going back and forth for nine days, and the verdict was published at 11pm in the UK, which was 5am wherever it was being held. She still remembers the tired-looking reporter trying to spin the limited information she had into something story-worthy, fleshing out the basics with increasingly inventive versions of the same sentence. *International per capita limits on carbon usage, to track an individual's carbon contributions across all categories, including, but not limited to food, travel, home, single use items, and retail.* A group of scientists from Bangladesh had run calculations for how much more the earth could handle in terms of emissions, and divided it by the global population. Which made sense, except some people already used a lot more than that, and some people barely used any. Follow-up articles in various right-wing tabloids had described regions of Asia and Africa where entire communities lived without electricity or petrol vehicles. Western governments had swiftly come to the same conclusion. The USA were the first to buy a portion of the quotas from the DRC, Mali, and Sudan. The UN had ruled the deal unlawful, and President Healy had issued a statement from the Whitehouse declaring that it was only a *temporary measure*, until his citizens could *adapt*. She wondered now if they might find it easier to "adapt" in the wake of the storm. "It should obviously be situation-adjusted for everyone!" Andrew had berated the decision-makers through the screen of his iPad. "Those people are fine with barely any allowance for carbon emissions. We've just had the pool put in." Alice had hated the way his words had sounded, unfiltered in the censorless perimeter of their family home - cringed at his example - but she had sort of agreed with the sentiment. It wouldn't change anything for those people. They *didn't* need as much as people in the West to carry on living the way they were. And even within the West, needs were different. Some people didn't have a car, or spare bedrooms, or underfloor heating. It was pointless to take that all away for no reason. Uneconomical, even. They all needed to be a bit more careful, she agreed, but the allowances should be proportionate to current usage, scaled down for everyone so that the total was low enough, but not just a flat rate. That was overly simplistic. The system had adjusted, of course, as it always did. There were always ways around things, for those with money. Only eight months later, the first scandals hit the headlines. MPs accused of putting their food and travel through a public carbon expense account, as if the sun's heat were selective as to which emissions would trap it in the earth's atmosphere, as if steak and a private jet after a political event were exempt from such mundane consequences as glacial melt. Later that same year, came the reports of *Magnetica*, the private company who had won the government contracts for the electromagnetic train network set to revolutionise UK travel and replace domestic flights, being discovered to have an entire division of ghost employees whose carbon allowances had been registered as bogus combined spousal accounts with the members of the Department of Transport; just by pure coincidence, the same six men who had awarded them the multi-billion pound contract four months earlier. And in early 2038, just fourteen months after 192 countries had signed the *per capita allowance* treaty at COP42, it was unearthed that almost 0.5% of the UK population, (primarily bankers, politicians, and barristers), had been allowed to make direct payments to increase their carbon quotas. There was a reshuffling in the government Environment Agency, and the Secretary of State for the department took an early retirement (full pension). Management of the *per capita allowance* treaty was privatised later that year, with the Prime Minister's (now former) Chief Advisor wishing OffSet luck, and making a scathing statement about the British Public's "*inability to ever think anything anyone does is good enough for them*." OffSet had taken over tracking and limitation of the population's carbon quota, and the strict individual ceiling was restored, for a time at least. But then they had devised new methods for carbon off-setting; advanced graphene production and carbon-capture sequestration, with a view to selling the off-setted amounts to the highest bidders. But at COP43, this was clamped down on as an immoral rule-bend by developed nations; the global carbon limit had been calculated assuming that all nations would already be maximising carbon sequestration, and so any increase in their ability to remove carbon from the atmosphere should not be negated by increased per capita allowances. The UK, as well as the US, China, and Saudi Arabia, were fined in the region of a total of $20 billion dollars. Alice and Andrew had got solar panels installed for the pool. OffSet had had to devise another way to make money. And so began the suggestion of *sharing*. Some people needed money. Some people *had* money, and wanted more carbon freedom. Alice had followed the news with only superficial interest; the developments of governmental rule-bending and accusations of corruption were nothing new. *To be honest, you kind of, just, would, wouldn't you?* She had said to Andrew over dinner one evening, within the security of their relationship. *If you were them, and you could get a bit extra, or shuffle things around, you would. People are annoyed because they didn't have the chance to do it. But I bet they would. 99% of people would have done it.* And he had said; *the things that people get most angry about other people doing are the things they secretly wish they could do themselves. That's why people get so irrationally angry about people who sing in public, or why skinny people get so cross watching fat people enjoying cake. It's your suppressed inner desires coming to the surface, and you get triggered.* He had mimed an explosion at either side of his temple with his hands. And she had asked him if he had been reading her trashy magazines that she kept by the bath, and he had put his finger to his lips, looking around their dining room as if his *mental-health-is-a-myth* work colleagues might be listening in, feigning embarrassment across his spag bol.

And now, here she was. "So you just install this app on your phone, here you go. Search *OffSet*. That's the one." The salesman pointed to the little green icon on her screen. "And then it tells you your combined limit for each category. You can increase yours by decreasing your Counter's with these sliding toggles on the screen. It tells you the cost of each change, and then you click to confirm. Really easy."

"That is easy. Okay. Thank you. So is this basic? Bronze?"

"We've actually upgraded the whole system to give users a more bespoke experience. So instead of fixed packages, you can just play with your limits for each thing."

"That makes sense. We will barely even use it." She wasn't sure why she felt the need to justify it to him, the very face of the system. "It's just a small amount in a couple of areas where things are tight, you know?"

He nodded like he knew but also like he didn't care.

"So what do you reckon? Shall we get you registered? There's a 50% discount on the sign-up fee if you do it on the same day."

"Oh, that's quick. Um."

The man tugged at the knot on his tie and leaned on one elbow, the epitome of blasé. "May I ask what your hesitation is? Because if it's the money I can assure you-"

"It's not the money." She snapped, irritated.

He nodded in apparent understanding, but didn't say anything. As usual, she felt compelled to fill the silence. "It's just… it just feels weird. Like slavery, almost."

He laughed then, and the laughter was laced with the same undertone that her mother's often was when she saw a news story about supporting minority businesses, or even women's rights in the workplace; the *isms* so internalised that she perpetuated them even against herself. The sort of laugh that was pitying, condescending, a little exasperated. *Hysterical*, it seemed to say, that short burst of air from both nostrils, the smile accompanied by an almost imperceptible *hmmph*.

"It's nothing like slavery. I find that word quite offensive. To be honest, it's patronising to suggest that these people, the *Counters*, are incapable of making this choice for themselves."

She thought about this for a minute. It made some sense. No-one was forcing them into it - if a world in which this program wasn't offered was better for them then they could make that a reality by just *not doing it.* She relaxed a little.

He seemed to recognise the weakening of resolve on her face.

"We have testimonials from Counters here who say this has changed their life."

"Well obviously."

"Not like that. Look - this couple say that they were able to buy their children new school uniforms." He pointed at the cover of a brochure on the coffee table between them, where a couple beamed out at them over the heads of three smartly-attired offspring. "And this mother says that her two daughters have started piano lessons and one has recently passed her grade seven." He flicked through the shiny brochure, smiles flashing out at their split-second of daylight before being whisked away, ready for the next time they had a role to serve. "There's a lovely man in here somewhere, describing how he is now able to pay for specialist medical treatment. Hang on." He rifled through a few more pages. "Yes, here he is! Diabetes, that was it." He snapped the brochure shut. "My point is, the things that the Counters sacrifice - if you can even call it that; really it's just better life choices, on the whole - are nothing to what they gain. And if they don't like it, they don't do it!" He looked at his watch, bulky and metallic. "I'm afraid the next appointment is due. Not to worry - you go away and think about it. Speak to the lady on reception about booking you in if you decide to go for it. The next available appointments are not for a few weeks. March, I think."

"Oh!" She felt herself drawn in by the retraction of availability, like a teenager whose love interest plays hard to get. And she thought about Maisie, lethargic, a lukewarm version of a dog. "Well couldn't I just sign up over the phone?"

"We need your signature, and just a few other bits. Fingerprints, that kind of thing."

"What? Fingerprints? What for?"

"Not for anything, really. Just standard procedure. A government requirement to finalise the off-setting process. It's all very boring really."

"Right."

"Well, it was lovely to meet you."

She thought again about the chill of the swimming pool at eighteen degrees. About the time she went to the zero-waste store and ended up pouring rice all over the floor. About the mother whose daughter had passed her grade seven piano.

"Wait."

The corner of his mouth twitched, and she thought she saw in it a crocodilian-ness, though it was probably just mild amusement at her predictability.

"Do we get to know who the person we are paired with is?

"Your Counter?"

"Yes"

"No. The process is fully anonymised. What I can tell you is yours would be a woman of similar age to yourself, or if you and your husband both sign up then you'd get an additional man to off-set him. Could also get a child if you went for a family account. They're a bit limited though, so most people just tend to share the extra with their kids, register some of their points against their own allowance."

His next appointment no longer seemed to be pressing as he relaxed back into his pitch.

"And I could just sign up and leave the allowances at equal and not use it if I wanted? While I decide?"

"In principle, yes. You'd still pay the base subscription and sign-up fee though."

"Sure, yes. Sure. Okay." She felt a small rush of adrenaline in her chest. Suddenly, it felt exciting. Like the idea of winning the lottery as a child. Or even like the idea of receiving twenty pounds for her birthday - she hadn't needed a whole lottery win in those days to feel extravagant, just a little extra to buy sweets or a new top.

"How do I do this then?"

"Did you know Roy Jenson has twenty-two Counters? *Twenty-two!*"

"Who?"

She was sitting on the sofa, beads of condensation forming around the base of the gin and tonic on the coffee table and the OffSet brochures spread across the footrest that she had pulled in between her knees.

"Ladylike." He nodded his head at her knees either side of the pouffe.

"Thank you." She burped, and blew it towards him.

"Lovely. Who is this Roy Jenson?"

"You know, the bloke behind the *Bin-cinerator.*"

"Ah! *Let the trash take itself out.*" He winked and made a clicking noise in the corner of his mouth like the man from the advert.

"Exactly. Anyway, twenty two!"

"It went well today then? Are we all off-*set*? 'Scuse the pun."

"That's not a pun. And it actually makes a lot of sense." She took a sip of gin and tonic, and pushed one of the open leaflets towards him. "The guy there explained it all to me. Obviously, as you know, it's all been worked out and divided up. And if everyone just stayed within those limits then we'd be all good with the old ice-caps and polar bears and whatnot. But obviously it's harder for some people because if you're just naturally a vegetarian, you're going to find it easier to have a low nutri-carbon count, right? So that's where it makes sense to…", she paused, flicking the page in the flyer, before jabbing at a line half-way down with her finger, "*re-distribute.*"

"I don't think anyone is *naturally* vegetarian, by the way."

"You know what I mean. Like, they were already, or whatever."

"Sort of like how we *naturally* have a pool, then?" He smiled to show he was joking, but she felt sensitivity prickling in her chest.

"It was you who was pushing for us to do this. Anyway, we left most of the categories on equal for now."

"No, no I know! I'm only teasing. I think it's good. We needed it anyway, for Maisie."

"There's a disposables option too which is about, like, single use stuff, plastic and packaging and stuff. But I didn't even register us for that."

She sat back on the sofa and pulled her knees up to her chest. She wasn't sure why she felt so defensive about it all. It was like the guy in the shop said - it would be patronising to *not* sign up just to… to what? To protect the Counters? If doing it was worse for them than not doing it then they could just… not do it. No one was forcing anyone.

"So – twenty-two eh?" He sat down next to her and nudged her in the ribs. "We've got some catching up to do."

She burrowed into his side until she had linked her arm through his.

"Hello." He said, resting his head on hers.

"Hi."

Chapter 7

Sam

It was hot in London. The kind of heat that makes you cough when you breathe in, when the hot air and moisture make contact with the back of your throat. A shelter-in-place decree had been issued. Checkers skulked in the shady strips along walls and beneath trees on pavements, silent green patrols. Menacing, more oppressive even than the intense heat. All the windows in the small pocket of Counter housing were flung ajar, its residents seeking the relief of a breeze like a plant's roots spread in the dry scorched earth of a desert in desperate search of water that does not exist. Rooftops and roads shimmered, adding to the general spacey feeling that the ground was swaying when you walked. Most people tried not to walk. The streets were empty, and the little boxy back gardens rang silent, the kind of silence that is louder than the usual shrieking of excitable children and the barking of dogs, its meaning pressing against the eardrums, reverberating in the skull. The narrow canal that ran along the backs of the houses was dry, for the first time in Sam's memory. Amongst the shopping trolleys, rotting dog leads, and even an old mobility scooter, police had found swampy stashes of firearms littered along the dried out bed, tossed into the water by unfortunate gang-members who could never have foreseen a drought to this extent.

She hadn't moved into the Counter community-housing at first; hadn't wanted to, hadn't seen the need. But eventually it had just been easier that way. Easier to manage her outgoings with the in-built controls, easier for certain things to be automatically off-limits to her, easier to be around people who understood. But also harder for all of those same reasons. In the end, OffSet had offered an additional financial incentive to persuade her to make the move. It had been touted as a choice, but not one she would have chosen, if she'd really had one. Now being a Counter was part of every aspect of her life, and her identity was unmistakable.

Running water was cut off to all three streets in the Counter estate she lived in. Thames Water were claiming there was an issue they were working to resolve, but Sam found herself wondering whether it was a directive from above to preserve what little water was available for those deemed worthy. She wasn't even sure whether she really believed that could be possible, or if she was turning into a conspiracy theorist, like the people in America who believe that the government wiped out all birds and replaced them with millions of disguised camera drones. But it was an easy way to decide how to ration it: Londoners geographically pre-divided, neatly grouped together on the water grid. Protecting those that could pay. Her mother thought she was being too cynical. Either way, they'd had no water since 6pm on Tuesday, and it was now 4pm on Thursday. On the radio coming from an upstairs window next door, a man in Westminster was talking about his peonies wilting. "It's a price we are willing to pay, of course. We all need to make cuts where we can." The audio cut back to the host, who repeated the government warning: *For your own safety, stay at home. Do not leave your zone unless essential.* Sam heard a muttered curse, and the radio went off.

She had filled the bathtub with cold water the morning before, a tip from Maya. *How did you know?* She had texted her last night, when the faint trickle in the kitchen sink had become drips, then nothing, when she was trying to fill the kettle. *Luck,* her mother had retorted, when she had presented this as evidence for her theory. *Or just good sense. The water could have gone out anywhere, what with the shortages we're seeing.*
Just a feeling. Maya had replied. Sam went to knock on the door of the houses immediately either side of her, while a couple of checkers eyed her suspiciously from the end of the street. She had hesitated before doing so, and she was ashamed of that. But she was genuinely afraid how long they might be without water, and she needed to think of Lucas. In the end her conscience had got the better of her, and she had gone round with two litre plastic bottles filled from the bath, and given one to each household.
"I just happened to have them filled up." She had responded to David, the old man from number 12, with milky eyes and a sour smell that was worse than usual with the heat. "Here, take it." She pressed it into his hands and made sure he was gripping it before letting go.

Later that evening, a young girl came and knocked on the door. Lucas hung behind Sam's legs shyly, peering around at the child who couldn't have been more than a year older than him.
"Do you have some water?" The girl's cheeks were flushed in the heat. She was wearing a faded vest and

loose cotton shorts that looked like pyjamas. Her feet were bare. Sam couldn't believe that she considered saying no, that she hesitated. How had this girl found out that she had water? What if the water stayed off, and the whole street came knocking on the door. What if she were mobbed? "I, er -" She was stalling. She heard a woman's voice calling from a few doors down. "Hannah? Where are you?"

"Please, don't tell my mum. She told me I wasn't allowed to come. It's for Wiggle. We haven't given her any water today."

Sam knew Wiggle. The small tortoiseshell cat that Lucas always looked for on his way to school. When they had first moved in, he had watched a cartoon about cats who liked to play with string, and the following morning he had tugged at the thread on his blazer sleeve until he had unravelled enough to dangle for the little cat, shrieking and running away when Wiggle batted at the thread with her little paws, over and over again, until Sam had shouted at him for making them late for school, grabbing his hand and dragging him away from the house and towards the bus stop, the little cat trailing at his heels, swiping at his laces and making leaps for his sleeve.

"Yes, yes of course. Hang on."

"Be quick!" The girl said, as her mother called her name again, more irritably this time.

"Here, here. She handed her a small 500ml bottle of water, and the girl hugged it to her chest, trying to conceal it with her arms as she padded back down the row of houses to her mother.

By Friday morning, with rain forecast over the weekend, the water was back on. The temperature had cooled by a few degrees. The shelter-in-place was lifted. *Checkers will be resuming normal duty.* No-one really knew what *normal duty* was meant to be. It seemed to be arbitrary, ever-growing, reactive. Initially commissioned by OffSet to check and enforce carbon counting through spot-checks, and still ostensibly doing so; but the more of the population became Counters - and thus automatically monitored - the less significant this part of their role seemed to be. *Particularly as it's all the rich people left for them to track.* She thought bitterly. *And they can be trusted to enter their numbers honestly, can't they. Easier to be honest when you're not fighting to put food on the table. Not that the politicians can use that excuse.*

She decided to visit her mother. She refilled the bath before she left, pulling down her blinds and double bolting the door behind her. She wasn't sure why, but paranoia prickled her skin.

Out on the main streets, fox corpses slumped in gutters. One had died with its paw stretched down the grill of a drain. When she closed her eyes, the vignette of its final desperate attempt to reach water blazed against the red of her eyelids, the horror etched into her memory. For the first time in well over a year, she scooped her son up to carry him, pressing his face into her neck so he wouldn't see. The road was littered with the frail bodies of birds, some perfectly formed, others flattened by passing cars, tiny skeletons and feathers and beaks ground into the scorching tarmac. A mother and baby badger, driven out of hiding by their thirst, lay in the bus stop. A crow pecked at the sightless eye-sockets of the cub, whilst its mother nudged at its small body with her blistered snout, unable to raise her body from the floor to run away as Sam and Lucas approached.

"Lu, I want you to look at this picture." She set him down facing an advertisement for a theme park at the bus stop. Someone had graffitied *ACAB* - 'all checkers are bastards' - across it in black paint but it didn't obscure the illustration so much that she couldn't use it for her purpose. "How many people can you count in the picture? Don't miss any out. Be extra careful, count them twice."

"Should I count the ones on the big dragon ride?"

"Yes, yes, all of them. Keep checking until I tell you to stop." Sweat streamed down her spine and the damp waistband of her shorts and the straps of her bra itched as her skin protested the weight of clothing in the heat. She searched around her for something to use and found a discarded coffee cup on the bench of the bus stop. She tore downwards an inch from the lip, and then parallel to the rim in a circle, so that she was left with a shallow cup, half of the original height. She took one of the bottles of water from her backpack, and poured some in, trying not to look at the ants crawling into the side of the cub's mouth. She crouched next to the mother, and placed the small paper cup of water beside her head. She continued to nudge at her baby. Sam dipped her finger in the water, and then shook a few drops onto the badger's snout. It jerked its head towards her, looking around for the source of the water. She moved the cup closer, so that it was pressing against her whiskers.

"Thirty-two Mumma. And twelve trees, and four bins."

"Four bins! That's a lot of bins for one picture." Her artificially cheery tone grated against her tongue. "Well done Lucas!"

"Can I turn around now? I haven't seen a badger before."

"This badger isn't feeling well. Come on."

She scooped him back up and moved away from the bus stop.

"How many rides were there in the photo? Which was your favourite?"

"The red one. What's wrong with the badger?

"Maybe one day we can go and ride on the red one, what do you think?"

"Then there will be thirty-four people in the park."

"Such good maths Lu! Such a clever boy."

They turned off the high street and onto the side road where her mum lived. Huge purple posters covered the walls under the railway bridge and circled lampposts in the carpark of the DIY store, lime font screaming denouncements. *END OFFSET. ENOUGH FOR ALL.* Evidence that someone had been out and about after all, under the cover of the intolerable heat. Uniformed Checkers were already circling, air-conditioned patrol cars crawling from post to post, officers exiting their cool cocoons to tear down the posters, purple shreds fluttering in their wake. Sam inspected one of the posters on a boarded-up shop window as she passed, careful not to draw attention by turning her head or slowing her pace. A small logo in the bottom-right corner with a picture of an old-fashioned weight scales and a stick figure standing in each of the suspended trays, and under it, in capital letters, the words: *EQUAL NOT NEUTRAL.*

"Nonsense Sam." Her mum set down two cups of tea, fishing the bag out of Sam's and adding it to her own as she always did, steeping it in the water until it resembled ink rather than tea. "Not a chance would the government do that."

"There were checkers stood at the ends of the streets leading into the OffSet estate."

"And? Making sure people are safe, is all."

Sam sipped on her tea, inhaling the top layer in a loud rasp of droplets because it was too hot to drink in a unified gulp.

"What's got into your head, making you all paranoid. Did anyone tell you you couldn't leave?"

"Not exactly, but it was just a feeling."

"A feeling. Honestly Sammy. I'd make you a foil hat if I had some to waste."

"I want a foil hat! Like a robot. Or a spaceman!" Lucas piped up from the floor, where he was lining up Lego bricks by colour and size.

"You're supposed to stack them on top of each other Lu. Here - oof, my knees - I'll show you."

"NO." Lucas screamed, shuffling around his bricks to block his grandmother from touching them as she clambered laboriously to the floor.

"Lucas! Don't shriek like that!" Sam shouted, exactly as she had read she shouldn't. Don't fight fire with fire, de-escalate, teach them to handle their emotions calmly. The manuals were much easier to read than to act upon.

"Don't touch! Don't touch my bricks!"

"Alright, alright, calm down, I won't touch your bricks." Sam's mother sat back and put her hands under his armpits from behind to pull him onto her lap for a hug. He twisted away from her, his body tense with fury.

"Don't touch me! Get OFF!"

One of his angry elbows connected with his grandmother's cheekbone, just below the eye. She recoiled and covered it with her hands, shocked.
"Lucas! Say sorry to your gammy!"
"NO!" His face seemed to implode, as if sight and sound and smell and touch were crushing him from all sides and he didn't know how to escape. He jumped to his feet and ran from the room, as if to escape from his own senses, fleeing the heat and the fear and frustration of the last few days, built up like flammable gas and ignited by the unsolicited advice from his grandmother. He slammed the door, and Sam could hear him wailing in the next-door room. Her mother sat on the floor, head in her hands. Sam stayed where she was, in the threadbare armchair, motionless, hardly blinking, so that her eyes blurred and burned in protest to the prolonged exposure to the dry air. And Lucas's wails rasped and strained, exhausting themselves into sad little coughs and low moans, and eventually into silence.

She carried him back to the house later that evening, breathing through his mouth as he slept, nose blocked with the remnants of misery, slumped over her shoulder. As she turned into the end of their street, a green-clad checker stepped into her path. "Excuse me, good evening ma'am. May I ask where you are heading? It's late."
"Not a crime, is it, being out late?" She hissed, bouncing her knees gently to rock Lucas through the exchange without waking him.
"Not at all ma'am. Just late to be walking into the estate, is all."

She heaved Lucas up and onto her other side so that his head no longer obscured the disc on her neck. "I live here, so I don't suppose you're too worried about me?"
"No need for attitude." His demeanour had clouded, syllables clipping. "Just doing my job. Move along."

The little girl from next door, Hannah, was sitting on the low front wall of the next-door house, kicking at the decaying brick with; the backs of her heels, feet not quite reaching the ground. Her face was streaked with dirt and tears. "Hannah? What are you doing out here? It's dark. Where's your mum and dad?"
"Mum took Wiggle's water."
"What?" It took her a moment to process. "Well the water is back on now. Yours is back on too, isn't it?"
"Yes, but-". Hannah looked up at her. She wasn't making any sound, but tears followed the channels they had drawn in the dust on her cheeks in a continual stream. She pointed at a shoebox on the wall beside her. Sam felt her heart thud, one big pulse against her sternum, and shock radiated from it, along her limbs, into her throat.

Chapter 8

Alice

It was sunny, the morning of Richard and Francesca's wedding. Durham University friends; mainly on Andrew's side, whom Alice had only seen a handful of times since, at reunion drinks events in the City. The remnants of the unbearable heat lingered, along with pruny fingers and small pieces of pink foam from the pool noodles strewn about the house, concentrated in guilty piles around Maisie's bed. The faint smell of chlorine emanated from towels slung on bannisters and repurposed radiators. In weather like this, it was hard to understand why radiators existed. How could anyone want to make the air hotter? She didn't think being cold had ever been as bad as being hot. Humans are not good at empathising with the future versions of themselves, or even with their past iterations through which they have already literally lived. Right now, she couldn't imagine a scenario in which she would ever want to be warmer. Tommy had been difficult to extract from the pool. He stomped his foot as she towelled his legs, folded his arms when she tried to tease them into shirt sleeves. "Come *on* Thomas! We're late!"

Andrew was sitting up at the island in the kitchen, wearing a light navy suit, and the polka dot tie her mother had given him their first Christmas together. She glared at him.

"Need a hand? Come on Tommo, behave yourself." He made to stand up from the counter.

"Oh, daddy is going to give us a *hand* now, is he? How very generous." Sarcasm and sweat dripped from her. She didn't want to leave the pool either. Although the peak was behind them, the heat was still unseasonable (if the traditional notion of *seasons* could not be considered obsolete). Oppressive, like the tailored seams of wedding attire.

"Sorry, I was in a world of my own. Here, you go upstairs and finish getting ready, I'll deal with this little tyke." He grabbed hold of Tommy's wrists and pulled them up and over his head, swinging him into the air so that he squealed, and forgot to be cross. It felt personal to Alice. Like he had made her look bad by failing to rise to her dig, and as though Tommy were taking sides. She already regretted her passive aggression. *Just ask me, if you need something.* He would always say. *Just tell me, I'm not a mind-reader.* Which sounded perfectly reasonable, on the surface. Except that was just it; she needed him to know, to take charge sometimes. *Initiative.* That was one of the key attributes he'd had to demonstrate in his promotion application. *'Easy!'* he'd exclaimed, laptop keys tapping out the rhythm of all the times when he had done at work what he seemed incapable of at home.

Florals and stripes vied for shade with a British decorum. Suede wedges and shiny Oxfords shuffled imperceptibly, torsos leant into the shadow of a parasol, feet maintaining a civilised distance from their neighbours. Tommy was sitting under a trestle table, neat rows of champagne above him. Small talk was batted away by fanning hands. Alice stood next to Sophie with their husbands, in a circle comprised of men she recognised as Andrew's old

University tennis team, their partners hovering like Remoras.

"It's a free bar, of course. *Free* free." Francesca's mother was explaining "That's very generous." She heard Andrew say.

"Hideously expensive, if it isn't crude to say so."

"How is it even possible? So much food and drink, the transport-"

"The fireworks!" Francesca's mother added eagerly. "Don't underestimate the carbon cost of those!"

"Don't ruin the surprise mum!" Francesca shimmied a gap between her mother. "God it's hot. Regretting all this lace!" She tugged at her sleeves.

"You look beautiful Fran." Alice offered. "This is all incredible, honestly." She gestured around at the weaving trays of canapes and teetering cocktails.

"Thank god, honestly, planning a wedding is a right pain in the-"

"Yes, thank you Francesca. Your friends were just asking how we managed it all, carbon-wise." *Were we?* Thought Alice. Sophie scuffed the side of her foot ever so slightly, conveying similar bemusement.

"It was an OffSet one-off bundle!" The mother announced, as if revealing a particularly mysterious answer in a pub quiz. "The venue organises it all. Very clever really. You just tell them your menu choices, entertainment, all of that malarkey, and they tot it all for you. I mean let's face it, you could *probably* get away with fudging the numbers a bit. Not that we would, obviously."

"Didn't you want to put that we were serving chicken instead of beef mum?"

"Har, har, very amusing Francesca. Beef for two hundred and fifty people is no small output, I can tell you. But that was just a joke. Anyway, it's lovely to see all of these old faces." She beamed around at them, mother-of-the-bride radiating out at each of them in turn. "So many people Richard and Francesca are friends with. Thank you all for coming. Cheers!" She clinked her way out of the group and beelined for the next shady cluster.

"I actually *did* put the beef down as chicken." Confessed Fran. "I know it's bad. It just feels counterintuitive to volunteer the information, you know? No-one's really checking."

"My cousin's friend actually got busted." Joey, whom Alice recognised from Andrew's tennis club, chipped in. "Checkers showed up at his daughter's christening. This friend was hosting a free-for-all too, but hadn't bought a bundle or anything. Just bought in all the food and drink off-record, never put it through their tracker. Checkers showed up at the christening and asked to see their account, cross-referenced it with the food."

"What happened to him?"

"Hefty fine I think. And an official warning. You get one life - if you get caught twice, they make you get a disc."

"Like a counter?" Alice asked, curious in spite of herself.

"Just the same." Joey patted the smooth side of his neck. "You've shown you can't be trusted on the honesty system."

"No-one is going to risk being caught twice then are they!" Andrew exclaimed. "That's barbaric. The return of corporal punishment!"

"Thou can take my money, but thou shall not brand me like a steer!"

The conversation had taken on the excessively jokey tone of people hiding entitlement under the cover of irony. The laughter smelled of champagne. Alice knew most of the men individually, but the effect of the pack regressed them, spurred them into caricatured versions of themselves.

"My godmother knew someone who threw a fortieth and bought all the stuff on the first day of the month, planning to pass on the output to the guests at the event, only none of them showed up. She'd used up her whole month's quota just to find she had no friends. Luckily OffSet let her take a loan against the following month. She was walking and eating tofu for weeks!"

"I'm going for more champagne." Alice cut in. "Who wants some?"

"I'll help." Sophie volunteered, and they set off across the grass, braving the early-afternoon sun. "I'd rather be cooked than listen to any more of their crap."

It was almost midnight by the time they left, bright pink strips of sunburn across their foreheads, just below the hairline. Andrew's tie was loosened and his sleeves rolled up, and the smell of a long day in forty degree heat permeated the taxi.

"We were joking Al! God, you can't have thought any of that was serious."

Tommy sat in the front seat; a rare treat. He poked his fingers into the Aircon vents and twiddled the volume button on the radio, up and down, up and down, so that it sounded as if the presenter were shouting through a window that kept being opened and closed. Alice and Andrew sat in the back.

'No, of course not, but it was just… in poor taste. I can't explain it. It's like it was said as a joke so that no one could judge you for it, but deep down you all kind of stood by what you were saying."

"Do you really think that little of me?" This coincided with the Radio 1 presenter's voice being spun to mute, so that the question echoed plaintively around the car, comparatively magnified. The driver shuffled, cleared his throat, adjusted his air freshener on its vent. Alice looked at Andrew, wondering how to respond.

"You're both little, that's why you're in the back, and I'm in the front!" Tommy giggled, and twizzled the dial back to max.

"It's not that." She said finally. "It just felt gross. Even to joke." She knew it was possible she was feeling bad about signing up to OffSet and projecting a little bit.

"Is it possible you're feeling bad about signing up to OffSet, and projecting a little bit?"

She glanced in the driver's rear-view mirror to make sure he couldn't see her face then turned and glared at Andrew. "Fuck you." She mouthed.

On Monday morning, the home system announced someone at the front door. *Shit*. She had forgotten that today was one of Sam's days working. In the five months since she had been employed there, Alice had managed to stay out of her way, other than a brief meeting to give her a key on her first day. She found it uncomfortable, skirting around someone cleaning up after her. She was fine when she couldn't see it, but lifting up her legs to let someone hoover underneath her - literally or metaphorically - was a step too far. She jumped to her feet, wiping a wet ring on the table from her tea mug with her sleeve, and gathering up the OffSet paperwork from where it was still scattered on the footrest, shoving it under the lid of the piano as the door opened. Sam was taller than Alice remembered, older. The image in her mind had been practically a teenager. She was wearing leggings that sagged a little at the knees, and a bright orange turtleneck jumper that Alice actually thought was pretty cool. She was wearing socks inside the sort of shoes that are halfway between slippers and flip flops - fluffy but open-toed.

"Oh! Alice! Hi!"

"Hey Sam. Sorry, I forgot you were in today."

"No, no, don't be sorry! It's your house!"

I should probably be the one to clean it then, shouldn't I? Alice filled in silently, though the sentiment was not detectable in the other woman's tone.

"Would you like a cup of tea?" She offered. "I'm making one for myself anyway."

"Oh, yes please, lovely, thanks."

"How do you have it?"

"Milk no sugar please. Oh, or, black, actually. Black is good."

"Milk is fine, we have lots. You don't need to worry."

She'd wanted to give Sam the box of clothes that Tommy had grown out of, but as they stood across from one other she worried about how the offer would be received. She ran through the best way to introduce the conversation in her head. In the end she settled on; "by the way, there are some clothes upstairs, nothing special, just some bits, if he wants them. I don't know if your boy is smaller than Tom, he's quite big for his age. No pressure, you might think it's a load of rubbish. Feel free to leave whatever you want. Or take it, sell it, give it away. It was just going in the bin. Not that it's bad stuff, some of it's quite nice actually. I'd definitely still have Tom in it, if he hadn't shot up over the last few months. Ankle swingers. Anyway, have a look." Smooth, concise. Really casual. *Not.* Sam caught her eye, and the corners of her mouth seemed to twitch a bit. "Sorry. I didn't know if you'd think it was rude of me to offer." She felt warmth in her cheeks.

"Yes, so rude to give me free things. How dare you." It took a moment before she realised Sam was being sarcastic. Another moment to decide if she was offended or relieved. It was a relief to choose to be relieved. She felt like their relationship had levelled up a bit, the formality of the power imbalance softened. She snorted, and the other woman began to laugh too. "Thank you Alice. I'd be glad to take them."

"Good." She paused, feeling a wave of loneliness that often comes after a brief connection. "Shall we sit and have this tea? Then I'll make myself scarce."

"What, *never*?" They were still sitting on the sofa. Cold dregs in matching mugs marked the passage of time between them.

"Nope, never. Never ever shouts, or even raises his voice, really. He's pretty relaxed."

"Oh, must be nice."

"I suppose. Sometimes… Oh I really shouldn't say this, it sounds crazy, but sometimes I wish he *would* shout at me. Just to mix things up a bit."

Alice couldn't believe she was talking to her cleaner about her marital issues. She wondered what the *gate mums* would think. But it was worrying about what they would think that made her hesitate to talk to them frankly about her relationship with Andrew in the first place. Andrew, the keeper, mender of showers. The need to justify her life, her choices, her relationship, jostling in the unspoken currents of social competition that even she was not consciously aware of - that she was both victim to, and also perpetuated - was exhausting, and kept her friendships superficial. Although it might have appeared flattering, the ease with which she was opening up to Sam was actually a little insulting: she felt little need to strut or rose-tint, so sure was she of her social superiority. Luckily these truths are too ingrained in the psychological infrastructure of humans that even those governed by them don't perceive them, or Alice would have clammed up in shame.

"I dunno, it sounds pretty great. Someone who never shouts. I know I'm supposed to just agree with you and say that that sounds bad, but, like, it doesn't really?"

"No, I know. It sounds perfect, when you just condense it into a summary like that. But when you think about it day in, day out… it's just not natural. It feels like he's sort of… given up? When a bit of shouting, a bit of confrontation, could actually deal with something, but instead he sort of shuts down, skims around it."

And that was it, she realised. Like when you find a big mat of knots in the back of your hair and you just can't be bothered, so you just brush the strands over the top, removing the teeth of the brush each time you feel resistance and re-joining below the problem area. But then the mat gets bigger, and you have to use a conditioning treatment or just cut the whole lot out. And a conditioning treatment wouldn't really do much to fix a marriage. She had never really realised why it bothered her until now, the simmering, the unspoken words, the calm.

"Yeah, I guess that makes sense." Sam shrugged, and reached forwards to pick up both mugs, her exit signalling that it made no sense to her at all.

"Sorry, God, listen to the state of me. Tragic. Sorry. Just still finish at your normal time obviously, don't worry if you don't get to all the rooms. We will still pay you." And just like that, the barrier went back up.

Later, she would replay the whole conversation with Sam in her head, mortified at her candidness, at how much airtime she had monopolised, analysing it like the percentage of possession in a football match.

"Oh, sorry Alice - do you mind, for the milk?' Sam came into the kitchen at the end of her shift, holding out her phone.

"Sorry, of course, no, erm, how does this work again?" She stalled, ashamed of her cluelessness. She'd assumed that Sam would just not program in the spend for the milk she had given her.

"It goes on automatically for us." Sam clarified, reading her thoughts. "'Cos of the disc. We have to claim the points back, from someone else's, if they're saying they'll cover them for us."

Almost like they don't trust you.

"It's almost like they don't trust us!" Sam laughed, and Alice had the exposing sensation of someone overhearing her gossiping about them.

"Oh right, of course, I should have thought. Here." She paused. "And I'm sure it's not that. The trust thing. It's just logistics."

She pressed her thumbprint to Sam's phone screen and watched the small red nutri-counter bar rise ever so slightly, as the imaginary points winged their way over to her. She imagined them arriving; rattling around, unaccustomed to so much space. Lonely, hardly touching the sides.

"Thanks." Sam took her phone back and pocketed it, and Alice noticed that she hadn't bothered to point out the obvious absence of logic in her dismissal of what she'd said about trust. "Sorry, I hate to have asked. I know it's basically nothing. Just, well, you know. Tight month."

"That was definitely my bad." Alice said firmly. "Much less than I owe you for the free therapy session I just made you give me."

They both laughed, and the awkwardness dissipated again, still hovering at the periphery, ready to reform at a moment's faux pas.

Chapter 9

Sam

It was dark as the shutter clattered closed, and a faint buzzing resumed as the first masking bubble resumed behind her. When the light turned green she stepped forwards out of the isolation chamber and the second bubble re-sealed itself, a continuous barrier to the outside. The music was loud, the bass thudding mercilessly. Maya was standing waiting for her, no longer in her grounds-woman's uniform, but in tight leather shorts and a baggy sequinned top, grinning.

"Welcome to the dark side! So glad you came. Yay!"

"It's loud in here! God! Not sure I've been anywhere this loud since I was about twenty-five!"

"What did you say?" Maya shouted back, pointing at her ear and pulling a face.

"I said-" Sam raised her voice further, cupping her mouth, shouting directly into Maya's ear- "I'm not sure I've been anywhere this loud-"

"Yes Sam I heard you, it was a joke! Fuck!" She jabbed a finger into her ear canal and rubbed it theatrically.

"It's so we can't hear the beeping." A man at the bar in a flowery shirt and brown chinos pointed at her neck, and then at his, which was flashing in protest at the temporary authority vacuum in which it found itself in the EatEasy. The smell of meat was giddying. Servers carried huge skewers of charred flesh from table to table, carving it onto plates. She'd never been a huge meat-eater, except for chicken, but there was something in its unavailability that lured her in, like a forbidden packet of sweets on the top shelf calls out to a rebellious child. She wanted to know that she still could, if she wanted to. She was still in control. The entry had cost her a quarter of her monthly payout from OffSet, but the victory danced in her stomach.

"I'm just going to go and finish talking to Daniel, over there." Maya pointed over at a slight, blonde man - maybe even a teenager - sitting on one of the leather sofas in the corner with a group of men and women of a range of ages, who seemed to be having a conversation that looked far too involved for the atmosphere. "Get me a drink will you? Whatever you're having."

Sam went over to the bar, over which hung a sign reading *LET'S GET WASTING* and ordered a couple of *fossil fuel*s from the barman, a young guy with blond curly hair in a ponytail at the nape of his neck, split ends illuminated by his flashing green disc. "I can see you staring honey." He said in a nasal voice, and flicked his hair theatrically, prancing over with her change.

"Sorry. I'm not used to seeing so many not covered up."

"It's a badge of honour here honey." He winked at her.

"Straw?" He rattled the box at her. She took one, and he poked two more into her drink, ramming them between the ice cubes.

"Thanks."

"First time?" Flowery shirt man hopped his stool towards her.

"Is it obvious?"

"No one orders the *fossil fuel* a second time. It's lethal." He raised his eyebrows towards her drink, straws bobbing.

"How does this work with the food?"

"Just place the card green side up and they'll keep bringing over the meat. Flip it when you're done. Remember you can't take any outside through the bubble, because it'll still get picked up by your disc. Even if you wrap it in foil and hide it in your shoes."

"You sound like you're talking from experience."

"Let's just say it didn't let me eat anything at all for a week." He pointed at his neck. "Electric shocks every time I tried."

"They told me those never actually get used!"

"Probably the first time anyone tried to smuggle a t-bone in their trainer."

She laughed - "no way was it a t-bone" - and took a long sip of her drink. Raw alcohol settled on top of his words, *electric shocks*, dissolving the discomfort.

"Alright, maybe a small strip of sirloin. But why ruin a good story with the truth?"

"I never used to even use straws you know. Before this." The shoulder nearest to her disc jerked involuntarily.

"Oh I'm with you. Pointless things. But you gotta get your money's worth here."

"I'm not sure that would be possible with five thousand straws, but I get your point."

"It's weird, I actually used to care about all this green stuff a lot. I would have cringed at the thought of wasting straws. Imagining them lobotomising a turtle, just to spare me a few mint leaves in my teeth. But somehow when you're being told you're not allowed, you forget the real reason you were doing something and it all becomes about getting away with it, their rules." He sipped at his drink, digging the straw down to the bottom to reach the last dregs. "Like when someone forces you to do revision and you start only caring about

84

convincing them you're doing it, and forget that a couple of GCSEs might not be a bad thing." He slid the now-empty glass away from him and raised a hand, signalling the barman. "And that, ladies and gentlemen, is how I ended up as a Counter. You don't get a good job with shit exam results. Another drink?"

"You talk a lot don't you. Yes please. I'll get the one after this. But something different, you choose."

"What did I tell you?" He looked at her drink and pulled a face of disgust, as though the ethanol burn of undiluted spirits were in his mouth, not his memory. "I recommend the *melting caps.*"

"*Melting caps?* Really going for it, aren't they."

"Oh yes, it's not subtle. But it has ice cream in it. And Baileys."

"God I miss ice cream!"

"I'll take that as a yes."

The server approached with a skewer of beef and a skewer of chicken wings.

"Say when." The girl instructed as she began to slide wings down the skewer and onto Sam's plate. She nodded as each one hit the plate to indicate that the server should continue.

"Never say *when.*" Flowery shirt whispered to her as he handed her the drink.

"You don't sound like you'd be here." She said, running a finger around the inside of the glass to collect up the creamy remnants of the cocktail.

"And what do people who'd be here sound like, exactly?"

"Well they don't use words like… what was it you said about the turtle and the straw?"

He laughed self-consciously. "*Lobotomise.* I went to a twatty public school. *Money down the drain*, my parents called it."

"Seems like they've got a point if you've ended up selling your right to eat eggs for a couple of quid."

"Never liked eggs anyway. Chicken periods - gross." She pulled a face. "You know what I mean. So you went to a posh school and didn't do any work, and then what? Parents disowned you?" she teased.

His expression seemed to mattify, the previous glow dulled. He sipped his drink.

"Oh. They actually disowned you? Shit, sorry."

"It's alright. It's pretty standard to put your foot in it after a fossil fuel. But yeah, sort of. It's a long story."

"I'm sorry. Here, do you want this one? I bought it for my friend, Maya, but I don't know where she…" She looked around for a sign of her, then pushed the glass along the bar towards him, leaving a wake of glacier-melt. "Peace offering?"

"It's all good. Generous as that is." He raised an eyebrow at the offending glass. "That's classic Maya. She's always bouncing around talking to people. Too much energy. She definitely doesn't need one of those." He thrust a thumb at the glass.

"Oh, you know Maya?"

"Yeah, I know the Ashtons. Her and her brother, Daniel. He was mates with my sister, before she decided she was too much of a posh twat. Pre-*disownment*, or whatever you want to call it."

Sam grimaced. "Yeah, sorry. Must be rough."

"Ah, I'm only where I would have been if I hadn't been born to filthy rich parents anyway."

"Yeah, but I reckon it's worse, having money and then losing it."

"That's what my parents used to say. He put on an exaggerated plummy tone. *It'll be worse for you, you know. You're not meant for that kind of life. Those people are used to it.*"

She snorted. "Well you can tell her that *those people* don't ever get used to not being able to buy their kid a birthday present, and we definitely don't get used to not being allowed to heat the house or drive a car."

"I would pass on your testimony, but they disowned me, remember?"

"Oh shit yeah. Sorry, - what was your name?"

"Mark."

"Hi Mark. Sam." She offered a hand self-consciously.

"Ooooh, you're on *hand-shaking* terms already." Maya's words barged between them. "You move fast Sam." She made a clawing gesture in the air and ran her tongue across her top teeth in mock seduction. "I've only been gone - what? 15 minutes?"

"I bought you a drink", Sam said, "but all the ice has melted."

Maya picked up the glass and drank it down in three long gulps. "I prefer it like that. Easier to drink. Efficient!" She slammed the glass down on the bar.

"Sorry for leaving you for so long Sam, but I can see Mark has been keeping you company. Not too bored, I hope?"

"I -" Sam faltered, sidelined by their obvious familiarity. Mark intervened.

"Ignore her. She's always like this."

Maya stuck her middle finger up at him and linked an arm through Sam's. "Come and dance!"

The light outside her bedroom window was still a navy-grey colour when loud thumping noise jolted her awake the next morning. She opened one eye and saw a flowery shirt in a heap on the floor. The thumping noise grew louder. Flowery shirtless - no, Mark - groaned and rolled over.

"What is that?"

"Front door. Sorry."

He pulled the duvet up around his ears.

"Make it stop."

She pulled on her dressing gown and stepped between discarded items of clothing, wondering who it could be. Lucas was with her mum, and she wasn't due to pick him up until 2pm. And she hadn't received deliveries before signing up, let alone now.

"Hang on!" The carpet felt so cold on her bare feet that she couldn't tell if it was actually damp. The heat of the EatEasy felt like a distant dream. She had some beef stuck in one of her molars.

"Did you get my text?" He demanded as soon as she opened the door.

"What text? I haven't checked my phone. I've been asleep." She noticed the immediate defensiveness in her voice. *You don't need to explain yourself.* She heard her mother's words in her head. She scraped at her tooth with her tongue.

"I sent it two days ago. Saying I miss you? Not to mention sending you those points."

"I'm sending those back. We don't need them."

He surveyed the small snapshot of her flat that he could see behind her.

"Sure. You have makeup all over your face by the way."

"Yeah, that's usually where it goes."

"Are you going to invite me in?"

"No Cal, I'm not. I was asleep, and it's not your day for Lucas so I don't know why you're here." She held the barely open door like a flat shield between them, and hoped Mark wouldn't materialise, with, and definitely not without, his flowery shirt.

There was a pause where his resolve seemed to sway between two approaches in response to her defiance; carrot or stick. In the end, he chose the carrot, cajoling, to reel her back in as he had so many times when he had sensed her strengthening.

"Sorry Sam. It's just I miss you, like I said. Don't send the points back. It was a gift. For Lu. And for you. Look, why don't I come in for a cuppa?"

"Want to come and use up your precious points on the kettle do you?"

"Jesus, Sam, are you that tight?"

"Yes, Caleb. Things are that tight. I need *a lot* of money, for this assessment for Lucas. The waiting times if I don't pay were going to be over a year. They're holding him back in school. He's a year behind already. So yes, I sold as many points as I could possibly spare. So no, you can't have a cup of tea."

He looked shocked at her outburst. She had only ever been passive around him, a product of his aggression, taking up only the tiny space that he left for her once he had filled the rest.

He held up his hands in surrender, as if the exchange had been in jest, undermining her win. "Okay, okay, keep your hair on. Take your makeup off though. You look like a panda. Still cute though."

"Please just leave Cal."

"I'm sorry. I just want to talk. Please." His tone had changed again and he looked like a child. She felt her resolve flicker. She knew that his regret for his outbursts was as immediate as his anger. It always was. He too was a victim of his anger, and as soon as the guilt came it felt as though he was transferred to her side of the fence, united against a common evil. "Please Sam. I just want us to go back to normal."

"So much so that you can't even stay off the drink? It clearly wasn't worth that much to you."

"It would be easier if I was with you. I need you."

He started to cry. She felt squeezed, trapped. She couldn't deal with him now, not with another man in her bed. A man on either side of her, blocking her escape routes. Frying pan in front, fire behind. She heard a noise in the corridor behind her. She shut the front door.

Chapter 10

Alice

As Alice was waiting to cross at the lights she could hear screaming coming from near the cafe on the green. A crowd of people had gathered, some crouching, others videoing on their mobile phones. She hated people who felt the need to do that, yet simultaneously always had to resist the urge to do so herself. Maybe Andrew had a point, when he said that the most aggravating thing to see someone else do is the thing that deep-down, you wish you could do yourself. As she reached the other side of the street, she paused. The cafe was not *technically* en route to the hairdresser, but it could also be incorporated into a roundabout way, at a stretch, without having to turn directly back on herself. She could just about justify the detour.

In the doorway to the cafe, on the pockmarked rubber matting, lay a man, panting, clutching at the neck of his t-shirt with one hand as if the light cotton were suffocating him, the other clawing at the skin of his throat. The screaming was coming from a woman who stood above him, casting wildly around as if a solution might be found in the vicinity. Two other men were kneeling over the prostrate man.
"Anaphylaxis, apparently," someone in the group of people filled her in, "One of those men says he's an off-duty doctor."
"Has someone called an ambulance?" A newcomer cried.

"They won't come." The woman looked deranged, frenzied. "They won't come." She began to sob; dry, angry, panicked heaves.

"Who won't come?" Alice demanded, pushing between a couple of teenage girls, the emergency replicated in miniature on each of their phone screens even as it unfolded in front of them. "I'll call an ambulance!"

"They won't send one! Fuck! I can't believe they actually won't send one!" The distraught woman bashed at the phone in her palm with her fist, as if she could punch right through to the emergency service call handlers who had now disconnected the call.

"What do you mean?" Alice demanded. "Of course they will." She pulled out her phone and called 999.

"999, which service do you need?"

"Ambulance.

"Connecting you now."

Alice felt her heart-rate slow slightly. *Of course* they would send an ambulance. This was exactly the call script that had played out when she'd had to call an ambulance for her great uncle on Christmas eve a few years ago.

"Ambulance service, what's your emergency?"

"Hi, yes, there's a man here. I think he's having an allergic reaction."

"Please could you tell me your location?"

"Yes, South London. The village green in Dulwich. Outside Roast. The coffeeshop."

"Please could you read out the victim's identification number? You'll find it on the home screen of his tracker. You won't need a passcode if you swipe up and follow the emergency access instructions."

"What? Can't you do that after you pick him up? We need the ambulance here right now!"

"Unfortunately this is procedure."

"Pass me his phone, quickly!" She jostled the shoulder of the off–duty doctor.

"Can you at least get the ambulance on its way while we do this?" She asked the voice on the phone.

"Unfortunately we cannot proceed with the call-out until we have this information."

"His phone! Pass me his phone!" She crouched and felt the man's pockets.

"I have his phone." The doctor stood up, so he could speak to Alice in a lowered voice. "There's no point. They're rejecting the request when we give them the ID." He pointed down at the man, whose rasping breaths were now interspersed with longer pauses, a semblance of calm, his eyelids half-closed. A small green disc was set into the skin amongst the hives on his neck. "They said he has an absolute-zero policy on vehicle transport."

"I'm sorry, how is that even possible? It can't mean for stuff like this!"

She stared down at the phone in her hand, the call still connected. She pressed it back to her ear. "You send an ambulance right now! Do you want this man's death on your conscience? There is no way this is what you're meant to do!"

"If you cannot provide the ID I am going to need to end the call, in order to open up the line for other callers. If he carries an EpiPen, please administer it now."

The other woman grabbed the phone from Alice and began to beg. "Please, please, you have to help us. Me and Matt are getting married next month. Please. He's only 29."

"An EpiPen. Does he have an EpiPen?" Alice grabbed the woman's upper arm, shaking her, trying to claw back her focus.

"No. No, he doesn't have one. He was waiting for the new refillable ones to come out. He can't have disposables. He gave up everything - *everything* - to try and get some extra money for the wedding." The woman fell to her knees and clutched at the man's shoulders, shouting his name in his face. Then she jumped to her feet and ran out into the road, waving her arms. Car horns blared, as their drivers swerved to avoid her. "Stop!" She shouted at them, her pleas barricaded by smooth glass of sealed windows. The man was no longer moving. His hands had fallen limp on his chest, which was now still. A car swerved around the woman in the middle of the road, into a blocked drain, and dirty water cascaded over the man's still body. A checker drone buzzed lazily above the scene, observing.

"It has to be strict, or there will always be exceptions, and then where do you draw the line?" Andrew looked up at her over the top of his laptop, perched on the white marble countertop of the island in the kitchen. She'd told him the whole story as soon as she came in the door, her shoes stained with the grey of drain water and her eyelids stained with the image of death. "I'm not saying what happened to the bloke was okay. It is obviously awful, and they need to make the policies more… I don't know, more nuanced. But there still have to be fixed rules, and there are always teething problems with these things."

"*Teething problems*?! Andrew, *teething problems* is a new restaurant forgetting to take your drinks order. *Teething*

94

problems is a train being delayed when they start running a new route. A man choking to death in the street because an ambulance won't come for him is… is-"

"Is what Al?" He stood up and put his arms around her. "What's happening to the planet is serious. Serious problems have serious consequences. They for sure need to iron things like this out, and they will. These things take time."

She shrugged him off angrily. "How would you have felt if that had been me, lying there in the street. Or Tommy?"

"But it wasn't. And it wouldn't have been. We would never give up essentials to save up for something as unimportant as a wedding."

Alice shrugged him off.

"Such a romantic you are."

"Oh come on, nothing romantic about risking your life for a champagne reception and a vodka luge."

"I didn't get the impression they were champagne-reception-and-vodka-luge kinds of people, but point made." She said dryly.

He held his hands up in surrender.

"It was a joke, Al. I'm trying to make you feel better. Sorry if I'm getting it wrong. I feel like I always get it wrong these days."

She sighed and picked at her nail varnish, buying time to decide whether she could be bothered to carry on being annoyed, whether she even stood by the standpoint that had caused her annoyance in the first place. It wasn't Andrew who had killed that man; who had refused to help him, who had written the laws. But she couldn't shout at those people. She felt angry at being confronted by the reality that she usually had the luxury of ignoring, and the anger and guilt needed an outlet. She knew it was hypocritical, that she was expecting him to be in exactly the same mindset as her at exactly the same time, when at other times she encouraged the jokes, even made them herself. Just as she was about to reach for him, offer an olive branch, Andrew sighed, and slid his laptop into his bag.

"I'll give you some space." He walked out of the room and up the stairs.

Alice had the sensation of narrowly missing a bus. She could have fixed it, could have apologised, but now the moment was gone, and now she was standing on her own, wondering when, or if, another would come along.

"To be honest, it doesn't sound like anything he said was out of order." They were back in their favourite spot, by the tinted window in the cafe at the gym, today having by-passed the exercise part and gone straight for smoothies. Sophie shrugged, apologetic for not validating her account of the conversation with Andrew. That was one of the best - and worst - things about Sophie. She told Alice when she was wrong. "But to be fair you had a pretty traumatic morning, so I'll give you a free pass this time." She waggled her finger, channelling a stern school-teacher. Alice rolled her eyes.

"Master of the get-out-of-jail-free passes now are you?"

"Master of everything. Obviously." She leant across and poked her straw into Alice's smoothie. "Yep. Still hate watermelon."

"Yep, just like the last hundred times you stuck your germy straw into my drink." Alice batted her hand away.

"Okay, but being serious for a minute." Concern etched Sophie's face. "It must have been pretty horrendous, seeing that."

Alice nodded, gathering her thoughts, determined to be honest with Sophie, but also with herself.

"I know this should make me more outraged at the system, and it does, of course. But honestly it also just scares me and makes me feel more like I want to do everything I can to protect myself, my family. God, that's awful isn't it."

"Yes."

"Thanks Sophie."

"Well it is! But it's normal too." Sophie shrugged.

"Normal just is awful, more often than not. Humans are selfish. Especially when they feel threatened. Feeling bad about being awful just makes you an honest awful person. So best of a bad bunch."

"Maybe. Or maybe *knowing* what you're doing is shit, but sticking with it, makes you the worst of all. You can't blame the people who are fully in denial, right?"

"Yes okay Alice, you're the worst person ever to exist. Happy? God, you just love to hate yourself don't you?"

Alice ignored her, saying instead "Oh! I saw my first checker drone today."

"Oh cool! Living in the future we are. What did it do?"

"Nothing really. Just sort of hovered and swooped. It was kind of creepy."

"Clever though. Soon no-one will have to work. I wish they could make a robot version of me to do all my chores."

"What, like drinking your smoothie for you? Or maybe getting its nails done so you don't have to?"

"That would actually be handy. I hate those appointments. All the small-talk. If it could have sex with Jack for me too, that would be perfect."

Alice snorted.

"What?" Sophie continued, laughing too. "Just imagine! It would never have a headache, never be on its period. He could download all his favourite sound-effects from his favourite porn sites, and away he goes."

The mundane simplicity of waiting at the school gates and seeing Tommy's face, as excited to see her today as he had been the first day she picked him up, and every day since, was like getting into a warm bath after a long cold run. She crouched to meet him, and he threw his arms around her neck, his bookbag bashing into her spine.

"Hello Tommo. How was your day?"

"I had sausages and beans for lunch, and Miss Lanter the dinner lady gave me three!"

"Lucky boy!"

He beamed at her, triumphant.

"How was your maths test?"

"Easy. I got twenty out of twenty."

"Well done my superstar." She squashed his cheeks between her hands and kissed his forehead. Sometimes she loved him so much that she had to overcome the urge to squeeze him too hard, shake him, overwhelmed with affection.

"Ben only got twelve, *and* he had to go home at lunchtime because something happened to his uncle."

"Oh no, poor Ben!" Alice took his bookbag and offered him a KitKat.

"He said his uncle is allergic to nuts, so maybe that's why. How can you be allergic to nuts? I know daddy is allergic to wasps, but nuts can't sting you, can they?"

Alice ruffled his head, outwardly reassuring, inwardly uneasy. The image of a man on the pavement taunted her. *Please, don't let that be Ben's uncle,* she thought, as if that would stop the man being anyone's uncle, anyone's brother or son, a social anomaly; as if that would mean no one would have been pulled out of school or work to receive the news. She felt heavy with confusion and contradiction, with self-preservation and guilt.

"Let's get ice-cream Tommo. And we can take some home for Lucas. He's at our house with his mum this afternoon."

"Who's Lucas?"

"You know, the little boy you gave some of your clothes to."

"My batman t-shirt?"

"Yes, your Batman t-shirt. What ice cream do you think he would like?"

"Chocolate."

"Do you reckon?"

"Of course."

He slipped his hand from hers and ran a few steps ahead, jumping cracks in the pavement, not questioning himself for a second, the world presented to him in black and white, and life all the more colourful for it.

Chocolate it is.

Chapter 11

Sam

The air was cool, the morning of the appointment. The kind of weather where the brightness of the sun contradicts the crispness of the air, so that you aren't quite sure how to dress. Jumper-round-the-waist weather, the extra layer pulled on and off with each transition between direct sunlight and shade. The coolness, unusual for September, was both a blessing and a curse. Lucas was calm, his atoms stilled after weeks of vibrating, ricocheting, in the oppressive heat. She never took his calmness for granted, the breathing room it afforded her, a long gap in a stream of cars to safely cross the road. But today, she needed him at his most broken. She needed to be taken seriously.

Six years earlier, heavily pregnant with Lucas, the hot water had gone. The boiler was throwing an error message that extensive YouTube troubleshooting and trawling through internet forums had diagnosed as an easy fix, but it wasn't playing ball. Cold showers, calls to the council, trying their suggestions, reporting back. Rinse, repeat. Eventually, they had sent out a boiler specialist. She had made him a cup of tea and taken him to the boiler cupboard in the hallway. *It really should be a simple case of restoring the factory settings,* he had said. *I know, and I followed the steps you gave me, but it just does this, look* she had said, confident, punctuating her words with the firm sequence of button presses that she could at this stage replicate without instructions. The green flashing light blinked on, smiled back at them; innocent, angelic. *I promise you that is exactly what I have done every time,* she had exclaimed, knowing he would claim to believe her, but would not. The lack of credibility that comes with being a woman casting doubt on the situation, and the situation in turn casting further doubt on the credibility of all women in the man's mind forever-more. Today, just today, she needed Lucas not to be on his best behaviour.

Advocate was what the websites told her to do. *Advocate* for her child. She hadn't really known what that meant, in practical terms, but it had seemed to involve two things: firstly, understanding more about learning needs and appropriate support than the specialists themselves, and secondly; money. What it always came down to. Acronyms flitted from the therapist's mouth, bounced off her head and drifted into the corners of the room, hanging suspended, unintelligible. She tried to track them, store them in their current form ready to unpick at a later stage, but they faded through the walls as new specialists, treatments, organisations, methods, documents, and potential diagnoses were proffered in a sequence of meaningless letters, crowding them out. In the corner of the room was the ubiquitous children's corner, faded foam mats joined together like giant puzzle pieces, small plastic chairs, and a few purpose-designed toys with no removable pieces that could be stolen or swallowed. The buzz of jargon was punctuated only by the click-clack of wooden beads as Lucas pushed them around a wire apparatus, backwards and forwards, backwards and forwards, only the yellow ones. She wished that she could sweep up the therapist's words and thread them onto one of the wires, locking them down, ready to sort through at her own pace. Dr Pederson had straight blonde hair and the faint hint of an accent, so subtle that it was hard to discern if it were foreign, or regional British. She was manically friendly, one of those people where you can sense volatility behind their smile, as if their excessive niceness were constantly on the verge of burning out. It was hard to put her finger on exactly what it was, but this type of person made Sam nervous, as though one wrong move would trigger a switch. A hint of impatience flashed in the woman's eyes at the end of each sentence. Sam felt dulled by contrast, sluggish, her brain slow to process.

"Fun night again on Saturday?" Maya clapped her on the shoulder when she opened the door to her later that afternoon, after she'd dropped Lucas off at school on the way back from the appointment.

It had been a long time since she had made a new friend; cleaning was not exactly a social job. But that's definitely what Maya was: a friend. It felt strange to have another adult to confide in. Someone who wasn't her mother, or her employer, or her ex. She and Maya had gone out four or five times now, sometimes with her brother, Daniel, and often with Mark too. She liked to feign indifference about the presence of the latter, but it was becoming increasingly difficult. They had even met up for the first time just the two of them the previous week; with neither alcohol nor Maya as a buffer. And it had been good - better than good - she had laughed, and felt listened to, and been relaxed.

On Saturday night they had gone to the EatEasy together for a second time, this time for a night hosted by Maya. The theme - *CheckMate* - was a fundraiser with donations and proceeds to victims of Checker brutality. A whole new world was opening up to Sam; one which painfully confronted her naivety and trust but was exhilarating too. She had trouble separating what was new information with what she was now sure she had always suspected, deep down. The whole experience was wrapped up in a Mark-shaped bow and carrying her along for the ride. Sometimes, she didn't recognise herself.

"Too fun. The next day was not." Sam mimed vomiting into a toilet.

"*Lovely*. It was pretty crazy stuff, eh? How did you find it?" Maya's usual self-assurance was replaced with the vulnerability of having exposed a part of her world, offering it up to be judged, like stripping off all of your clothes in front of a new partner and standing, goosebumps on your breasts, waiting for the verdict.

"It was amazing. I loved it. You nailed it." She mustered, compressing the doctor's prognosis into a dense icy layer in the bottom of her stomach to make space for the enthusiasm. Maya's face collapsed into a grin, and her trademark coolness returned.

"Good. Come in. I can't wait for you to meet Scoot. *Finally.*" She paused and looked back at her. "What's the matter? Not still hungover are you?"

After introductions, she sat at the table across from the two women and summarised the therapist's diagnoses. Maya's girlfriend, Scoot (as she had been introduced to Sam), had kind eyes, and a calm, teasing energy that complimented and corrected Maya's unfiltered brashness. Sam hadn't planned to confide in them so openly, or at least not straight away. It felt alien, the self-indulgence of it.

"... so, basically," Sam concluded, "she said there's some Autism, and maybe ADHD as well." Maya and Scoot were sharing a bottle of beer; they had given the other bottle to her. She exhaled, blowing air up over her top lip so that it lifted her fringe. "Honestly, I just don't know how to deal with this. It's too much." She put her head in her hands and slumped her weight into them, so that her elbows pressed into the vinyl of the tabletop and began to throb. Scoot and Maya's flat was small, and eclectically decorated. Colourful cushions and throws jarred with macrame wall-hangings and chic candles, centres hollowed from use. Sam pulled a large ceramic one towards her now and picked at the skimming of wax that coated the inside of the jar, avoiding looking at either of them. It was uncomfortable to complain. She wasn't used to it. But it was like she had started running down a steep hill; she couldn't stop now, even if she wanted to.

"I just never get a break." She burst out, slamming the candle against the table, flakes of wax scattering. "And it makes me feel like a shit mum, complaining about it because it's just him, isn't it, and it's not his fault. And I'm meant to say I wouldn't change him. But maybe I would. Just parts, you know? It would make both our lives easier."

"Who wants an easy life eh?" Maya shrugged. "Easy is dull."

"Yeah, real helpful Maya." Scoot nabbed the beer from her and took a swig. "Look," Maya said, more seriously, "it can feel like shit stuff keeps happening because when

104

stuff is already shit, then everything that comes next automatically gets coated in it."

"What does that even mean?" Scoot asked, trying to leverage another gulp while Maya tried to wrestle the bottle back off her, so that the neck of the bottle clipped her teeth.

"Ouch!" She passed Maya the bottle, who took a swig before continuing. "What it means is, right, imagine if your fancy lady friend, in the palace where you clean. Let's say this was her kid. Do you think it would be such a stress for her? Do you think she'd be having to starve herself, basically, to pay for him to see doctors, or whatever? Doubt it. She'd probably just get a whole team of them with a click of her fancy little fingers, poof," Maya mimed clicking and conjuring, "and if that didn't work, she could just get him a private tutor."

"To be fair, you wouldn't want to home-school Lucas anyway would you, even if you could afford a private tutor. Makes kids weird, that."

"It's not going to come to that anyway. He won't get kicked out of school. She's getting him help now, aren't you Sam."

"The worst part is," Sam pinched the scattered flakes of wax between her fingertips, working them into a ball, "the woman said his problems aren't even that bad, or they shouldn't be. He just can't regulate his emotions, and with a little bit of help he should be able to have a normal life. I just don't know if I can get him that help."

"You will, you're a trooper Sam. You'd do anything for the kid."

"I just don't know if I can sort it in time. They said he's on a waiting list. But they said it could be 3-6 months. And his school said he's on his final warning. They called me to collect him yesterday because he was caught going through the other kids' lunchboxes in the cloakroom."

"Who didn't try and nick some sweets at school when they had the chance?" Maya asked with a glint of pride.

"The kid that told on him," Sam went on, "Eleanor. He sits behind her in lessons. Later that day, he cut off one of her plaits with scissors."

"Oh, wow." The expressions of the two women opposite her mirrored one other: amused, appalled, impressed. In isolation, the incident was almost comical, but the resulting warning was not. *This behaviour cannot continue. It is affecting the other children. If something like this happens again, we will unfortunately have to look at a temporary exclusion.*

"He's just so stressed out, from all the changes. The stuff with his dad, not being able to eat some of his safe foods, being different from the other kids with all the new rules. All the walking everywhere. And then when it was so hot, it really tipped him over the edge."

"Can't blame the kid. It's a lot."

"I just feel like crap. Like I'm failing him. And if he gets kicked out of school it'll mess with his routine even more. He'll lose his shit." She drained the warm froth at the bottom of the bottle of beer and set it down. "And the woman I work for, Alice. She cut my hours already, and she's started talking to me when I'm meant to be working."

"Not *talking* to you. *Shocking.*"

Sam pulled a face. "I can't get everything done because she keeps going on and on. And her problems are just ridiculous. Her husband doesn't shout at her enough apparently. Honestly, I feel like a free therapist."

The words tasted different when she said them, to how they had sounded in the awkward warmth of Alice's living room. Spiteful. She regretted them.

"She sounds awful to be honest." Scoot pulled her scarf around her shoulders and her knees up to her chest, a small ball of a person huddled on the chair.

"Oh, she's not that bad. Just different to us, I guess."

"Yeah, bad different." Declared Maya. "Don't defend her. Some people need a reality check."

Sam thought of the bag of clothes that Alice had painstakingly sorted through and left for her, her desperation not to offend.

"She's generous, too, though. She gives me stuff for Lucas, and she-"

"Oh they are always like that. Generous in ways that suit them, to make them feel good. Playing the hero. Bitch."

Sam must have looked shocked at the bitterness in Maya's voice, because Scoot elbowed her in the ribs and said "give it a rest," before turning to Sam. "Maya hates the system. In case you hadn't noticed."

"I had, actually." Sam smiled, trying to lighten the air around them, which felt charged with tension suddenly. "But Alice isn't all that bad, really."

"Alice *is* the system. They all are. You sound like you've got - what's that thing where you've been kidnapped and you start caring about the maniac who abducted you?"

"Stockholm Syndrome," Scoot supplied, "God Maya, you're so dramatic."

"It's not dramatic. Or no more dramatic than how fucked up everything is."

Scoot placed a hand on Maya's upper arm. A subtle gesture, but one that conveyed a relationship's worth of empathy. "I know it is, M. I know." Maya leaned sideways so that their shoulders were touching, and rested her head in the crook of Scoot's neck.

Sam looked between the two women, feeling a flicker of envy, of loneliness. And something else: a sense of something unsaid.

Scoot answered the question without her needing to ask it.

"Maya's brother was *disappeared*."

"What? Daniel? Why didn't you say?"

"No, not Daniel." Maya sighed, and straightened back into her chair, taking back her bodyweight and story. "Not Daniel. There were - are - three of us. Billy. He's the youngest. He got into trouble with the Checkers last year. Stole some nappies for a friend of his who'd run out of allowance and got caught. Gave some of the Checkers who caught him some lip, and they roughed him up a bit. He came home with a black eye and a split lip, ranting about how he was going to bring down the whole system. You know what eighteen-year-old boys are like. Full of it. Anyway," she exhaled sadly, summoning Scoot's hand back to her thigh, "the next day, he left for work in the morning, only he never arrived. Haven't seen him since."

"So, she told you about her little bro, eh?"

She and Mark were walking along the side of the canal near Camden. She was very aware of her hand in his. The warm pressure points of contact. His thumb tracing gentle circles on her knuckle, as if to say *yep, still wanting to be here, still glad your hand is in mine.*

"Yeah. I had no idea. I didn't know stuff like that even happened."

"*Serious situations demand serious actions!*" His imitation of the Prime Minister - bumbling, toffee-tongued - was cruel in its precision. She laughed bitterly.

108

"I know, but, like… what do you think happened to him?"

"Who knows." He shrugged, but his imitation of nonchalance was less convincing. "I reckon they've decided to nip stuff like that in the bud, show people they mean business. Because what they expect of people, you know, the restrictions, they're only going to get worse. And the harder people are pushed, the harder they push back." He slipped his hand from hers and made a motion like squeezing a balloon, then an exploding noise with his mouth.

"I just don't understand how it could even be allowed to happen. In this day-and-age. It's just hard to believe it's possible, even though we literally know it has happened." He fed his fingers back through hers and pointed out a small garden area next to one of the canal boats, a makeshift barbeque and some furniture made from pallets, fairy lights.

"That's nice, look." He turned back to her. "It's happening all over. More and more reports."

"I haven't seen anything about it on the news."

His half-smile was laced with pity.

"Of course you haven't. It won't ever be in the news. But *the powers that be* are shook. It's like even they have gone into survival mode, and they're willing to risk things they wouldn't have before. And that includes looking out for their own when it comes to running the numbers and rationing stuff like water and power, even if that literally means people dying. And getting rid of people who challenge them."

"Do you think he's dead?"

"That's what we're trying to find out. It's difficult though. The secrecy. It's like we're in a war but we only have half as many guns, and on top of that we can only fire ours while they're not looking."

"Men and their guns." She said, but some of his words were like needles, and her hands tingled with adrenaline. "Who is *we*, though?" She pushed. "You and Maya? And Scoot? That doesn't sound like even half as many guns."

They had reached the lock in Camden, where the canals opened out. A huge willow tree drooped over the water, its fallen leaves distorting the reflections of its branches. People sat on the decking drinking beer and eating food from the nearby market with plastic forks, unblemished by green discs or worry.

"No, not just Maya and Scoot. Come on Sam." He turned to face her, put his hands on her shoulders. "*Equal not neutral*....?"

She wasn't sure what to say, or what she wanted him to say, so she just looked at him and waited, giving him nothing. He sighed. "Who do you think is behind the EatEasies - yes, *EatEasies*, plural," he clarified when she started at this. "You don't think *Maya* developed the technology to block the tracker emitters do you? There's loads of us. *PowerCut*. We're a resistance group - well, more of a network really. It shouldn't be like this." He traced the uneven skin around the disc in her neck with the tip of her finger. "We're fighting back Sam."

And she wasn't sure if she was surprised, or if she had known all along.

110

Chapter 12

Alice

On 31st October 2042, the Thames flooded its banks.
People had thought the news was a Halloween prank at
first, because tabloid newspapers had been creating
clickbait with rumours of the river's imminent flooding
for decades. The huge, *indestructible* polycarbonate
barriers that had been constructed along its banks, had
indeed not '*destructed'*, but rather been ripped from the
very concrete foundations in which they were rooted,
smashing into the first rows of buildings along the
Southbank and around the tube station at Blackfriars. The
construction of these barricades had been yet another
example of the billions of pounds of budget that the
government was able to source for plans that seemed
almost to have been devised by a child - *let's just 'contain'
the water: as if water were not the single most powerful force
on earth* - rather than actually taking the long-term
preventative measures suggested by the UN.
Hypocritically pushing sustainable initiatives in the
developing world but being unwilling to change
ourselves, as if the climate would respect the arbitrary
geography of borders, as though all of humanity would
not eventually burn on a planet oblivious to social
construct. If the world were a human body, then each
government blindly focusses only on their assigned
finger or toe, applying band-aids to their own locality
whilst sepsis spreads through the heart and major organs,
as disease attacks the brain. *Not our responsibility,* mutter

their policies, blinkered, building sea walls, a soothing balm to a papercut as rainforests are incinerated in the lungs that supply their precious finger with oxygen.

Sophie's apartment block, a short walk from Waterloo Station, had to be evacuated because the entire ground floor lobby had flooded. Her concierge, Linh, a sullen Vietnamese man who had often tutted at Alice for traipsing muddy footprints across the shiny marble floor in winter, had drowned in the storeroom where parcels were kept for residents. Two high-rise buildings in the Cherry Tree estate, a series of high-rise council blocks situated across a small park from Sophie's building, had collapsed vertically: their structural integrity (or lack thereof, as it transpired), essentially washed out from underneath them layer-by-layer as each set of walls disintegrated, gaining momentum with the assistance of gravity, the horizontals of the floors coming to rest stacked immediately on top of one another, walls blown outwards, bed frames, lamps, refrigerators, and residents crushed within.

With a great heave of effort, Sophie swung her suitcase onto the bed in one of Alice and Andrew's guestrooms and pulled the zip open around three edges with a flourish, flipping the lid. Sienna and Tommy were in his room, engrossed in an elaborate migration of a herd of Stegosaurus, dolphins, and unicorns across his long-suffering carpet, fleeing whatever predators and natural disasters the imaginations of two five-year-olds could conjure. Incongruous sound effects drifted down to them: machine gun fire, lasers, the roar of tigers.

"Grim." Sophie said, rifling through for her slippers and tossing them to the floor, before turning to sit on the bed, lying back and staring up at the ceiling. Alice lay on her front next to her, resting her cheek on Sophie's outstretched arm.

"Seriously grim," she agreed, closing her eyes, breathing in the scent of her best friend, and the florals of fabric conditioner from the duvet cover. "Like something you see on the news, in India or something."

"Or Wales. Always rains a ton there."

"Yeah."

They lay there without speaking for a while, looking up at the ceiling. It was Sophie who broke the silence.

"You made the right call, moving to the sticks."

"I'd hardly call Zone 4 *the sticks*."

"*Sticks* enough to dodge the flood."

"This time, yes."

The implication hung in the air like a swollen water balloon, one that might burst upon them at any second.

"This is actually scary. Like, hard-to-get-your-head-around, scary. Part of me is like *everything will obviously be fine, because the people in charge will sort it out before it gets really bad, like they always do.* And then part of me is like *maybe not this time. Maybe things are going to be too big, too bad.*"

"I think people in the Cherry Tree estate would say that things are already pretty bad." Alice pointed out. "If they were still alive to say it."

"And Linh."

"Yeah."

"I'm going to send some money to his family. He has four kids, and his wife can't find work."

"That's nice. Poor woman."

113

Silence again. Alice started at a tiny hairline crack in the ceiling near the window. She imagined water trickling through it, the crack widening. She rocked backwards on the bed to build momentum, before rolling herself forwards and onto her feet. "Come on, let's make dinner. I'm thinking Tacos."

"And Margaritas?"

"Of course."

Once the kids were in bed, with sincere promises that all droughts and meteors and ice ages would be put on hold overnight, at least in the world inhabited by the eclectic group of plastic beasts on Tom's bedroom floor, the women regrouped in the kitchen. While they chopped and stirred, the men completed the domestic cliche in the living room, watching football and drinking beer.

"It's like something from a 90's TV commercial." Sophie huffed as Alice carried two more beers through to the sofa.

"Wouldn't catch Brighton winning the league in the 90's!" Jack retorted, as Andrew half-stood from the sofa, hands to his mouth, suspended, before slumping back and throwing his arms in the air in despair. As the Brighton keeper lined up the goal kick, the screen went black, and all the lights in the house turned off.

"Wouldn't get power outages like that in the 90s either." Andrew said grumpily. "Almost as annoying as Brighton playing well."

"Such a bad loser." Sophie rested the base of her cocktail glass on Andrew's head and pinched his cheek like you would a small child having a strop. Alice held her breath, but he simply laughed at the chiding. Whether it was out of the necessity of social etiquette or if he was genuinely not offended, either way it stung. If she'd done that to him, teased him when his team was losing, she was sure he would have fallen silent, maybe even got up and walked out of the room. *What had happened to them?* The sound of the backup generator clicking into gear signalled that she should compose herself; the cover of darkness ending. Around them, appliances whirred back to life. The sound of the crowd rattled out at them from the television once more.

"It's 2-0 now, look! Unbelievable scenes!" Jack clinked his bottle against Andrew's.

"Typical, the power had to go out just as there was a goal."

"Bound to happen when we're scoring every other minute mate." Jack winked at him before returning his gaze to the screen. "Have you got any crisps Al?"

"Seems to be happening more and more now, the blackouts." Back in the kitchen, Alice shook tortilla chips into a big wooden bowl. "I think there's some guacamole in the fridge, can you have a look?"

"I know, I think that's the fourth this week." Sophie dipped a finger in the guacamole before sliding it across the counter to her like a hockey puck.

"Gross." Alice spooned out the corner with the indent of Sophie's finger and flicked it into the sink.

"Sorry. Quality control." She sucked her finger.

"Guacamole has passed all checks." She gave a salute.

"What would we do without you?" Alice picked up the dish and the bowl of tortilla chips. "Yeah, you're right, that was the fourth."

"Someone in Jack's team at work said they think it's sabotage."

"By who?"

"Whom." Sophie darted another finger into the guacamole.

"For God's sake, I nearly dropped it all." Alice set the bowls back on the counter. "By *whom*? Environmentalists?"

"Nah. PowerCut. You know - '*Equal not Neutral.*' The anti-OffSet people."

"What is the point in them messing with the power? What does that solve?"

Sophie helped herself to a handful of crisps, and tipped some guacamole directly on top of them in her hand.

"It doesn't solve anything, for them. Classic dog-in-the-manger tactics really. If they can't have it, they don't want anyone else to either."

Alice took a handful of crisps too, the men forgotten now. "But surely it just cuts it off to them too. Everyone loses."

"They're saying, apparently, that a lot of Counter housing up North has had no power for days at a time, but it is still being taken out of their allowance." She transferred crisps to her mouth while she spoke. A splodge of avocado dropped onto the countertop. Alice swiped it absent-mindedly with her finger, and licked it off.

"Apparently the numbers are not adding up, at the top level, Jack's colleague says. Something about the way it's been working with government expense accounts, and big corporations putting stuff through for their employees without recording it, but at the end of the day the totals on the trackers for the whole population have to match the output from all the energy providers, otherwise the UK is gonna get fined again next COP."

Alice licked her fingertip and pressed it into the edges of the bowl, hoovering up the last crumbs.

"What so they've been fiddling the numbers by screwing over these Counter people up North? To balance the books?"
"Basically yeah. Same old story really."
"Yeah, same old story. Except people are literally dying now."
"You mean Linh?"
"Well, yeah, Linh. And the guy outside the coffee shop."
"Oh! That reminds me, I've been meaning to ask you ever since you told me that story. Was that the one we used to take the kids to as babies? With the amazing banana cake with salted caramel? Because we should go back there, that cake was honestly the best cake ever. I still daydream about it."
"Sophie! I'm talking about someone dying here."
"Sorry."
"Forgiven. Anyway, it's just made me think about stuff."
She drained her margarita and reached for the jug, taking a deep breath.
"It's always dangerous when you think. I prefer to just go with the flow. Love that lobotomy life." She made a peace sign and pushed her glass across the counter for a top-up. Alice shook her head and poured her one. "When you've finished talking crap, and decided to let me speak, let me know won't you."
Sophie pretended to consider, stroking her chin with her thumb and forefinger.
"Okay I'm done. What were you saying?
"Well, it's just all this stuff Andrew was saying. *Where do you draw the line?* As if it's some kind of impossible problem. But like - it's obvious isn't it? You draw the line at not letting someone die in the street. It's just all gone so far."

"It's so simple when you put it like that, but I don't know, after today, and after the heatwave, and everything that's going on, it has made me agree with him even more. Things have to be drastic or loads of people are going to die. More people." Sophie swirled her drink as she spoke, careful not to let it spill over the rim of the shallow glass.

Jack's voice drifted through from the living room over the distorted sound of fans cheering and booing, winning and losing, always hand-in-hand, one impossible without the other.
"Alice, where have those crisps got to?"

Chapter 13

Sam

"I get to play with Tommy's toys again? Really?"

"Come here, you've got a bit more." She scrubbed at his face with the corner of a towel. "How on earth did you get baked beans on your forehead?"

Lucas shrugged and wiggled away from her, running in a circle with his arms out like an aeroplane.

"Do you think he'll let me play on his console? Or maybe this time we can even go swimming!"

"Lucas, you can't swim! And you need to do something quiet because Mumma will be working."

Lucas the aeroplane parked up abruptly next to her and his wings drooped in confusion. "Working? I thought you were coming to Tommy's house too?"

"Tommy's house *is* work for Mumma. I clean their house, remember? That's my job."

"Oh yeah." His engines roared back to life and he began to fly laps of the room again, fuelled by his elation at the prospect of a second visit to Greenfields Manor. Sam did not share his enthusiasm; she hated asking for favours, but with Lucas on half-term, Caleb's mother being unavailable to supervise her grandson, and her own mother recovering from a cataract removal, she was left with little choice.

"Come on", she channelled her best air traffic controller energy, "choose a jumper, we're going to be late."

"Hi Sam, hiya Lucas!" Alice's welcome was warm, but Sam's self-consciousness about her lack of childcare placed a cynical film over her words. *She's over-compensating. She feels sorry for me.* "Come in, come in!" Lucas was bouncing on the spot, his eyes searching for his new friend.

"Take your shoes off Lucas." She turned to Alice, determined to be gracious. "Thank you so much for this Alice. Lucas's dad couldn't get out of work. Important meeting."

"Oh honestly it's no bother. Tommy had a great time hanging out with you last time Lucas."

"Really?" He looked up from where he was carefully lining up his shoes against the wall. His earnest expression squeezed Sam's heart. Lucas didn't really have any friends at school; his last invite had been to the disastrous football party earlier that year. Alice didn't seem to notice.

"Tommy's friend Sienna is staying with us at the moment, they're both in his bedroom playing. You can go upstairs and join them."

Lucas looked up at Sam. She knew he was thrown off-kilter by the mention of an unexpected third child. He hated the unexpected. It felt as though he were standing in the middle of a seesaw, his shifting weight tilting it one way, then the other, testing the options before committing one side to crashing down. Explosion, or acceptance. She held her breath.

"Okay." He said, shrugging, and scampered up the stairs, using his hands like front paws. Sam exhaled and smiled at Alice.

"I'd better get to work then."

As she mopped, she began to go through her worries, like thumbing through the spines of books on a shelf, cataloguing. She found the cleaning work therapeutic sometimes, the physical exertion of it. The way in which it occupied her hands seemed to free her mind. *I need to get a second job.* This book was getting worn, its cover faded from being examined on a daily basis since Alice had cut her hours. She had sent out another burst of applications last night, but her circumstances were limiting; unable to drive or take public transport, and challenges with childcare. And for a lot of jobs she now needed a background check and a specific licence because of her Counter status; anything involving food, clothing, fuel, cosmetics or household products was strictly regulated because of the risk that struggling Counters would somehow cheat the system if they had unregulated access to any of those things. This, it turned out, limited a lot of the jobs that she might once have applied to, in retail or hospitality. In fact, the Counter-friendly section of the job site was now reduced to a handful of private cleaning jobs. The next title on her shelf of anxiety was Lucas. This book was five years old, and was extensive, encyclopaedic, with chapters covering every topic imaginable. How was she going to manage looking after him during school holidays without Caleb; or, worse still, if he was expelled permanently? How was she going to deal with this new chapter, crammed full of medical jargon and unknowns? How could she afford to pay for him to get support quickly enough that he could stay in school, whilst also protecting his fragile little world from further twists and turns of offsetting? She polished the induction hob in rhythmic circles, removing traces of cooking grease, before turning her attention to the hood of the extractor fan. Then, there was a brand-new book on the shelf, the cover shiny, colourful. *Mark*. She hadn't had a chance to read it thoroughly yet, but she had just hit a twist that filled her with trepidation. Mark is part of PowerCut. So is Maya. Should she stop reading? She could just return that book to the library, leave Mark so he could be with someone else, someone who was unburdened, free to take risks, to fight against the system with him. The thought of him with someone else was like acid in her throat. No. She would just have to read slowly, page by page, at arm's length. Until she had found out more. She tossed the greasy rag into the washing machine and went to get the vacuum cleaner. She wondered what books were on Alice's shelf. *Princess stories*, she thought bitterly, as she looked around the utility room, which was bigger than hers and Lucas's shared bedroom. *Finding treasure chests, winning tickets to magical chocolate factories and adventures with handsome princes who never shouted at you, and were definitely never, ever, in dangerous revolutionary groups and trying to convince you to join them.* The sound of the hoover filled her ears and she thrust it backwards and forwards across the delicate patterns of oriental rugs and herringbone wood. She allowed the roar to enter her ears, and flow through her skull, sucking the anguish and resentment with it like the dust from the floor, until her mind was numb.

A loud crash, a scream. She was shaken free from the cocoon of the drone and the dust. She stabbed at the power button and her ears squinted for the sound, searching for it amongst the fading whir of the machine. Lucas's unpredictability coupled with her societal insecurity had inverted her maternal instinct: where once her first thought would have been please, don't let anything have happened to him, now it was please; *don't let him have done anything*. She took the stairs two at a time, listening for further clues, envisaging a broken television that she could not replace, a cut ponytail that she could not explain; maybe even Tommy or Sienna with a bloody nose or a black eye, though he had never actually hurt anyone. The gravity of the *what if* seemed to magnify its probability in her mind.

Three children smiled back at her as she burst into the room. The impression they gave was one of people who have rushed into position, presenting a freeze-frame of innocence, teetering, breathless, pretending that they were there all along.

"What was that noise?"

"What noise?" Tommy blinked, the angelic self-assurance of the host, of a child who eats free-range beef, who gets driven to school in one of two cars, whose parents have a cleaner. She turned to her son.

"Lucas, I heard a loud bang. Can you tell me what it was, please."

"Tommy threw the ball and it knocked over the fan." He pointed to the corner of the room. "But we put it back." The fan and the children appeared mercifully intact, but Tommy looked outraged at the betrayal. She flailed to repair the damage she had done to her son by putting him on the spot.

"That's okay, it doesn't matter. It's only a fan and it's not broken. No one is in trouble." She let her hands fall from her hips. "And I know Tommy is a good boy, and he was going to tell me what had happened anyway, weren't you Tommy?"

"No."

Right. Lucas looked between the two of them, cowed in the fear of having failed them both, desperate to please. She felt helpless, a blundering diplomat in an embassy of five-year-olds.

"What are you playing?"

"Dodgeball." Piped up Sienna. "Boys vs girls. I'm winning."

"We're switching teams now." Tommy announced. "Sienna, you play with Lucas."

"Actually it's nearly time for Lucas to go home now. Lucas, why don't you come down and help Mumma finish up?" He shrugged, lips sealed to prevent further mistakes.

"No! Lucas, stay. We need three people for the game." The tension fell from Lucas's shoulders, his faux pas forgiven. He nodded vigorously, his eyes pleading for a few more minutes of play.

"Okay, well I'll come and get you in…" She looked at her watch and decided to stay an extra ten minutes to allow Lucas time to end on a high. "…fifteen minutes, okay? Be careful with that ball, kids." The three of them nodded, reunited once more against a common grownup.

"Haven't you finished Sam?" Alice looked at the clock above the fireplace, Roman numerals and wrought iron. "The kids seem to be getting on well. Tommy can be a bit cheeky. I hope you didn't mind too much."

She and her friend, Sophie, were sitting in opposite corners of one of the big white sofas in the living room, feet tucked underneath them. "We're keeping an eye on them through the home system." She nodded her head at a small screen propped on the coffee table. "Make sure they don't kill each other."

She and Sophie laughed. Sam did too; not at the joke itself but rather at its levity, incongruous with the residue of her own fear which still seeped from her pores.

"Yes, just finishing up. It seemed a shame to drag Lucas away mid-game. I'll just put this stuff away and then I'll go and fetch him."

"Leave that, let me get you a cup of tea. Milk, no sugar, that's right isn't it?"

"Erm, sure, thank you." She hovered by the vacuum cleaner, reluctant to leave it in the middle of the rug. Alice picked it up as she walked through to the kitchen, and flapped her hand to indicate she should sit.

"Alice told me you had to leave your place, because of the floods. I'm sorry." She offered to the woman still seated on the sofa.

"Yeah, pretty rough, but we're coping. Luckily Sienna is on half-term this week or it would have been a nightmare getting her to school from here. So much traffic."

Sam nodded.

"I suppose traffic isn't much of an issue for you. Silver linings eh?" She indicated the disc on Sam's neck.

"Mmm, you could say that." She looked at the screen. Lucas and Sienna were running across the room, and Tommy launched the ball at them, missing, and hitting the fan once again. She dragged her eyes away from the screen.

"When will you be able to move back in?"

"The water's all drained out. It just needs cleaning now. The whole downstairs is like a swamp."

Alice reappeared with a mug of tea for her and sat down between them. "Did you ask her Soph?"

"I was just getting to it!"

"Ask me what?"

"Well, Sophie was thinking - I was thinking - I know you were looking for more work, and the company in charge of cleaning her building are looking for people." She looked nervous, unsure if she was overstepping. "You've probably found something now, you're so good at what you do…."

Sophie nodded in agreement. "It's always spotless here. And it's definitely not this lazy lump." She jabbed a toe into Alice's bottom. *Being good at cleaning is just a case of needing to do it enough,* thought Sam. *It's not rocket science. You'd be good at it, if you had no other choice.* But she needed the job, and though patronising, and another handful of dirt to her ego, she could see their good intent, their eagerness to help, to not offend.

"That would be great, actually." She said, "I do have a few other things lined up, but just not starting right now."

"You could start straight away if you wanted?" Sophie offered with relief. "I can drop a note to John, the guy managing it all."

"Maybe on Monday? It's just difficult, with half term, and Lucas…"

"Her husband works a lot." Alice explained.

"He's not my husband, he's my ex-boyfriend. Lucas's dad. But yeah, he's very busy. Working all the time."

"Okay, Monday it is. I'll message him now." Sophie reached for her phone on the coffee table.

"Thank you."

"No need to thank me. I'll be the one thanking you if you can help get that place fit for living!"

"Me too, the sooner she's out of my hair the better." Alice added.

There was another bang from upstairs. All three women looked at the screen. The children seemed to be playing a sword fighting game now, leaping around, from bed, to chair, to floor. The fan was on its side again. Alice rolled her eyes and pressed a button on the screen, before speaking into it.

"Time to come down, kids." The game continued, un-interrupted. Alice paused before dangling the bait. "There's biscuits!"

Three pairs of footsteps thundered down the stairs towards them. Alice leaned across and squeezed Sophie's shoulder affectionately. "Can you go and grab the biscuits from the kitchen?"

The children appeared at the bottom of the stairs, panting, socks slipping on the shiny floor.

All three women spotted it at the same time. There was a beat, where all three seemed to be deciding how or whether to react. Their three children stood opposite them, oblivious, waiting for biscuits. Sam didn't know what to do, what to say. Shock and anger fought against the boundaries of her status as an employee on an employer's territory.

"I'll go and get the biscuits." Sophie broke the silence. "Come and help me Sienna. Come on."

"It was just part of the game. So they knew which team I was on in the fighting game." She and Lucas were walking home, hand in hand. Back on neutral ground, back where she was a whole adult, a real person, and the hurt and humiliation were no longer suppressed by practised subservience. Lucas, however, seemed genuinely unfazed by the big green circle that had been daubed on his neck in permanent marker by other children. "It was a fun game. I was really good at dodging. And fighting." He re-enacted it now, jumping around drains and over litter that was strewn on the pavement of their street, jousting invisible foes.

"We'll wash it off as soon as we're home."

"But now I'm matching with you. I like it." He complained.

Her phone buzzed. A message from Mark. She allowed herself to be distracted by the giddy rush of seeing his name on the screen. She swiped it open.

We are meeting tomorrow night. Give it a chance, see how you find it. No pressure after that. Promise x

She looked at Lucas, kicking a can along the street and then pretending to jump out of its path, still elated from the excitement of his day. His friends who, at five years old, knew no better. A green circle the obvious choice for branding her son. To make it clear he was different. She tapped out a response on her phone.

I'll be there.

There were more people than she'd expected, huddled in the small apartment near Peckham Rye Park. She'd dropped Lucas at her mum's for a sleepover. His neck still had a faint greenish hue, now framed with the pink irritation of scrubbing. She'd told her mum she was going on a date. She looked around at the group of unfamiliar faces, hollow cheeks and bags under their eyes like bruises. The sky outside looked bruised too, dark blue but with the faint ripple of smog still detectable, omnipresent. She regretted her decision to come already, wished she had joined Lucas at her mum's, snuggled up tight against this harsh world. Mark put a hand on her thigh and gave it a squeeze, sensing her discomfort. Maya winked at her from across the room.

"That's Billy." Mark murmured in her ear, jerking his head towards the wall to their right. "Maya's little brother. See the photo of the guy with the motorbike?" She scanned the wall of photos until she saw a faded snap of a young man with a smooth face and mirrored sunglasses making a peace sign at the camera, a blue motorbike propped behind him. The other photos seemed to crowd in too, vying for her attention.

"Who are all the others?"

"People who have disappeared, or been arrested."

"But… there's so many of them?" The faces pressed against her eyeballs, and pressure built behind them.

"These are just the ones we know about; friends, friends of friends, people from South London."

Maya jumped up and pulled a curtain across the window.

"Checker drone." She said, "Scoot, have you got the muffler?"

Scoot rummaged in a box under a long table against one wall, and pulled out a small black device which she plugged in and placed under the window.

Sam looked at Mark, questioning, as seemed to be her default state these days.

"It interferes with the drone. Stops it recording."

"It was designed by a couple of Cambridge PhD students as a side project. Didn't like the idea of Checkers being able to swoop in and make sure they were tallying everything up properly at their dinner parties and drinking societies."

"Not that they ever would." Scoot said with a sigh, dropping into the empty seat beside Mark. "I reckon you

can count on one hand the number of times they were
actually used for spot-checking rich people. What they
were supposedly made for."
"Alright everyone, enough chit-chat. Time to get started. I
was going to bring chocolate but well - you know how it
is."
A ripple of laughter moved around the group. She had
not seen Maya like this before; she had always been
bolshy, self-assured, but now she was commanding the
room with ease.
"We've got a couple of newbies here tonight. People
stupid enough, or just damned *fed up* enough to give up
their Thursday evening for this sweaty little meeting."
"We're just here for the chocolate." A man in a leopard
print tank top heckled. Sam recognised him as the
barman from the EatEasy.
"Sorry to disappoint Raj." Maya called to him.
"Ah, same as ever." The man flicked a hand at her
affectionately. "Might as well stay, now I'm here."
Maya rolled her eyes. "As I was saying. Two new joiners.
Over here, we have Bricks, a friend of Scoot." A bald guy
with tattooed biceps raised a hand to the group in
greeting. "And over here, is a good friend of mine, Sam.
A big fan of the EatEasy, is Sam. Lured her in with the
fossil fuels and a good time."
"Guilty." Sam raised a hand to the group. "Hi everyone."

"- so what we need to work out," Maya was rounding up,
one foot up on the chair which she had spun so that the
back was facing into the circle. "Is where best to hit them.
Where will it hurt most. But remember," She put a hand
on the back of the chair and leaned into the group,
looking around at each of them to impress upon them the

importance of her point, "inequality is the enemy. OffSet is the enemy. Those rich fucks who are buying your freedom - your health! - and pretending they're doing you a favour? They are the enemy. We support climate action. We recognise the need for change. It just cannot continue to be only at our expense!"

The regulars seemed to recognise this as the end of the speech.

"Down with the rich fucks!" Raj stomped a leather-booted foot on the floor. "Off with their heads!"

Sam whispered to Mark. "That was pretty impressive. Like she's giving a speech to her soldiers before they go into battle with their horses or something."

"That's basically how she sees us, I think. Minus the horses. If only there were horses. That would be much more fun." He leant back in his chair and stretched out his legs. "She starts all our meetings with that same speech. I could mouth the words along with her, but Scoot got told off for doing that a few weeks ago."

"I can hear you Mark."

"Yes ma'am." He gave Maya a curtsy from his chair.

"So, let's recap on the last week. Raj, do you want to kick us off?"

"You bet I do." He clambered onto his chair and cleared his throat. "As you all know, this week we disrupted the power supply to the whole South-East and South-West of the UK." Sam was taken aback at the scale of what he was describing.

"There are other PowerCut units all over the country. It's a big operation." Mark footnoted for her, as Raj continued, and again she was confronted by her own naivety, her London-centricity.

"This was in direct retaliation to the carbon scamming that OffSet and the government colluded to carry out against the Counter housing estates in Liverpool and Manchester, and most importantly people were making the connection between these two events on social media which is a big win for us."

Raj spoke for another ten minutes or so, fielding questions about various initiatives across the country, and then climbed down from his chair. Another woman stood up. "I've been working with Anonymous - the hacking group, in case any of you don't know - to try and push forwards on getting access to government communications. They're hoping we will have some good stuff by the end of next week. Then we just need to try and convince a paper to actually publish it."

"Sounds great Jenny. What sort of things are we looking for?" Maya asked.

"Anything that links them to the power scams in the North, or anything to prove the Counter estate water-cuts all around London were intentional."

"Good stuff Jenny." Maya gave her an appreciative nod. "Keep pushing that. And keep us posted. Going forwards, I think we need to ride the wave of successfully getting these things in the public eye, and apply some pressure around the loopholes with carbon counting for non-Counters. It's one thing that rich people can tip the scales, but even then they're not sticking to their side of the bargain." The group nodded their assent. Two more people got up to speak, sharing ideas for possible plans to put pressure on the government, to expose carbon-corruption, or to shine a light on the suffering of life as a Counter. Maya stood back up.

"Thanks guys. Lots to think about. And just before we finish up, we've had another five reports of disappearances this week." She pulled an envelope from her back pocket and fanned a set of photographs like those on the wall: different faces, same stories. Mark stood, silently, and moved across the room to take the photos and pin them on the wall. Sam felt the space beside her as if there were a draught, exposing her. What was she doing here? This wasn't her. This wasn't her life. She was normal. Boring, even. All this talk of disappearances and hacking and campaigning: it was as alien as Lucas's therapy. But then, before she had time to follow that thought too much, Mark was sitting down beside her again, his hand on her thigh, and the draught had gone.

"So, what did you think?" They were cutting through the park, lit only by the reflection of light pollution in the smog that blanketed the city.
"Not as fun as the EatEasy."
He laughed and put an arm around her shoulder, pulling her close.
"No. But they're a nice bunch. Bit weird, some of them. But good people."
"Yeah." They walked along for a bit in silence, footsteps falling into rhythm. "It was nice, how passionate everyone was. Nice to focus on something other than my shit parenting and rubbish job."
"What about that other one, the flood cleaning one. Are you going to take it?"
"Yeah, I mean I have to. Not exactly going to set the world on fire though, is it."

"I can see the headlines now!" He marked out the statement across the sky ahead of them with a swipe of his hand. "Front-line angel saves the day for horrible rich people whose perfect lives have been blighted by the tragedy of a wet carpet."

She pulled a face. "Making me feel so much better about it."

"Sorry. That was meant to be a dig at them, not you." He stroked her arm with his thumb. She wondered if this was what it felt like to be Alice, for someone to back down when they upset you.

"I know." She bent her arm up to link a couple of fingers through his so that her arm hung from his hand, his arm still draped over her shoulders like a security blanket. "I don't think a boyfriend has ever said sorry to me before. Not unless they've hit me first."

"I would have pretended to be terrified that you just called me your boyfriend, but that sentence was way too sad for making jokes."

"I guess that was a clever way of slipping it in then. Note to self: always reference past abuse to get my own way."

"Sounds healthy. But yes, I guess I am your boyfriend. Can't exactly strong-arm you into a secret rebel society and claim we are still casual, can I?"

Chapter 14

Alice

"Now is not the right time to talk to him about it."
Andrew rarely overruled her, but today he stood firm.
"All the family will be here tomorrow, you don't want to
set him off. Plus it was harmless."
"You weren't the one who had to deal with it. Trying not
to blow everything out of proportion and upset the kids,
but making sure it didn't seem like I was downplaying it
to Sam. Sophie hid in the garage it was so awkward! And
you know nothing ever bothers her."
She had been putting off dealing with the issue for a full
week since the incident with the green ink had taken
place, but with Sam's imminent arrival for her weekly
clean, she needed to decide whether to address it, or bury
her head in the sand. Andrew smeared the mixture of
butter, sea salt, and finely chopped rosemary and garlic
over the lamb rack.
"I just don't think it's a massive deal. You said the kid
didn't seem fussed. And if Sam is upset by something a
five-year-old does then she needs to get a grip."
Sam had seemed to pre-empt this view, donning it as if it
were her own. '*It's fine. It's fine! No big deal. Kids will be
kids!*' She had insisted, hoisting Lucas onto her hip like an
oversized toddler. They hadn't stayed for biscuits.
"I just think it's sensitive, that's all. I reckon she has a
pretty tough life. I don't think her ex is very involved
with Lucas."

"Lots of people are single parents. A guy at work has four. Takes them skiing every year with no support." He stood back to examine the lamb appraisingly. "Are we doing an egg hunt tomorrow?"

"By *are we doing*, do you mean *have you organised?* In which case, yes, I have."

"I'm literally prepping the main part of the meal! The *pièce de résistance*."

"It's just the way you always get around directly asking me to do things, to try and pretend you're not being bossy. *Are we having a salad with this Alice? Are we bringing wellies? Are we writing Christmas cards to my parents?* Just ask me to do it, for crying out loud."

He held his hands up in surrender. "That feels like semantics to me, but I'll try and take it on board."

"Semantics are important, Andrew. And so is the way our son is brought up to think about the world. It felt like, I don't know, like he was putting a Star of David on him or something. Marking him out."

"Do you realise how ridiculous that sounds? You're comparing a voluntary - paid - energy sharing scheme, to Nazi Germany?"

"Well sometimes that's how it feels!" She burst out, surprising even herself. "Sometimes, I feel like... I don't know, the guy who mowed the lawns at the concentration camps and never reported them. Not exactly shepherding people into the gas chambers, but definitely not doing anything to stop them!"

"I don't think the concentration camps had lawns, Al." He pointed out, carefully covering the tray of lamb with clingfilm, before placing his palms face down on the counter. "Is this still about that guy outside the coffee shop? Maybe you should talk to a therapist. It must have been awful to see." He came around the counter, testing the waters for a hug. She let him, because it was easier to talk into his armpit than facing him. "Some problems can't be fixed by therapy, Andrew. Some things need fixing in real life. Not just for me to feel better about them."

The relevance of this statement to their marriage hung in the air, intrusive.

"Sam is working this afternoon, right? Why don't you have a chat with her. Woman to woman."

She picked up the tray of lamb and carried it over to the fridge, balancing it wedged between the edge of the bottom shelf and her stomach while she rearranged jars and bottles to make space.

"We have six different jars of mustard. *Six*." She shoehorned a squeezy bottle of American in between a jar of jalapenos and an apricot jam in the fridge door. Her mobile phone vibrated on the countertop. She dumped two jars of mustard in the bread bin behind a packet of bagels and slid the tray of meat onto the empty shelf.

"It's from Sam." She waved the phone at him, triumphant, the bad news softened by the vindication of being right. "She says she can't come to clean today. Says she's ill."

"I'm sure she is ill then." He passed her a potato peeler. "Honestly, I think you're looking into this too much. Let's just get through Easter with my parents, and I'm sure she'll be back next week."

Little clouds of oil from the lamb fat collected on the surface of the red wine in their glasses. Gravy and the novelty of one another's company grew tepid, congealed.

"I wonder if, in a hundred years' time, they'll look back on us and think we were so weird and gross for eating meat." Alice pondered aloud, tipping lamb ribs from the edge of her plate into the communal bone bowl. "Like, you can imagine, if they have totally stopped eating animals, they would look back and be like 'that is disgusting. *They used to literally eat the flesh of other living things.'*"

"It's natural." Andrew selected one of her discarded bones from the bowl and nibbled at the fat she had left on it. "We're top of the food chain."

"In Japan they've fully transitioned to lab-grown meat. And somewhere in Scandinavia I think? Where was it, Andrew?"

"Norway."

"It's always Norway." Andrew's father rolled his eyes in the way that old men do at objectively positive concepts that for some reason feel threatening to them.

"Ooh, what about that stuff in Berlin that you were reading about this morning, Hugo?" Alice's mother-in-law cued her husband dutifully.

"God, yes, now that is absolute madness." Andrew's father took a sip of wine and leant back in his chair, shaking his head without elaborating, as if to build suspense for his anecdote.

"What's happening in Berlin?" Hosting the in-laws was an annual Easter tradition, and she would play her part.

"Nukists." He declared grandly.

"Oh for God's sake Hugo, tell them what they are, before they fall asleep." Andrew's mother had little time for his theatrics. Alice poured her another generous glass of wine with an unusual wave of affection for the woman.

"I'm getting to it Charlotte." He cleared his throat. "*Nukists* are what this group are calling themselves. Sympathisers with countries like India. A terror organisation, in essence. Standing in solidarity with the VNCC."

"What's the VNCC?"

"'*Victim Nations of Climate Change*'. Basically all the big-hitter countries who claim they are being worst-affected by all of these natural disasters that keep happening. Rumour has it that at the next COP they plan to give Western governments another ultimatum. If we don't fix things, they are going to start targeting what they call the major carbon culprits in the West. Aviation, oil rigs, beef production, fast fashion warehouses. Disable them in some way. Interfere with air traffic control, blockade the rigs so they can't operate, that kind of thing. You must have read about it. *The War on high-emission infrastructure*, they are calling it."

"Oh I read that article. It was in The Times." Without breaking his flow Andrew reached over and took the ketchup from Tommy, who was drawing a dinosaur with it on his plate. "Weren't they talking about an electro-magnetic pulse that could take out entire networks, communication systems, bring us to our knees basically?"

"That's the one. All seems pretty uncouth to me. Especially given it's only with *our money* that they've sorted out all of this green stuff in their own countries anyway, money we've basically been forced to give them to have any hope of not breaching our carbon limits. Well, anyway, these *nukists* are a bunch of extremists who are threatening to take it one step further. Bring down planes mid-flight, blow power plants up, that kind of thing. A less subtle approach, if you will."

"Get to the nuke part of nukists though Hugo!" Charlotte tapped her finger tips impatiently.

"Well, as well as all of this, this group are lobbying the VNCC to threaten the West with nukes. A sort of 'if we're going down we'll take you down with us' approach."

"Is there any chocolate?" Tommy had dabbed up the half-dinosaur ketchup sketch with his finger, licking it off in little red blobs.

"Chocolate? At Easter? Why would there be chocolate?" Charlotte scooped him off his chair by the armpits so that he giggled and squealed. "Come on. I'll take you out for the Easter egg hunt." She turned around as he dragged at her arm, already through the door. *"Siblings.* He needs *siblings."* She mouthed at Alice. And then at a normal volume. "And I don't think this talk of war and *nukes-"* she said the word as if they were something that only existed in a sci-fi film, "-is appropriate for a small child." Alice reached across and took Charlotte's glass of wine, tipping it into her own.

"How would it help anyone, though, nuclear war? That can't exactly be great for the old ozone layer or greenhouse gases or whatever else?"

"This group in Germany - and I think it is gaining traction elsewhere in Europe - are basically saying that if we don't make changes - like, right now - then it is game over for all of them in those VNCC countries. This nuke thing wouldn't be to save themselves. It's a last-ditch attempt to scare people into action. The nukists' stance is - and this is what they are trying to tell these governments to say - is that those people are all going to die anyway. So they have nothing to lose."

"Nothing to lose is a dangerous thing."

140

"But it's just selfish!" Hugo exclaimed. "Why hurt someone else just because you are hurting? And isn't the whole point that we should all be working together? Us humans, united against the problem?" His teeth had a slight purple sheen from the wine.

"Do you think we are?" Alice asked, unable to help herself.

"Are what?"

"Being united. Against the problem. Can you, hand on heart, say we are doing everything in our power to slow down climate change? And what about letting people from the worst-affected places move here? Isn't it selfish, saying no to that?"

"Oh, we have our very own nukist right here do we?" He laughed as he said it, but his eye contact held no mirth.

"Don't be ridiculous dad." Andrew said, standing to stack the plates. "Alice isn't saying the nuke thing is okay. She's just playing devils' advocate."

"I'm not actually." And she realised it was true. "If something someone was doing was putting Tommy, was putting our family's lives, at risk. I would do anything to make them stop. Threaten them with anything. I don't blame them for saying whatever they need to, to make people sit up and listen to them. Isn't that what we are doing, really, each time we get in our cars when we could walk, each time we turn on the heating instead of putting on a jumper, isn't that just us slowly building a nuke of our own, that at some point will destroy them? Destroy us too, eventually. Already even - look at what's been happening here with the heat and the flooding." She held her plate out for Andrew to stack, but he didn't seem to notice.

"Alice, you're not even willing to give up your swimming pool."

"I know. I'm not saying that I'm not in the wrong. In fact, I'm saying I am: we all are. And that's exactly why I can understand what this VN- what was it?"

"VNCC." Andrew supplied, noticing her plate suspended above the parsnips and taking it from her.

"Yes. That's why I could understand if they went along with it. I get their point. Even if I don't like it, I understand."

"I found forty eggs mum! Nine blue and nine pink and nine yellow and nine green!" Tommy burst back into the room, Charlotte and the faint smell of sweat trailing behind him. "I even found the ones in the hole in the tree!"

"That's thirty-six eggs. Don't they teach you maths in school?" Hugo rounded on his grandson, mathematical truth and a five-year-old opponent an easier win than a moral debate with his daughter-in-law.

Alice stood up. "We should be getting on. Tommy has homework for his first day back." She moved towards the hallway as she spoke, the implication clear. "Thank you for coming, Hugo. And thanks for taking him on the egg hunt Charlotte. What do you say to granny, Tommy?"

Tommy turned to her, a couple of pink eggs dropping from his arms and rolling under the table. "You said it was forty eggs granny. Don't you know maths?"

The corners of Andrew's mouth twitched. Alice caught his eye, and they shared a rare moment of synchrony: love for their son. He winked at her.

"Grandad can teach granny maths in the car home. Say goodbye Tommo."

In the bath that night, Tommy seemed lost in thought, his sea creature bath toys remaining beached on the floor.

"We do learn maths, with Mr Connors. Every day after lunch."

"I know you do. Grandad was being silly." She splodged a spot of bubble bath onto his nose. "Behind your ears, come on Tom. And the back of your neck. Scrub properly." She dipped and wrung out the flannel and handed it back to him.

"I'm going to give some eggs to Lucas."

"That's lovely Tom. I'm sure he would be very happy to get a couple of yummy chocolate eggs."

"Eighteen eggs." He looked up at her, worried he'd made a mistake. "That is half isn't it?"

"Yes Tommy, that is half."

Chapter 15

Sam

It had been terrible timing to have to call in sick. She knew that Alice would link it to the Lucas incident. The Lucas incident. Maybe she should start numbering them, to make it clear which particular incident was being referred to in each instance. Except, for once it hadn't been his fault, and anyway, he didn't seem bothered. It was unfortunate that she actually *was* sick. She had been vomiting all week, after waking up, behind a skip on her first day cleaning the flood damage in Sophie's building, ducking into a bush as she walked Lucas to school. The stress was clearly catching up with her, she thought. She had powered through at the new job, keen not to give them an excuse to fire her in her first week. But by Friday, she was wiped out. Alice had sent her the money for her shift anyway, and had also sent her some carbon allowance. *For some chocolate eggs for Easter*, the accompanying message had read. Mark had dropped round potato and leek soup this morning, for Easter lunch. He had leaned through the door and kissed her. *Stop, I'll infect you!* She had laughed, kissing him back. *I don't think being overworked and overstressed is contagious.* He'd said. *Then how come it seems to spread through counter-housing like wildfire, be endemic amongst my friends? 'Endemic'*, he had teased. *Big word. Growing up through the Coronavirus decades made scientists of all of us, eh?*

The new job was hard work. The commercial grey-blue carpet in the building foyer had to be ripped up and got rid of. Apparently, this was classed as cleaning; in an economy suffering from the worst labour shortages in almost thirty years, companies like this were not being picky about qualifications and regulations. She had abrasions on her knuckles. The skin around her nails was peeling. People who said papercuts were the most disproportionately painful injury had clearly never had those tiny snags of skin around their nails curling upwards, the area raised and pink, burning. It was unreasonably sore. The scrapes and the peeling skin stung with the harsh chemicals used to combat the traces of sewage in the contaminated flood water. Her eyes were bloodshot, and her knees and lower back ached. Lucas was back at school after half-term, and seemed to be coping. He'd had a private appointment with a psychiatrist yesterday to come up with a care plan for school. She'd felt pride, sitting in that waiting room. She'd washed her hair for the occasion; put on a smart shirt, an Alice cast-off. *I'm providing for my child*, she'd thought, smugness in her cheeks and chest. *He deserves the best, and he will get it.* Lucas had been exhausted from the four mile walk to the clinic. Catatonic, almost. He'd sat sullenly on the chair in the doctor's office, the backs of his heels drumming against the metal legs, refusing to stop, refusing to answer. *It's hard to get a proper picture*, the doctor had concluded. *It's probably best you book a follow-up.*

Lucas was not tired now. He was bouncing around the small flat. "Can we play dodgeball Mumma?" He threw a rolled-up pair of socks at her where she sat huddled on the sofa, a skin of potato and leek soup crusting in two bowls in front of her. "Mumma's not feeling well Lucas. Why don't you come and sit down and we can read a book?"

"Can I watch TV?"

She didn't need to check the meter.

"Not today love. What about doing some drawing."

She reached under the coffee table and pulled out the box with a blackboard and a small pot of chalks.

Her phone flashed on the table. Maya pestering her for a night out at the EatEasy. She turned it face down so that the screen was hidden, and sat back on the sofa, pulling the blanket up to her chin.

"What are you drawing Lu?"

"Wiggle. I'm going to draw a picture to show people so they can help look for him."

A stick cat with a round belly and smiling face was etched in powdery white lines. White powder dusted the coffee table, collateral damage of Lucas's concentrated pressure with the chalk. An innocent recreation of his father's own scenes involving the coffee table and white powder. She ruffled his hair, willing him in that moment never to grow up.

"That's so kind Lucas. We can show it to Hannah's mum later, if we see her." *And if we want her to think that we've lost the plot*, she thought sadly. She reached for her phone, her willpower short-lived. A message had come in on the app that had been installed on her phone after the first PowerCut meeting, secure and encrypted. She tapped in the password they had given at the meeting and opened it, feeling like an imposter in this world of secret codes and illicit updates. She glanced at Lucas, who was busy adding a sun, a tree, and a bowl of water for the cocaine

146

cat. His tongue scrubbed at the corner of his lips in concentration. She scanned the body of text. A date, location, and list of topics for the next meeting. *Tracker shielding, parliament sit-in, n*kists*. The last word was censored, presumably to keep the message from being picked up by government monitoring, but the missing letter eluded Sam too.

"Sam? Sam! You gotta come see this!"
Peter from number 62's voice carried through the open window twenty minutes later, even as the body it came from was already a few houses down, the last words trailing behind him and then regrouping, like a swarm of bees, as he called out to others living on the street. She pulled the blanket over her head and shuffled down into the sofa so that she wouldn't be visible through the window. Peter was well-known on the street for being the proud owner of a small solar-powered television. He had stolen the device from his manager's desk when he was fired on suspicion of stealing a punnet of strawberries when he worked in the VIP section at Wimbledon tennis tournament. *They still think we steal food to eat*, he'd said to them, during the neighbours' first huddled screening of the Eurovision song contest last summer. *Even though we literally cannot consume a thing without our trackers counting it*. He'd tapped the disc in his neck with each syllable for emphasis as he spoke. *Still, they trust us less than the rest of them, the people who've got all the reason to steal: no transaction, means no need to type it on their little 'honesty' apps.* And so, he'd explained, he had stolen the TV, because *when you do the time*, he'd said, laughing, *you might as well do the crime*. He stroked the top edge of the screen lovingly, as Greece awarded Italy thirteen points.

There was commotion outside: Peter's roundup gaining traction.

"What's that man saying?" Lucas had put down his chalk and was kneeling up on the sofa, peering out to the street. Half-drawn suspects in the mystery of Wiggle's disappearance floated around the edges of the chalkboard - a bear, an alien spaceship, a vampire. All less far-fetched, to Lucas, than the truth. "It's Peter, the man from number 62."

"TV-Pete, he said we have to call him, remember?"

"I don't think so, Lu." She hissed, distractedly. "Here, come out the way of the window."

"He did!", he agitated, pitch rising, "remember, 'look what I've got ladies'" he pranced, an imaginary television set under his arm as he strutted across the sofa, "just call me tv-Pete."

"Did I hear my name?" TV-Pete's antenna had picked up the sound of his nickname. He approached the window.

"Alright lad. You're up for a bit of TV-Pete, aren't you?" Lucas looked down at Sam for guidance, giving away her furtive position. She sat upright, just as Pete was peering through the window, trying to spot her.

"Hi Peter. What's up?"

"Big news. Big, *big* big. Live coverage now. You've got to see this. You have *got* to see this."

Yes, you said that already, she thought, as she got to her feet in resignation.

Huddled around the set were David from number 12, Hannah's mum from next door, and a handful of other neighbours that Sam knew by sight from the street. At first, she wasn't sure what she was looking at. An aerial shot of the ocean, perhaps. But as she looked closer, she saw the tops of buildings, upside down cars, and then, closer still, bodies. Dozens of them, and as the camera panned outwards, hundreds, bunching at points where the flow of water was blocked by a high-rise block or an electricity pylon.

"Where is that?" She asked, appalled by the scene in front of her. "*What* is that?"

"Tsunami. Tokyo." To Peter, the horror was a form of social currency. He thrived on being the one to supply it. "They haven't found any survivors yet." He added, almost proudly. "None."

"Terrible." Murmured Hannah's mum, shooing her daughter and Lucas into the other room as the drone hovered over an adult and three children, bodies bloated, swollen with water, being knocked against what looked like a concrete motorway bridge. Sam felt the nausea which had swilled in her stomach all week rise, threatening at her gullet. She swallowed and looked away from the screen, at David, the old man whom she had given water to during the drought, his gaze transfixed by the horror unfolding, dark crinkles of skin around his eyes rising and sagging as the images flashed. She imagined a giant wave ripping through London, tearing along this street. David would stand no chance; none of them would. That last thought filled her with some small comfort. No one would survive it, not even the people in charge: so they would never let it happen. The thought of it was too absurd. On the screen, a reporter was giving an update on the events in Japan. "Yesterday's earthquake in the Pacific Ocean, off the South-East coast of the country, caused this monumental wall of water to move up towards the Tokyo Bay where it gained speed and volume, devastating the capital. A rise in sea levels meant that the city's tsunami defences were largely ineffective, and heavy casualties have already been confirmed, with projected deaths expected to reach three million, making this the most devastating tsunami since records began. Leading seismologists are attributing the increasing frequency of this kind of earthquake to rising atmospheric temperatures putting pressure on fault lines under the ocean. The city, with a population of forty-two million…" Sam had seen enough.

"Lucas!" she called, and his head peered around the door frame into the room. "We're going home. Come on, quick quick."

"But the report hasn't finished." TV-Pete spoke as if they were leaving before his favourite scene in a movie. "You should stay, to be informed about what's happening. And there'll be some tips coming up," he insisted, hovering as if to block their exit. "Keeping yourself safe in a Tsunami, that kind of thing."

"I've seen enough. Thank you, Peter." She said firmly, guiding Lucas ahead of her.

"Okay, well if it happens, be sure to climb to the top of something high! Or get in a boat!" He called after them.

An hour later, the doorbell rang. Maya was brandishing a white paper bag.

"Pretty horrendous stuff in Japan eh? Take it you've heard the news."

"Saw it. TV-Pete." She offered by way of explanation, then pointed at the bag. "What's that? Sweets?"

"You wish. Come on, take it." Maya thrust the bag into her hands, and she tipped out the neat white box. She looked down at it.

"Oh don't be so ridiculous."

150

"It's not ridiculous. And I'm having to go without toilet paper for a week to cover the disposable points for this, so you'd better not drop it down the toilet."

"I want one! What is it?" Lucas ran into the hallway, using the back of her legs to stop his momentum, and peered at their visitor from behind her.

"Hi mate." Maya crouched to his eye level. "I don't think you want one of those. But you might like…", she whipped a lollipop from behind her back like a magic trick, "one of these!"

Lucas darted forwards, all shyness forgotten with the prospect of sugar. He busied himself with the wrapper, all adult conversation muted to him.

"Maya I can't be. There's no way."

"Throwing up every morning? Tired for no reason, -"

"No reason! You try scrubbing sewage out of concrete. I'm not exactly sitting around on my arse-"

"- stroppy and, dare I say it?" She took a step back, laughing, and held up her hands in mock-defence, "- hormonal?"

Sam snatched the bag from her. "Come in." She said grudgingly. "Make yourself at home."

"Top host, your Mumma, isn't she Lucas?"

He considered, earnest.

"I don't think so." He said, deadpan. "I think she's being a bit rude."

"Don't you think she seems pleased to see me?"

"Not really." He ran to the sofa and did a forwards roll over the arm before lying stretched out, sucking on his lolly. He shrugged, matter-of-fact. "I think she wants you to leave." Maya turned to her and mimed a broken heart, but her eyes brimmed with suppressed laughter.

"You asked for that." Sam told her. But amusement flickered at the edge of her mood, lightening it slightly since the dark panic had poured from the mouth of the pharmacy bag and enveloped her. "We're working on the sarcasm thing. And the white lies."

"That's alright, I've got thick skin." Maya shooed at Lucas's feet so that he would make room for her on the sofa. He bent his legs a fraction, freeing up a six-inch gap. "Jeez thanks Lucas, so kind of you to share."

"You're welcome." He said seriously, spinning the lolly in his mouth so that it rattled against the back of his teeth.

"Wow, no kidding on the sarcasm thing." She perched on the armrest nearest his feet and pointed at the package in Sam's hands. "Now you can just round off the welcome you've given me by pissing on the gift I brought you. Go on."

Chapter 16

Alice

"This is pretty big. I mean, I really didn't think they could ever do something like this. I actually couldn't believe it when I heard."

It was the end of April. Hot again, even in the air-conditioned sanctuary of the department store. They were perched on the sofas in the shoe section, drinking milkshakes, half-heartedly pretending to look at sandals while they sought refuge from the heat.

"Insanity. I always assumed it was just scare mongering, when the media was going on about this being on the cards. I cannot believe they've actually gone and done it."

"Well there goes our covert mission: same age babies round two. I was quite warming to the idea of a little mini Sienna and Tommy running around."

Alice raised an eyebrow. "And how, exactly, did you plan on having another baby? Immaculate conception? Or were you going to let that robot version of you that you're planning to have shagging your husband carry the baby for you?"

Sophie kicked Alice's shopping bags, knocking them over, so that cans of deodorant rolled over the floor. "That is *so insensitive*." She paused, reaching for a bottle of conditioner that had scuttered under the bench. "You know that I'm sad I haven't managed to make the robot sex machine happen yet."

Alice laughed, and held open the bag for Sophie to return the wayward toiletries.

"Things still that bad then?"

"I don't know what's wrong with me. Maybe I'm asexual. Like a strawberry plant.

"Maybe it's the menopause."

"Give it a rest Al, I'm only 34. Have you finished your milkshake? Shall we carry on?" She stood up before Alice could answer, marking the question as rhetorical.

"Although I might as well have all that stuff down there shrivel up now anyway, I suppose, what with the government saying I can't use it." Sophie imitated a flower wilting, tongue drooping from the side of her mouth.

"You could, though. 4500 points to have a baby. What is that,-" Alice counted in multiples of five hundred across her fingers, "-like 500 points a month? It's just to put people off, really. A deterrent. And a kind of tax, to scrape back some points for the government to recoup everywhere they've been fucking it up."

The news had been on the BBC website this morning, on the home page, above an article about the bid for hosting the next Olympic games, and next to a small update that read '*from 1st May, disposable points for items deemed 'non-essential', including materials for campaigns and protests, will be charged at two times the standard rate'.* The main headline: '*Flat fee of 4500 carbon-points for any pregnancy to be allowed to go to term.*'

"If you think I have 500 carbon points spare each month you're having a laugh." Sophie retorted. "And limits are definitely going down again next COP. Gotta show them we're playing ball."

"What do you think happens if you get pregnant and don't have the allowance?"

154

"You'd just have to buy some, I guess. You could sign up for another Counter, if you really wanted one. Just for 9 months." Sophie stopped to examine a display of reed scent-diffusers by the department store exit. "Or one of those one-off things, like Richard and Franny did for the wedding. Plus I don't think there's much risk of an accidental pregnancy for me, is there?"

"Yeah I reckon as a born-again virgin, you're safe." Alice placed a hand on Sophie's elbow as she spoke to propel her away from the display and out of the sliding doors. "Celibacy is a pretty good contraceptive."

They turned onto the high street, past a young boy busking outside a shop selling camping gear. A man threw a cigarette butt into his open guitar case as he walked past. The busker stuck his middle finger up at the man mid-chorus.

"I'm not sure I'd be keen to have another one either right now. Not with how things are, with Andrew."

Sophie transferred her shopping to her left hand and put her right arm around Alice's shoulders, giving her a squeeze, so that their feet tripped over each other.

"Things haven't seemed too bad while we've been staying with you?"

Alice sighed. The prospect of trying to explain something that even she couldn't put her finger on felt insurmountable suddenly.

"Things aren't too bad. I know it sounds stupid, but I think that's part of the problem. If they were, we would just split up. They're just not *great*."

"To be honest, I've been aiming for anything from middling to better than average." Sophie shrugged. "I think you might be expecting too much from life."

"Maybe. It's just, things did use to actually *be* great before."

"Before… you had a tiny human demanding your attention at all hours of day and night? Before you quit your ultra-cool graphic design career to be a kept woman? Before the government started pitching us against each other and limiting our every move? Before London started having weather like the apocalypse? Before your tits started getting saggy and you started getting greys?" She selected a strand of hair in Alice's ponytail and brought it round for her to examine, before yanking it out.

"Ouch!" Alice batted her away. "Remind me not to come to you when I need cheering up. But yes, I suppose, before all of those things." They had just got back to the carpark and stood by their respective car doors, handles half-pulled, shopping balanced against their feet on the concrete floor.

"Sounds like you need-"

"- don't say quality time. I'm sick of people recommending that." She thought of Andrew's mother, of the mums at the school gate; even Sam, all prescribing the generic remedy, with no suggestions of how to get there. As if that wasn't the exact issue: the time they spent together, no matter what they did, never ended up being 'quality'. Like telling someone who wants to know how to swim faster: oh, you've just got to *swim faster*.

"I wasn't. I was going to say a boob job."

Sam had called in sick for two consecutive weeks, but she had texted to say she was coming this afternoon. Alice paced up and down, and so did the thoughts in her mind. But when Sam had come in, swapping her outdoor shoes

156

for slippers and tying her orange jumper around her waist, Alice's quandary about what to say to her evaporated.

"Hi Sam. I'm so sorry about the last time we saw you. I really hope Lucas is okay. How are you feeling? Sounds like a nasty bug you've had."

The other woman looked grateful and relieved, and Alice wondered for the first time if she too might have been feeling anxious about the awkward last encounter and the consecutive sick days. Sometimes we are so focussed on our own role in an event, playing prosecutor, defendant, judge and jury in our own mental court case, that we forget that the other person might be doing exactly the same thing.

"Honestly, don't worry about it. Lucas wasn't bothered, and kids will be kids. He had a great time. He had no idea what the fuss was about, to be honest. Must be nice, being a kid. Simple." Sam smiled at her, but she looked drawn.

"Are you sure you're up to working? You're still looking a bit peaky."

"Yeah, yeah, I'm fine. And listen, thanks again for sorting out the extra work for me."

"Oh, yeah, I forgot about that.' She let it slide that Sam had clearly been up to working the other job. "Sophie said they should be moving back in next week. Does that mean it's almost finished?" She moved towards the kitchen, slowly, to suggest that Sam should follow.

"Not exactly." Sam shuffled after her, putting her backpack by the radiator. "They're moving us to night shifts next week, so that the residents can move back in and we don't disturb them."

Night shifts. Alice shuddered internally as she clicked on the kettle and pulled two mugs from the cupboard. She wasn't sure whether to express her horror, to offer sympathy, or whether this would make her look privileged and naive. Maybe for some people, night shifts were normal. Maybe you got used to it.

"Oh, right." She settled on neutral. "How is that change for you?"

"A bloody nightmare to be honest." Sam picked at a scab on the back of her hand. "Caleb - Lucas's dad, my ex - he used to do them in a supermarket. Killer. He never got into a proper sleeping pattern. Messed up his meal times. Everything, really."

"Sounds awful. Are you going to quit?"

Sam looked at her, considering.

"I don't know. I need the money for… for stuff. I don't know. I'll work it out."

She passed Sam the tea and pointed through to the living room. "Take your time today, and don't do more than you can manage. Drink your tea first. Maybe you could do an extra shift for a few weeks - only if you have time that is."

"Where are the kids today?"

"Oh, the dads took them to the zoo. It's Sienna's birthday. There's an exhibition about The Extinct Five. Sounds pretty depressing to me, to be honest. Andrew and I saw a tiger, on our honeymoon. I think that was the year before they went extinct. Sad the kids will never see one, isn't it."

Out of habit, she glanced at the photographs on top of the piano. She and Andrew grinned back at her from the open top of a safari jeep in Northern India, tanned, smooth skin. Pert breasts.

Sam looked at the photograph too.

158

"I doubt Lucas would have seen a tiger anyway. He hasn't ever been abroad. I guess that's a silver lining. Of, well, you know." *Of being poor,* Alice finished the sentence in her head. *Of the fact that we made your lives so difficult even before the planet decided to stick its oar in.* For some people, there are two enemies, two causes. The climate *and* the system.

"A lot of this stuff going on doesn't really change much for us." Sam continued, "I haven't ever been on a plane."

"Not all it's cracked up to be, to be honest. Overpriced sandwiches and tiny seats with other people's fingernail clippings on. I don't miss it." She often wondered whether in trying to downplay her experiences and thus the extent of the wealth divide, she instead conveyed an air of ingratitude or flippancy. "We've given it up, of course." She added, pre-emptively defensive.

"Well, maybe soon no one will be flying at all." Sam said. Whether it was a platitude or a loaded statement Alice had no idea, but she wondered how Sam felt about the aggressive inequality of their lives, and, for the first time, what she thought about *Nukists*, or *PowerCut*, or any of these other resistance groups. But Sam was shuffling her feet, clearly keen to draw a line under the conversation.

Chapter 17

Sam

"I'd better be getting on. It's a right state in here. You'd think I'd been off two years, not two weeks."
Alice raised an eyebrow. Sam had always envied people who could do that, without the other one so much as quivering. She wondered if Alice was waiting for her to apologise for the dig. She didn't; instead turning on her heel, and heading up the stairs.

Last night's meeting, she reflected, as she folded clean clothes in the laundry room, separating out a pile of shirts for ironing, had ramped things up a notch. The operation, which at first had given her a sense of amateurishness (or perhaps she had seen what she expected to see, because when you meet the people involved, put faces to the idea of it all, see them meeting in a dingy flat with wobbly chairs and tattered photo collages, it is hard to imagine that it can be anything but) was bigger and more powerful than she had first thought. Over the course of the meetings, she had discovered that the people with whom she was meeting were just one small part of something bigger, something slick and entrenched and serious. Discussions about forming an alliance with these so-called nukists had shaken her. *They don't have the same goals as us anyway*, she had reasoned to Mark on the way home, where he would always detour to walk her to her door. *They're climate activists and we are fighting against inequality*. Because she struggled to see climate change as the enemy, even now, faced with extreme heat and deadly flooding in her home city, because the day-to-day struggle of life as a Counter, and the outright *unfairness* of the way the rich were mitigating the pressure of carbon limits on themselves, made the focus feel much closer to home. *But their message is the same*, Mark had explained to her, as they crossed the boundary into the Counter neighbourhood and paint peeled on the walls, and inside the houses, fridges were empty. *They care that the people that have the most, with the most power to change things, do the least. But more than this: they suffer the least. The whole world agreed to make change, but instead the rich nations just pushed the responsibility onto the poorest countries in exchange for money. But if these wealthy countries: the US, Japan, the EU, us - yes, us -* he had repeated when she'd looked at him, picking his way along the Counter street with no cars and disconnected street lights, noting the irony, *if these places don't actually make the changes, as much as is humanly possible, instead of just bending the rules and muddying the water, then that's it. And the VNCC countries will be first. Are first - it's happening already.* And she'd asked him, with no hint of irony, why these countries didn't just say no to the money, say no to the deals that would make life impossible for them? Make the rich suffer through it like everyone else? And he had looked at her in the dark night and asked *why didn't you?*

She reflected on their conversation as she plugged in the iron and waited for it to heat up. It hadn't seemed like the right time to tell him about the baby. It hadn't seemed like the right time for her to find out she was having one either, but some things would not wait for the perfect moment: and for others, the perfect moment did not exist. She thought back, now, to the thudding of her pulse in her ears, the only evidence she'd had that time was not, in fact, standing still, as she waited for the pregnancy test to return with its verdict. The two lines, when they'd appeared, had been like two bars growing across an open window, trapping her inside. She had no more capacity, physically, emotionally, financially, as a Counter. She'd turned and vomited into the toilet before splashing cold water onto her face and unlocking the door. From where she'd stood she could see Maya, still on the arm of the sofa, expectant. She'd given one, brief nod, and then buried the information and any emotion in the bin along with the test.

Only now - three days on from Maya's visit, and with the rhythm of her work - did she have space to process what was happening. *Pregnant*. The sadistic irony of condoms being inaccessible within disposable limits for most Counters - the group that could least afford to have a child. Raj had shared an article at a meeting a few weeks ago which reported a huge rise in STIs and pregnancies in sex workers - an industry which is comprised of 90% Counter women. "Are the government fucking idiots?", he had exploded as he concluded his dark show and tell. "How much do they reckon a single condom fucks up the environment compared with a WHOLE FUCKING EXTRA HUMAN?" And he was right. Whilst condoms were a struggle within her quotas, a baby was impossible. She placed a hand on her stomach in apology at the thought, and closed her eyes, travelling inwards from the neat room with its piles of clothes and pleasant smell of laundry powder, to the tiny mass of cells inside her. *Hello*, *little human*, she thought. *I wonder what you'd look like. I wonder what music you'd like. Would you ever taste real cheese or ride in a car?* She thought of Lucas. *I can't have another child. I barely have enough for the one I have. Our lives are small, so small.* And her hand squeezed at the soft skin of her belly as if reaching inwards to comfort the foetus, or perhaps to rip it out of herself. As she thought of Lucas, his earnest little face and his small hand gripping hers, her mind's eye formed an unbidden but picture-perfect scene of big brother carefully holding a baby, bundled up in soft blankets. And then Mark appeared on the scene, also unbidden but not unwelcome, and she allowed herself to wonder.

Her phone buzzed in her back pocket, and she answered it where she knelt on the floor.

"Mrs Allywood?"

"Miss, yes."

"Lucas's mum?"

An impulse, for a moment, to deny it, to run from whatever Lucas's school was going to tell her, to throw away the phone and dive into the freshly laundered clothes and curl up into a ball and sleep, safe and warm. Just for a moment.

"Yes, that's me. Is everything okay?"

"It's Miss Brockley here, Lucas's form tutor. I'm afraid there's been an incident and we need you to come and pick him up."

"What kind of incident?" She fought the urge to lead with an apology, with an assumption of his guilt. "Is he okay?"

"*He* is fine, don't worry." The woman's emphasis implied that not all parties had come through the incident unscathed. Sam usually liked Miss Brockley; a patient,

163

energetic woman whom Lucas seemed to trust. But today it was clear her patience was wearing thin.

"It's just - I'm at work. It will take me an hour to get there, I don't have a car and…"

"I'm afraid he does need to be collected and taken off site as a matter of urgency. He has destroyed a display made up of a number of children's end-of-term artwork and they are extremely upset. And we haven't been able to calm him down either."

Define "*okay*", then, she thought, but focused on flicking through options in her mind, trying to work out how to solve the problem.

Caleb accepted her request with nothing short of glee when she called him. "Of course I can collect my son from school, I'd be happy to. I'll just need to rearrange a couple of things and I'll be right there." He'd paused, to add effect to the blow. "Oh, but - of course, I can't pick him up because mum is in Liverpool visiting her sister, and it wouldn't be safe for him to be alone with his own father for an hour, would it."

She had hated him as she gritted her teeth, swallowing her pride along with the bitter retort that first presented itself to her.

"I was thinking, actually, that maybe it's about time we had a think about all of that."

"Ah, I thought you might be. Convenient timing."

"Yes Cal," *this is all extremely fucking convenient for me, can't you tell?* She wanted to add, but instead she said, "so, can you go now? It would really help me out."

His smirk seemed to drift out of her handset and linger in front of her face. It was as though she could smell it over the ocean breeze fragrance of the detergent.

164

"I'll be there in ten." He'd said, as though he'd just been invited to receive an award for Father of the Year, and hung up.

"We're moving back in tomorrow!" Sophie greeted her as she came into the kitchen at the end of her shift. "Such an amazing job you've all done with the building. We are so grateful."

'Oh!" Sam realised that she was talking about cleaning the flood water in her building. "That's great news! You must be relieved!"

"Well to be honest, the insurance company has been pretty good in terms of compensation for the inconvenience. Travel points for extra journeys or commuting, disposables in case we're having to get takeaways all the time. Standard stuff. And luckily we've been staying here," she put her arms around Alice and gave her a loud kiss on the cheek, "so it's not been too much of a hardship."

"Oh I'm so glad that it hasn't been too much of a hardship for you." Alice teased, and perched on one of the sleek leather stools by the counter. "What did you decide about the night shifts Sam? Are you going to carry on?"

She thought of the money. She thought of the baby growing inside her, fumes and fatigue carried to it through her blood. She thought of life without the money. She thought of the baby growing inside her, unfurling itself ready for a lifetime of struggle, of resentment, lack of freedom - or maybe, even, (though it was something that troubled her less frequently), dying in some freak weather event, drowning or burning or being crushed into nothing. Impossibility burned her eyes. She clenched her jaw and looked upwards, as if to tilt the impending tears back into their ducts. It was as though all of the stress were condensing in her eyes, the sheer injustice of it. There was no winning. Nothing she did, no matter how hard she tried to make the right choice, would bring her out on top. Alice glanced over at her, as if to check that she had heard the question, seemingly confused by the lack of response. And then she did a double-take and her mouth opened with the certainty that a woman crying in your kitchen needs addressing, then closed again with an absence of anything to say. Sophie was scrolling through her phone, oblivious, and Sam gave a small shake of her head, both to signal to Alice that she shouldn't draw attention to what was happening, and as if to physically expel the sweep of tears passing through her. She cleared her throat, the first time with a trace of a sob and the second time with more purpose. Pull yourself together, she thought.

"Erm, yes, I'm going to give it a go. See how it goes. It might only be for a week or so anyway and then we'll be finished."

"Right, that's good. I suppose." Awkwardness was syrupy in her throat and in the air between them. Sam pulled out her phone and sent Mark a message asking him to meet her at Just Coffee, an enterprising Counter-friendly coffee stall that served cheap black coffee into reusable cups on the North-east corner of Dulwich Park. By the time she'd sent the message, she'd composed herself. She cleared her throat one more time, this time into an airy smile.

"Ah, well." She looked around the room. "That's me for the day. I'd better be off." She picked up her bag off the floor. "Good luck with the move back Sophie. And thanks again, you know, for hooking me up with the job."

"What? - oh - no problem. Happy to help. See you around Sam."

"I'll see you out." Alice said decisively, walking into the hallway.

She stepped ahead of her to open the door for her but paused with her hand on the handle. "Is everything alright Sam? I mean, it obviously isn't but… is there anything I can do?"

Sam traced a finger along the bottom row of eyelashes under each eye, checking for traces of weakness. "No, honestly. I'm sorry about that. I'm just emotional at the moment."

"Time of the month?" The question that from a woman is empathetic; from a man, diminishing.

"Something like that." She felt a sudden urge to confide in her employer. Perhaps it was having sons the same age: perhaps it was the openness with which Alice had shared her own problems. But if she was honest with herself, it was more than that. The same power imbalance which she so despised also somehow gave her a feeling of deference, of security in her company, as if the other woman's financial and social omnipotence could protect her too from anything. She felt for a moment like a rebellious teenager who is wavering on the brink of conceding that they do, after all, need someone older and wiser to take control of the situation. Like she wanted to fall to her knees at Alice's feet and beg her to tell her everything would be okay. To wrap her in a blanket and stroke her head and tell her she never needed to worry about anything ever again. And then she felt disgusted at herself for feeling that way. She imagined what Maya would have to say about that. Scoot might understand, she was softer, more forgiving, but not Maya. She pulled her shoulders down and lifted her chin. "Honestly, everything is fine, thanks Alice." *Everything is fine.*

Mark was waiting for her on one of the small wooden stools by the low wall that ringed the church behind the coffee stand. It was their favourite spot at that shop; they could rest their cups on the wall and watch busy shoppers, and late commuters, and other people hurrying for no good reason at all, as they sipped on their drinks. Usually, the sight of him made her feel calm, but today it spiked her blood with anticipation. She had to tell him. He stood to kiss her on the cheek when she arrived. "Hi babe."

"Babe? Since when do you call me babe?"

"Oh." Embarrassment reddened his cheeks. "It was just something I thought I'd try out. Not a fan of that one then." He plucked an imaginary notebook and pen from the air and made a careful note, full-stopping the memo with a dramatic flourish. "Noted."

She snorted with laughter. "You are such a goof."

"That's what you love about me, right?"

"I see what you did there. You're not going to trick me into saying it." She settled on the stool next to him and placed a hand on the outside of the cup to test if it was ready to drink.

"Ah, it's only a matter of time."

"What, before I fall in love with you, or before you trick me into saying it?"

"I'll take either." He shrugged. "So, if you didn't ask to meet so that you could declare your undying love - which is a huge blow for me, obviously - what's up?"

She cupped his cheek with her hand and stroked his forehead with her thumb. Gold flecks dotted his irises in the sunlight. She knew she did love him. It was a different love to the one she'd had for Caleb: it didn't need the extreme lows to create the extreme highs. It didn't eat her up inside like it had done with him, where the only possible thing worse than being with him would have been being without him. With Mark, it was mutual: it included her. Love, she had learned, existed in many forms, and came from many sources. It could come from someone making you feel bad about yourself, or from someone making you feel good about yourself. One was obsessive love; infatuation, fuelled by the fear of losing it, of being tossed aside, of being lesser. And the other was peaceful love; appreciating and being appreciated, wanting things to continue because they are so *good*, not because you are trapped by fear of the alternative. And it is impossible to recognise one without experiencing the other.

"I'm pregnant, Mark."

"I know I've been asking you for more commitment but I think you've taken it a little far."

"I'm serious."

"I know. This is how I react to serious things. I make bad jokes."

A trace of coffee lined his upper lip. He looked into his cup as if it might provide him with a more appropriate response. His other hand squeezed his thigh through his jeans.

"What do you want me to do?" She prompted.

"What do you mean?"

"We don't have to keep it."

"We *can't* keep it Sam."

It was as though someone had opened a valve and was deflating her. The sharp edge of the wall cut into her back. She shifted her weight on the stool.

"Right, no of course." She knew he was right. It was madness. They'd only known each other for seven months. And they were struggling to survive as it was. "I was just making sure you were on the same page." She went to stand up, her vision blurring with tears for the second time that day, as if recognising she was at her limit, protecting her from having to see any more of the shit around her. "Of course I didn't really think that you'd want this, that we could do this, I -"

His hand closed around her wrist.

"Sam, sit down. You have seen the news, right?"

"Quite frankly I don't give a fuck about the news right now Mark. And no, I haven't. I don't have a TV, or a car with a radio, and in case it hadn't crossed your mind I've been a bit preoccupied to sit and scroll through my phone." She jerked her arm hard to shake him off her, but he released his grip easily, not willing to keep her there by force. The ease with which he let her go surprised her, almost disappointed her, because she didn't really want to leave and had thought he wouldn't let her. She stood for a moment, breathing heavily, looking at him.

"Sam?" He half-rose too, and now it was the gravity of his voice, and not his physical strength, which kept her there. "Can you just sit down? You need to listen for a minute. Please."

Finding out that she had no choice, that she could not keep her child, made her cling to it all the more. The phrase *you always want what you can't have* sounds petty, too trivial to apply in this situation, but the psychology behind it is solid: often only when faced with the reality of life without something, do you realise its true importance. Her previous indecisiveness was unfathomable now. This was her baby, Lucas's brother or sister.

It was two o'clock in the morning. Lucas was in bed, and Mark had gone home. She'd said nothing to him after he had told her about the new rule. Not a single word. It was like her mind had shut down completely. She sat on the floor of the kitchen, leaning against the cupboard under the sink. The same place she had been for the last five hours. *They're going to kill my baby.* The words went round and around in her head. *They're going to kill my baby.* Mark had explained it to her, gently holding both of her hands as they'd sat on the hard wooden stools and their coffees had gone cold. *They'll already know that you're pregnant. From your tracker. It can detect the hormones. It's illegal to carry it to term without the points.* He'd pulled up the government website on his phone, checking the facts. "We have until twenty weeks, apparently. To arrange to… to *deal with it.*" He'd paraphrased the last part with obvious disgust. She'd asked the question with her eyes: *what happens if I don't?* And he had scrolled down a bit further, eyes flicking from side to side. He'd darkened the screen and pushed the heels of his hands into his eyes for a moment before looking at her, and giving a small shake of his head. But she had known how to read his silence, and the unspoken words were etched into the space around her as she sat in the darkness. *Then they come for you. They come for you both.*

Chapter 18

Alice

7th June marked Andrew's thirty-fifth birthday. Birthdays were always celebrated in a big way in the Leverton household. This year, because birthdays divisible by five are more significant than those with lesser factors, and far more than prime number birthdays, they were hosting a barbeque for his university friends. Tommy was staying with Andrew's parents, despite much protest. When she'd come to pick him up, Charlotte had grudgingly dropped off a bubble machine, replacing her customary annual offering of confetti, and had conceded that at thirty-five, her son no longer required numbered balloons to remind him of his fading youth. Alice had never truly considered just how bad birthdays were for the planet. Balloons, banners, party hats, glitter, unwanted gadgets and clothes wrapped in reams of single-use paper and ribbon: a veritable tat-fest. She looked out at the garden now, the 2025 Durham Tennis Team sprawled around in various stages of undress and inebriation. Richard had filled an upside-down garden gnome with Champagne and was overseeing an elaborate competition involving a badminton racket and a tangerine to see who had to drink it. His new wife, Francesca, was trying to teach some of the women - including Sophie, whose pink granny knickers were on display for the world to see - how to do a headstand. A snapshot of a bygone era's intellectual and sporting elite: past their prime.

As the day progressed, and even attempting a headstand seemed a long-gone implausibility, Alice found herself on the rattan corner sofa under a parasol with Francesca and Sophie, and a couple of other wives that she recognised from the wedding but had not met otherwise. She was lying with her head in Sophie's lap, and Sophie was stroking her hair like a baby. On the coffee table beside them, half-devoured salads curled and browned, and crescent edges of burger-bun lay discarded directly on the glass table-top, smears of ketchup opaquing the surface. Talk had turned, inevitably, to OffSet and the growing tensions surrounding it.

"I'm giving it up." She announced, partly for effect, but partly also because saying it out loud made it one step closer to reality. She reached for Sophie's hand and placed it back on her head. "Keep stroking my hair please."

"You're so needy. And what do you mean *giving it up*?"

"OffSet. I'm going to go cold-turkey. The whole family is."

Francesca's laugh was one of disbelief, almost scorn. "As if. They've suckered us in now. Once you're signed up, you're hooked. It's impossible to do without it."

"I hate to say it, but Franny's right Al. Look around you. It literally could not be done."

"I'm seeing this as a sort of 'last hurrah'. I've been looking at everything, and I think we can do it. It'll take some changes, obviously-'

"- some changes? Alice, it'll be a lifestyle lobotomy!"

"Don't be so dramatic. Pass my gin and tonic please." She sat up enough to take a gulp, and passed it back to Sophie to return to the table.

"To be honest," Sophie topped up her own glass, equal measures of gin and mixer, before wiggling the bottle to offer them a refill. "I feel like they're setting us up to fail. It would be easier for everyone if they had just made us stick to the limits from the start."

Franny snorted. "And how would they have made money from that? Good old-fashioned communism wouldn't line the pockets of the people at the top."

"Alright, don't start guys, I'm way too drunk to be talking about all of this political stuff."

Alice clapped her hands together: "Oh yeah Soph, I forgot about you and politics. Remind me what you got in your GCSE?"

"Oh give me a break. It's not my fault Mr Vickery was a complete moron. I came out of those classes not even having heard of Capitalism."

"You did not." Francesca egged them on.

"I did! We had a question in our GCSE paper about *the downsides of Capitalism*, and I wrote a whole answer about how it was the process of deciding which city should be the capital, and that the downside is that sometimes they pick cities that don't make sense, like Brasilia or Canberra, when it should obviously be Rio and Sydney, and that this has economic disadvantages for the country."

"I'll give you that, that's pretty creative to be fair." Francesca reached over and clinked Sophie's glass.

"Oh come off it Franny. Guys, I'm losing brain cells in this conversation. Top me up please Soph." Alice reached for her glass, sitting up with an effort. "Look, I'm not saying it's going to be easy, but the whole point is it's meant to be doable right? They said that at the COP meeting, when they announced the limits. They've tested it all out."

174

"I bet you one hundred pounds you don't make it through a month." Franny stuck out her hand.

Sophie batted it out of the way, offering her own instead. "I'll make it two hundred."

"Yeah, thanks for the votes of confidence ladies." She lay back against the cushions and rested the edge of the glass against her bottom lip. The alcohol was giving her conviction, but the seed had already been there. She wanted to try.

"Looks like you enjoyed yourselves yesterday."

It was the next morning. The party hadn't ended until around 5am, and she hadn't counted on such imminent outside judgement of the aftermath. Sam looked around the kitchen now, empty bottles and crisp packets, the fug of beer and body odour, a room with a hangover.

"I feel as bad as it looks. Don't touch this room. It's on my list for tomorrow."

"It's no prob-"

"I mean it. If I could lock it I would. Probably would just throw away the key to be honest, throw away the whole damn room, cook on a camp stove in the hallway. It looks how I feel."

"You look how it looks."

"Ouch."

Sam smiled angelically back at her. "I'd better get to work. You should go and nap. I'll leave your room till last."

"Sam?" She hadn't planned to say it: wasn't sure if it was the alcohol still charging through her system, or that Sam had brought her guard down with her obvious familiarity, or, perhaps, whether the sight of her receding back made her feel as though it were her last chance. Sam turned slowly to face her, mop and curiosity hanging suspended.

She shouldn't ask her that. Certain lines shouldn't be crossed, certain things had to be kept separate. Some things just needed to stay where they belonged.

"What is it?"

She took a deep breath, regretting having called her back even as she ploughed forwards, her alcohol-steeped brain unable to contrive an alternative topic.

"Do you - I mean, have you -, have you heard about these people, this group, who are against carbon sharing and checkers and stuff? Anti OffSet."

Sam seemed to consider for a moment; as if weighing up how much to tell her, perhaps wondering how much she knew, or maybe wondering whether to answer her at all.

Chapter 19

Sam

Surely she couldn't talk to her employer - her employer who was, almost certainly, relying heavily on offsetting through a Counter of her own no less - about PowerCut. The mop dripped onto the floor, like seconds on a clock. It was a secret. At least, parts of it were. They wouldn't exactly achieve much if no one was ever aware of their existence: the whole point was to disrupt, to make noise, to change things. But no one outside it was supposed to know the details about the '*what*', the '*how*', and definitely not the '*who*'. But maybe it was madness to think that Alice would believe that she knew nothing about any of it. *How much to tell her?* To convince her that she was being open without giving anything important away. She didn't want to lose her job, but she definitely didn't want to put PowerCut at risk. She stalled for time.

"People who are anti OffSet… I suppose there are a few people, you know, people who struggle with the contracts they've signed up to," she tried.

But Alice pushed on; "I mean more than that. Rebels - activists, I guess you could call them. An organised group. I've seen the symbol, the set of weighing scales, and the slogan. *Neutral not equal*. I just wondered if…"

Sam considered whether she could continue to evade until Alice felt awkward enough to retract the question. Her employer looked uncomfortable, out of her depth, like a male teacher giving a lesson on menstruation. Unsure of her tone, unsure how forward to be: unsure, even, what words to use. She could let her flounder, she was sure, until she garbled an apology, changed the subject. She waited, playing for time. The other woman waited too, and Sam wondered if she had underestimated her. Maisie, Alice's golden retriever, mooched between them, a ball with a plait of rope dangling from her mouth. Her claws clicked against the wooden floor.

A game of chicken. Finally, she conceded: "I've seen that symbol dotted around too."

"Right." The two women looked at each other. "So do you… I was just going to say, I was thinking I could do something to help in some way." Alice bent, and took hold of one end of the rope, causing the dog to clench her jaw and lean her bodyweight backwards, taking up the strain of the rope. That was the best thing about dogs, Sam thought. They were dependable. Always hungry, always ready for a tug of war. Alice pulled the rope from right to left, diverting the attention from the conversation, trying to appear off-hand. "Something small, I don't know. If you knew of anyone with a link to them. It's just, well… I saw about the restrictions on materials for protesting, for example, and it just made me think. Andrew has a printer. He gets an allowance through his work. Or something else, I don't know, maybe it's stupid. I just thought…"

Sam's silence was not intentional, though she took some small satisfaction in watching her employer continue to say words, even as each new utterance grew more uncertain and incomplete than the last, like a coffee machine that has delivered its shot of espresso and was now spewing and sputtering hot water to fill up the cup. It was that she wasn't prepared for this conversation. All of the possible answers jostled against one another so that none could rise to the surface and form a coherent response. Maisie's tail was thumping against her leg as she geared up into the battle, back legs slipping on the floor as she struggled for traction. Finally, she said, "she loves that toy, doesn't she."

Alice gave her a searching look. "She sure does."

Sam scratched Maisie's back and smiled back at her.

She was walking back from Alice's, and was almost at her house when she saw them. Two of them, hovering outside her house, green boiler suits like badly thought-out camouflage in the grey concrete of South London. Waiting for her. It struck her how tall one of them was, and how short the other, superlatives, comical, like a pair of cartoon detectives. *They know.* She thought. She considered running, or even turning down another street, keeping walking, pretending to be someone else. Lucas was with his dad, as he often was at the moment whilst she was at work, his suspensions from school becoming more regular even with the weekly occupational therapy sessions which seemed to be making things worse rather than better: *all part of the process*, the therapist had assured her after Monday's incident which had involved him throwing his tray across the room at school after becoming frustrated to find out that the only meal option he was allowed to eat was finished by the time he had got to the front of the lunch queue.

Why did I get so comfortable with Alice? What did I give away? How could I have been so stupid?

The Checkers were looking at her now, wondering, she was sure, if this was the woman they were looking for. The woman whose employer had reported her. She wondered if they would arrest her on the spot. She still had time to turn around. She could go to Caleb's now, and collect Lucas, and… *and what?* Where would she go? They couldn't even get on a bus or a train. The Checkers were approaching her now, only a few steps away.

"Mrs Allywood?"

"It's Miss." She corrected them by force of habit, as though her martial statement mattered in the face of imminent arrest.

"Right you are. Miss Allywood, mother of Lucas Allywood?"

The question shocked her out of her mental image, in which she was already sitting in the corner of a cell, pregnant belly starting to swell against the prison uniform, no way to earn the points needed to keep her baby.

"I, err. Yes. I'm Lucas's mum." Different panic now.

"I'm afraid there's been an accident, involving your ex-husband."

"He's not my - what? What's happened?" She clutched at the short man's arm, but the other tugged her hand free.

"No touching."

"Sorry." She swallowed her impatience out of the necessity of keeping these men onside, but was inwardly furious at their nonchalance. "Where is my son? *Please*."

"That's better." The tall man cleared his throat and looked down at his notes. "It appears that the father - Caleb? - had been drinking heavily. He'd been driving under the influence, and then it seems he went inside and fell asleep but left your son locked in the car. Forgot about him, he says. Anyway, it's been a hot day as you know and-"

Black spots appeared at the corners of her vision. His words floated down her throat and were met by rising bile. Her brain seemed to focus on a smaller, more immediate detail, to keep her present.

"But why you? I mean - why are you here, why not the police? I thought…"

The short man shifted uncomfortably. "Well, we were closer, so it made sense, it was quicker. The police are busy with…" He didn't finish his sentence, and in her distress she didn't care that he would have said 'more important things'. *More important than the son of some poor Checker woman.*

"Is…" she made a strange noise, somewhere between a wretch, a gulp, a cough; fear and air trapped in her chest, "is he alive?"

"Yes, he's alive. He's at Guy's hospital, being treated for dehydration and heatstroke."

She began to cast around wildly for a way to get there, a miracle, physically looking from left to right, as though a teleportation machine might appear from thin air beside them on the chewing-gum-spotted pavement. She felt like a fish, hooked and tossed away to gasp and flap, unable to move, unable to speak, unable to breathe. The Checkers seemed to consider the message delivered, and were communicating through a sequence of glances and cuff tugs that it was time to move on.

"We do wish your son all the very best."

"Wait!"

"Yes?"

"Can you give me a lift? I mean, to the hospital. It's just I-"

"I'm afraid not. It's not protocol."

"But - how am I meant to get there? I need to be with my son!" Even the time it took to say these words felt like a betrayal, and she wrapped her arms around her body, clawing at her upper arms, the pain giving her something to focus on, keeping her present. The tall man was already a few paces away, scrolling on a tablet, but the short man seemed to soften.

"I wish we could help you out. But even if you weren't a Counter, we've got another call out to head to. Is there someone you can call?"

His partner called out to him and he too moved away down the street, and the two of them headed off like tankers after an oil spill: light, unburdened, leaving utter devastation in their wake.

Alice had arrived to pick her up and drive her to the hospital in less than ten minutes. Her hair was dripping wet and she was not wearing makeup, and her top had white spots of toothpaste down the front. It had been over a year since Sam had been inside a car, but neither this, nor her employer's unprecedented un-put-togetherness, penetrated the bubble of shock that wobbled around her, threatening at any moment to burst and force her to feel.

"Thank you for coming." She managed.

"Don't be silly. Of course. I - I'm so sorry Sam. I can't imagine."

Sam placed her hand flat against the window, looking out. An image flashed back at her from the glass; Lucas thrashing, bashing a small fist against the glass, his messy hair stuck to his forehead with sweat, manic with fear and pain.

"They say he had a seizure. At the hospital." She'd called them while she waited for Alice, demanded an update, wished she could crawl through the phone and be beside him. "His brain. From the heat. Swelling."

She could only manage broken fragments of sentences, as if her brain too were swollen, fragile soft tissue pressed up against unforgiving bone, crushing the very essence of her. She pressed the button to wind down the window, hoping the image of her son cooking in a metal cage would slide away with the glass. Alice reached across and took her hand. It felt uncomfortable, but also like a lifeline. When the other woman squeezed it, she squeezed back.

Lucas was asleep when they arrived. His cheeks were still flushed, and a drip hung next to him. Caleb grabbed at her shoulders when she came into the cubicle, shook her roughly, as if from within her he might dislodge the forgiveness he was looking for.
"It was an accident!"
Alice stepped forwards to intervene, but Sam stopped her, shrugging him off.
"Get out of my way Cal." She pushed past him, to Lucas's bedside. She stroked the hair from his forehead, placed a hand on his chest to feel his breath, picked up his tiny hand and pressed each one of his fingertips, the colour fading and returning, needing to see for herself that he was alive. When she was satisfied, she rounded on Caleb.
"Why are you still here?"
"I - he's my son." Even now, his indignation prickled.
"Why haven't they arrested you?"
"They're waiting outside. They let me stay with him until… until you…"
"Well I'm here now, so he doesn't need you. We don't need you. Not ever again Cal."

And she meant it. Even if she had to lie, or steal, or kill, she would not let her precious baby spend another second with this man.

He raised his hands to his face and began to sob, great heaving breaths.

"You're bleeding.' She pointed to his wrists. She felt no pity, no emotion at all to see that he had once again slashed at his arms in guilt or self-loathing. When he had done it before, after crashing the car, after losing money on a bet, even after hitting her, it had always drawn her back in, shifted her mindset into one of protector, consoler. But not this time. "And if you're going to have a panic attack," she continued, as his breathing became faster, shallower, "do it outside."

Lucas had to stay in overnight for observation. Alice stayed with her, on fold-down plastic chairs in the corridor outside his room. Caleb was taken away shortly after they'd arrived, and a policewoman had come to speak to her. *Five more minutes, and he'd have been dead*, she'd told her. *The temperature inside the car was likely to have exceeded 65°C. If it hadn't been for a passing neighbour raising the alarm, he wouldn't be here. He was very lucky.* The woman had concluded. *Lucky*. Sam looked across at Alice, mouth slightly open as she slept, hair still slightly damp. She thought about the other woman's son. *Lucky* was having two sober parents who loved you and looked after you. *Lucky* was doing well in school and finding it easy to make friends. *Lucky* was coming from a family with enough money to buy you everything you wanted, everything you needed, not having to worry about what you ate or whether you could turn the lights on in the dark of night. She couldn't have made it to the hospital without Alice, didn't want her to leave. But still she felt resentment. Resentment for all that she couldn't give her son. Resentment that she should have to feel grateful at all, like thanking someone for throwing you a life ring, when they're the one who pushed you off the boat in the first place.

Chapter 20

Alice

It wasn't until the end of October that she had *The Idea*.
Her cameo for PowerCut had begun with a hundred
posters. She had printed them for Sam while Andrew was
at work, sliding them into the backpack that she always
propped by the radiator, feeling like she was a secret
agent in rather a dull action movie. Wonder Woman and
the forbidden flyers. In the weeks since she had first
approached Sam about PowerCut, and as her
involvement had grown, she had often wondered if she
was now just a bored housewife, playing at heroics,
meddling without getting her hands dirty. She was
simply not under the same scrutiny as Sam. She wasn't
taking the same risks. Drones did not target her, and the
presence of Checkers gave a sense of security: they were
on her side. But she had become obsessed with the drama
of it all. At night she lay awake beside Andrew and the
ideas and plans she mulled over became more and more
outlandish as sleep drifted in, such mundane
practicalities as prosecution and mortality - or even basic
feasibility - smothered by the trance of hypnagogia. One
night, she'd imagined them kidnapping OffSet's CEO and
forcing him to live by the quota of the most restricted
Counter; the next, she half-dreamt a scheme in which the
whole country switched everything off for seventy-two
hours each week, and everyone took sleeping tablets to
block out those three days, leaving ample carbon
allowance for remaining four; and the night after that,

that they should just kill everyone off over the age of eighty, when people were too old to really enjoy their consumption anyway, leaving plenty for the rest of them. But finally, one October evening, when the weather was just beginning to flip between the soft mildness of autumn and the sharp cut of winter - no two consecutive days the same, a jacket discarded one moment and insufficient the next - she thought of it. It was an article she'd read in The Times that had given her the idea: a long-read titled *How Russia Almost Lost The War*, which detailed an elaborate operation by a Polish anti-War effort, in which they managed to contaminate the fuel supply for Russian tanks during the illegal invasion twenty years previously, destroying their engines and tipping the odds firmly back in Ukraine's favour. Phrases like "levelled the playing field", and "previous unfair advantage" jumped out at her, as well as the international public support for underdogs who had managed to gain so much ground with zero casualties. *This could work*, she had thought. *This could really work.*

There were no tanks in this scenario, of course. No tangible weapons at all, only systemic ones. And air travel was not exactly even an example of a systemic weapon, but more a symbol of toxic disparity. Air travel was a luxury that only the wealthiest, only the most environmentally indifferent, continued to enjoy. And its continuation - in an era where high speed rail connected all of Europe - along with all of the most extreme examples of carbon-profligate activities that the ten percent refused to sacrifice - was one of the biggest enemies of both Counters, and the planet. After all, they could continue to dedicate the same portion of their wealth to OffSetting, whilst requiring a far smaller additional carbon allowance in return - or better yet, none at all, but simply adhere to the philanthropic concerns that they had used for so long to validate propping up the OffSet system, but expecting nothing in return. *We should let them make the choice for themselves* - she was guilty of perpetuating this idea herself - that if she didn't pay a Counter, their family might starve. *We're doing them a favour*. Why did so few people consider the idea of a secret option C: a world in which people were not forced to decide between their freedom and their basic needs at all? That was how the EU had finally agreed on the blanket embargo on importing anything produced in a sweatshop in 2032, stopping all the *would-you-rather-those-people-were-unemployed?*, virtue-signalling, cheap-slave-tailored-jeans-wearing in their tracks. People still wanted clothes, so conditions were improved and pay increased, and exporters simply passed the additional costs on to the consumers. And people paid more, and bought less. So yes, air travel was a worthy target on which to focus efforts, she'd decided. Without these big hitters, the carbon quotas would be manageable as prescribed per capita by COP, or at the very least the super-carbon-spenders would get a small taste of *life without*.

Sam had, predictably, appeared dubious. She had not even put down her bag before Alice had ushered her into the living room that Wednesday morning, after little sleep. Sam lowered herself slowly to the sofa, backpack still in hand, but she paced in front of her, excited by the idea about which she was so certain, desperate that it be well-received. After asking after Lucas, and establishing that he was recovering well from the hideous business with that awful ex-husband of hers and the car, she had launched straight in.

"Aren't all those places, like, pretty well-guarded?" Sam had asked, picking up one of the patterned cushions from the sofa and hugging it to her chest like a shield. But Alice had thought of that, as she had tipped water over Tommy's curls and shampooed his soft scalp in the bath while he squealed and screwed his eyes tight shut.

"They are. And who do you think guards them? Who does all of those jobs?" *The shit jobs*, she thought, but didn't say this. "Who drives the tankers from the ports to the airports? Who cleans the tanks and checks the fences? Who does the night shifts and who manages the hoses and hauls around the equipment to refuel the planes? Which people do all of the jobs that keep this country running, but still don't get paid enough to survive without selling part of themselves to the system?" And Sam had looked at her blankly, still not quite getting it.

"*Counters do*. And that's the whole reason why you guys have a chance. When so many people - and such key people - are treated like shit, then they have the power - and the motive - to really screw things up for the rest of us. I am just *sure* you could get enough people onside to make the plan work. All you'd need to do would be to convince enough people in the chain of custody for the fuel. Get the stuff in there at Calais, or wherever it comes in. Those same guys who search the trucks for illegal immigrants, they could help you with that part. And the best part of it is no violence. Maximum disruption, no one gets hurt. Well, except perhaps my in-laws who would consider the cancellation of their annual trip to the Caribbean to be a physical attack." She laughed, partly to lighten the mood, and partly to show that she was now firmly *not* part of the demographic of people who considered a holiday abroad a basic human right, but rather of the group that scorned them for it. Although, it had transpired upon checking, she herself was tied into her OffSet contract for another three months - a discovery about which she did not know whether to be frustrated or relieved.

"I don't know, it sounds difficult." Sam looked small suddenly, her shoulders curled forwards on the sofa, looking down. But Alice felt possessed by her plan, as though it would somehow undo the role she had previously played in this subjugation. And the cleverness of it: inspired by history, peaceful, symbolic.

"Have a think about it. It's just an idea." *The most brilliant fucking idea in the history of ideas.*

"Actually Alice," Sam began, and she wondered if the woman might accuse her of a saviour complex, tell her that she should mind her own business unless she was willing to put her money where her mouth was, but instead she said: "I'm pregnant."

She had not been expecting that. She opened and closed her mouth, before turning and sitting beside her. "You're - you're having a baby? That's -"

"Not *having a baby,* no. Just pregnant. I take it you've seen the update."

"Oh, right. Fuck." She wanted to ask if Sam would have wanted to keep the baby regardless - was that awful man from the hospital the father? But she was worried it would sound crass to ask.

"A right mess, isn't it." It was not a question, but Alice nodded anyway. Sam leant her cheek on the edge of the pillow propped in her lap, and looked back at her.

"How are you feeling? Oh", realisation dawned, "the other week, you actually were sick then? Morning sickness?"

"I knew you'd think I was avoiding you."

"I didn't -"

"Yes you did, and it's fine." It should have been an accusation, exposing, but instead it was just matter-of-fact, like it really was fine.

Sam continued, "I did kind of want to avoid you anyway. But yeah, I was actually throwing my guts up. I didn't know what was causing it at that point though."

"What are you going to do?"

"Not much I can do. I got a notification this morning, look." She pulled out her phone and passed it across to her. "I need to confirm that I am aware of the update and provide a decision within six weeks."

"What happens if you ignore it?"

Sam pulled a face.

"If you haven't booked a termination or submitted the carbon fee by nineteen weeks, they come and 'support' you in doing so." The word support, usually with such positive connotations, was sinister. "Oh, and do you know what the funniest part is?" Sam continued, as if she had been running through a list of increasingly comical statements, rather than describing the steps leading up to a forced abortion. "There's a carbon charge for the termination itself."

Chapter 21

Sam

It was Mark's turn to host the meeting. They'd taken to changing the location for each meeting, since OffSet had turned on location tracking in all Counter discs as part of the government crackdown on resistance groups. He'd offered to cancel, to stay with her and Lucas, but the truth was he had recovered well from the incident with the car (far better than she had herself, in fact). He was back at school, and, far from being devastated at the news that he would no longer be spending time with his father, neither for his weekly visitation nor if he needed collecting from school in an emergency, he seemed somehow more settled. Her mother had been desperate to spend some time with her grandson after the recent events, and Sam had been grateful for the time off. Since the incident, and probably compounded by knowing the fate of his sibling, she had become an obsessive mother; sick, fearful, watching his chest rise and fall as he slept, checking his temperature over breakfast each morning and before he went to bed, reluctant to allow him out of her sight. She was suffocating him, and suffocating herself. She needed to give him - and herself - space to breathe.

It felt strange, seeing all of these people crowded into his familiar living room, an uncomfortable melding of two parts of her lives: love, and fear which - though inextricably linked by Mark - she had managed to compartmentalise up until now. But not anymore. Raj was lounging sideways across the arms of the armchair where she herself had sat a week previously and told Mark she loved him for the first time. Scoot was drinking squash from her favourite mug; the one Mark had bought her as a birthday present from the Southbank Market. Somehow, she had gone from an outsider, to a non-committal guest, to now all of this being hosted in the apartment where she had slept and made love. And tonight, she was not simply going to be listening. Tonight, she wouldn't be able to lurk in the background. The more she'd thought about it after their conversation, the more she'd liked Alice's idea. Her immediate reaction had been to reject it as insane. Too big, too difficult, *too involved*. But although she had shut Alice down, and although her employer still thought that the suggestion had been deflected in its entirety, there had been a small, flickering moment, like a light deciding whether to turn on when you press the switch, where she had allowed herself to consider: *what if?* And suddenly, the floodlights were on, and all of the possibilities were illuminated, and she'd begun to run with the idea, hypothetically, almost as a joke or a game, something to distract her from the knowledge that soon she would be forced to swallow a poison that would kill her unborn child, or have it cut from her with a knife. And now, here she was.

"So basically, it would be the perfect non-violent attack. Hundreds of planes would be ruined as soon as the fuel gets put in. The engines wouldn't even start, and they'd just be sitting there, blocking all the airports. It would be chaos. They wouldn't be back to normal for months." She concluded, looking around at the group, trying to gauge their response. She felt self-conscious, suddenly. Like she'd told a joke and no one had laughed. They had sat silently while she had relayed the details of Alice's plan, repackaged as her own. She hadn't told them where the idea had come from – they would never go for it if they knew who'd suggested it – but she had impressed upon them the key to the plan: "their weakness lies in how many of us there are, and the types of jobs we do". *The shit jobs,* she thought, but didn't say this.

She had gone over the plan and what she would say over and over again in bed with Mark the night before, and at intervals had pleaded with him to be the one to tell the group, but he had insisted it should be her. He took her hand now, and nodded his support, and repackaged the essence of her message so that it was at once simple, and powerful. "Basically, we – and by *we,* I mean all us poor bastards, and all Counters, obviously – however you want to group us – we are the backbone of society, and that means we are uniquely placed to bring them down." His hand sla"ped his thigh –ith the last three words, so that they rang around the room after he had finished speaking. No one spoke for a moment as they considered the proposition, and she thought that perhaps they hated the idea; thought it stupid, or impossible maybe. Then Maya laid her hands, palm-up, on her knees, shrugged, and said quietly: "You ain't shit without a backbone."

"Any fucker who still travels by plane while I can't even get on a pissing bus is fair game as far as I'm concerned." Raj declared. "I'm in."

"You're always in Raj." Scoot clipped him playfully on the shoulder. "Your vote's not exactly discerning, is it? Didn't you vote 'yes' for the goat plan?"

"Erm, yes, because we share 98% of our DNA with goats and they only eat grass. Stick ya tracker on a goat and you're good to go! I *still* vote yes for the goat plan."

"Don't ask." Mark whispered to her as she sat back down, and one of her legs shook with the delayed effect of speaking in public, so that she had to cross it over the other one to still it.

When everyone had left, and they stood in the empty room, he took her hand and pulled her into him so that his face was hidden. "You were amazing. I'm so proud of you."

"Do you reckon they'll go for it?"

"I don't know. It's a good plan, but it's a pretty big ask." She tried to see it as win-win; either they would like her idea and go ahead with the plan, or she would be allowed to continue to simply exist between the lines, without exposing herself to danger or the potential to fail. But by the same logic it felt to her like a lose-lose; the only outcomes now were rejection, or the risk of being responsible for vandalism on a national-scale, neither of which much appealed to her.

Despite the positive reception from the group, Sam's excitement was fleeting. Over the next three weeks, she felt herself withdraw from PowerCut, her focus shifting inwards – onto the hardships and inescapable tedium of everyday life, and of the countdown in her womb.

She was four months pregnant now, and the word *deadline* had taken on a new, sinister meaning. She felt powerless, angry, mourning a loss that had not yet happened but that she could do nothing to prevent. And at the same time she felt compelled to enjoy what little time she had with her child, safe inside her for the

195

moment, protected and oblivious to its impending fate. She had read a series of interviews published on the PowerCut protected network in which the first families who'd been victim to the new regime had shared their stories. Two couples had been intercepted trying to board the train to France, pregnancy status in their Counter discs triggering an alert when they passed through the barriers at the international station. Another woman, in Newcastle, had been imprisoned for 18 months for attempted evasion (but not before her compulsory abortion was completed). A fourth pregnant woman had died after her sister had hit an artery whilst trying to cut the disc from her neck to prevent the Checkers from locating her during the twentieth week of gestation. And then there were the stories of the procedures themselves – wrists and ankles bound, sedatives, fathers forcibly restrained. And the aftermath – bleeding, cramping, crying – body going against heart and mind to expel the fragile ball of cells that cannot yet survive on the outside. An unceremonious end in the u-bend. A lifetime of sadness and remorse.

And so it was that one morning in December, after she dropped Lucas at school, she found herself heading back along the long road, under the bridge where she had first seen PowerCut's symbol scrawled on the crumbling brickwork, and up past the station to the supermarket in the town centre. She didn't go through the automatic doors, but instead cut around the back, through the car park, and round the corner to the alleyway at the back where the bins were kept. Movement from inside one of the large plastic containers where the supermarket dumped out-of-date ready meals and fruit that was past its best made her jump, stepping into a puddle that flicked grimy grey water up the back of her leggings. But it was just a man rummaging for something to eat, and after lifting the lid to peer out at her for a moment, he returned to his mission without a word. *Dumpster diving*, the press had coined it, as though it were a trendy quirk, rather than a tragic irony, a symptom of a world in which food waste and starvation could simultaneously vye for the top spot of *society's biggest issues.* She cast around for what she was looking for. A group of men stood in a circle at the end of the alleyway, smoking cigarettes and talking in accents she could not place. There was no-one else around, and these men seemed perfectly at ease in their shabby surroundings. *This must be them* she thought. When you are not sure if someone is who you are looking for, you have to attempt to catch their eye with just the right level of confidence. Too much, and they will engage even if they have no reason to, your certainty erasing their doubt. Not enough, and they won't notice you at all. You need to give them just enough that they will know you are looking for them only if it is indeed them that you are looking for. And so she threw them a glance, and then another one, and when she caught one of their eyes she quickly gave a confused half-smile coupled with a questioning shrug.

"You looking for us love?"

"I don't know - I mean, I think so? Are you -?"

"Who are you looking for?"

Desperation had bestowed upon her a warped notion of invincibility in the way that rock-bottom can do. It had propelled her to come here, to try this, but this feeling faded fast as the man searched her face.

"I - uh - is one of you *Gregg*? I read online that-"

The men laughed, and she felt the skin across the back of her shoulders prickle.

"We're all Gregg, if the right person is asking. New here, are you?"

"Sorry, I think I'm in the wrong place. I should go." She began to walk back the way she had come, half-sideways so as to give them a chance to respond and not to appear rude.

"We're only messing with you love. Are you after our services?"

She considered saying no, but the images in her mind's eye flashed before her once again. Hands, gripping her upper arms. Holding her down. Unidentifiable instruments; a metal hook, a knife, a big serrated ladle, and chemicals, bottles and tablets with terrifying warning labels - she wasn't sure of the details of an abortion, so the images were generic, hedging their bets across an array of primaeval looking options for forcibly removing a foetus - floated in her periphery where they waited for the next opportunity to crowd her thoughts in their entirety.

"Yeah. I am."

"Then you're in the right place." The man smiled at her and stepped away from the others. "How much are you after?" He asked her, as though they were discussing a casual purchase in a shop. She took a deep breath.

"4500."

"Ah." He said knowingly. "Been bringing us a lot of business, that has."

"Right."

"It's a straightforward process, not to worry. You'll need to give me some basic information, name, address. So's I know where to find you, that's all."

198

Her phone rang, and she stepped away to answer it, grateful for the precious extra seconds before she had to tell this man, from whom she was going to borrow points that she had no way of repaying, where she lived with her five year old son. It was Lucas's school, calling her to ask her to pick him up. She apologised to the man, conscious that it seemed like she had lost her nerve. "Oh I'm not worried. You'll be back.' The man pointed at her stomach. "You haven't got long. You're starting to show."

"Promise me you won't go back there Sam. *Promise me.*" It was evening, and she had put Lucas to bed after a game of cards in which Mark had let him win three times in a row. She'd picked him up from school after a melt-down because the teacher wouldn't let him open the window in his maths lesson, and the sun was shining in his eyes. *Not exactly rocket-science is it*, she had shouted at the school nurse, in her head, as she ushered her son out of the sick room, *that he would be afraid of being trapped in a hot space behind sealed glass, after what happened to him.* But she had smiled, and apologised, once again, for her son. "I can't Mark. I can't promise that. I'm sorry." She was tucked under the crook of his arm on the sofa, leaning into him, and he kissed the top of her head whenever he was stuck for what to say. The need to protect this baby was consuming her, as though her life depended on it, as though it were her heart that would be cut from her rather than her unborn child. The love she felt was even more potent than it should have been, strengthened by defiance, as if her fear and anger were also masquerading as love, so that she felt protective instinct like nothing she had ever experienced before. It burned in her chest and

her womb and made her restless, agitated, and she felt as
though she would be able to run forever if it would save
them. His arm stiffened around her.

"You don't know what they're capable of, Sam. Those
kinds of men. I know people who've borrowed from
them before. You just end up owing them, and owing
them, and you can never pay them back, the amount gets
higher and higher and-"

"I might not know what they're capable of Mark, but I
don't think it can be much worse than the alternative, do
you?" She sat up and shuffled around to look at him,
wriggling free of his arm. "I have to try." She was crying,
despair running down her cheeks and soaking the neck of
her sweatshirt. His eyes were wet too, and she realised
for the first time how hard this was for him.

"Can you just give me some time Sam." He dragged his
knuckles violently across his eyes, as if to reassert his
masculinity. "Give me until Friday. And then if not, I'll
come with you."

Chapter 22

Alice

She didn't recognise the man on her doorstep. He had an air of uncertainty about him, and also somehow the sense that he was not used to being uncertain; that being outside of his comfort zone was, in itself, out of his comfort zone. Perhaps a door-to-door salesman, or fundraising for a charity. He wore brown chinos, battered trainers, and a green disc. She opened the door with the chain on.

"Hi."

"Hello?" She waited for him to elaborate, irked by his initial greeting not being accompanied by explanation of his presence.

Battered trainers shuffled against terracotta tile.

"I - erm - I'm a friend of Sam's."

"Oh - is she alright?"

"Yes. Well, sort of. Not really. Can I come in?"

She hesitated. Anyone could claim to be a friend of Sam's - and even a legitimate friend of Sam's didn't necessarily fill her with confidence. Giving her wild ideas to take out of the house was one thing, but inviting Sam's wider world into the house was another. The cowardice was hypocritical, given what she had suggested Sam - a pregnant, marginalised woman with few resources - should attempt to do. But her status afforded her the luxury of being a coward, and she was accustomed to it.

"Sorry, my son's asleep. Could we…" She made a small circular gesture at the narrow gap between them to indicate that she would prefer to stay as they were.

"Yes. Of course."

"Sorry." She was careful to pull a mild face of apology, that befit her excuse - *child asleep, no big deal* - rather than one that said: *sorry, I don't trust you because I'm a bigot*, even though she knew this was the truth. "What can I do for you?"

"I don't really know how to start this." A small clearing of the throat. "Okay. Has, uh, has Sam told you her news?" His hand flickered, almost imperceptibly, towards his stomach, so that she was almost certain of what he meant. But given the stakes, she was unwilling to give anything away.

"Could you be more explicit? I'm not sure…"

"Has she told you she's pregnant?"

"Ah, yes. Yes she has." She wondered for a moment if he was here in an official capacity, but his Counter status and general demeanour suggested otherwise.

"Right, good. That's good. She doesn't know I'm here. It would be even worse if she hadn't -"

"Who are you, sorry?"

"My name is Mark. I'm the father. Of the baby, I mean." She laughed. "Yes I didn't think you meant hers. Well, congratulations, I suppose…?" The end of her sentence a double-question; *is congratulations an idiotically insensitive thing to say?*, and also, *why are you here?*

"I suppose, yes." He spoke with an accent incongruous with the disc on his neck, and she felt slightly more at ease. "Well, aha, it should be congratulations, shouldn't it, except - well - that's sort of why I'm here."

"Yes, I'm so sorry, about the new rules. What does she - what are you both planning to do?"

"We - well, I, actually. Like I said, she doesn't know I'm here . I'm not sure she'd be impressed, to be honest, but I'll worry about that later. I wondered if you could help us."

"Sam knows I would help if I could. She's a great employee, a friend, too." And she knew it was true, even though the realisation had taken far longer because of social circumstance.

"Well, you can, actually. This points fee. It's just that - a fee. Anyone can give her the points, just by sending them to her account, so that she has them available at the twenty-week mark, and again when the baby is born, so they can take them. I'd pay you back, I swear. I'll do whatever it takes, we can work out a plan -"

It was so obvious now. This was what she could do to help. Not some crackpot idea to destroy planes. This was how she could make a difference, how she could use the extra points that would accumulate with her plan to scale down their usage whilst still in contract. *Offsetting her OffSetting*, as it were. How she could save a life.

"I'll do it. Of course I'll do it. Hang on." She closed the door and slid off the chain to open it properly, emboldened by purpose. "I'm so glad you asked."

"Don't you need to check? Have a look at your account, or maybe speak to your husband?"

She prickled at the suggestion, as though the man were cheering for the patriarchy, rather than mere marital democracy.

"No. I'll do it. I just need to know the logistics of it all." The logistics, it transpired, were simple; transferring the points from one account to another. He showed her how to go to the right section on her app, looked away as she entered her passwords, and set up the transfer for her. "You'd just have to click *approve*," he pointed at the blue button at the bottom of the transaction screen, "right here. You don't need to do it right now though, I didn't want to put you on the spot,-"

She clicked *approve*, not waiting for him to finish speaking. "Done." A thrill ran through her.

"It says you've gone into debt of twelve hundred points?" He looked alarmed. She was warming to the man - *much better than the ex.*

"Don't worry - I have an overdraft limit, I get interest-free credit."

"Oh right. That's good." Something in his tone suggested it was *not good*, and she tried to scrutinise what she had said.

"Oh. You don't get credit, I'm guessing." She tapped her teeth together awkwardly.

"Can't even get an official loan." He shrugged, as though talking about the supermarket having run out of eggs. "Pretty hard to pass basic eligibility checks when you're already selling them half your soul." They both laughed then, just a few syllables of a laugh, but it expelled some of the tautness. In that moment, she could see what Sam saw in him. Emotional intelligence. The ability to correctly pitch a joke to a stranger in an uncomfortable situation and make it a little less uncomfortable.

"I'm sorry. The system is awful. I'm getting out, I don't know if Sam said. I have to do my notice, which is why I'll have enough to do this. But then I'm out." She felt pride as she said this, her conviction renewed. So, when Mark left, she listed the car for sale on a local buy-and-sell page, made an appointment for someone to come and decommission the pool, and ordered a vegetarian cookbook online. *She was doing this*. She wondered what Andrew would say about it all. She knew he hadn't really taken her seriously, especially following her failed resignation from OffSet. Maybe this would finally piss him off enough for a real argument, or maybe he would get on board, and these changes - the challenge of it all - would be enough to shake things up in their marriage. Make or break. She would take either at this point.

Chapter 23

Sam

"What the fuck, Mark?" Sam hissed at him that evening as she threw open the door, the latch hitting neatly into the indent in the wall, a small shrine to years of Caleb. The points had flashed up on her app before Mark had arrived at hers, and she had realised almost immediately what he had done. And she was pissed off. She was also immensely grateful to both of them. And then she was pissed off all over again, angry that she should have to feel grateful to anyone at all for the simple right to keep her baby. "What happened to '*no secrets*'? How the hell am I meant to show my face at work after this?"

"It wasn't exactly a secret, more a *delayed truth.* It wasn't like I didn't think you'd ever find out." He stood on the doorstep, feet not quite fully planted, as though expecting to be invited in at any moment.

"It's kind of fucked up though, don't you think? These are points she's got from another Counter. Imagine if that person is pregnant too? Or desperately needs them for something else."

"Well Alice has that person's points already anyway. And you can't think like that. This is not your fault."

"I didn't say it was my fault Mark. It's *yours*. You went and stuck your nose in. I had this handled." She thought again of her meeting in the alleyway behind the supermarket, of the warnings and horror stories on the forum where she had found out where to look for those men, of him asking for her address. She heard Lucas's voice calling down the stairs and looked up. He was kneeling on the worn carpet of the landing, his head poking through the bannisters.

"You'd better come inside. For God's sake." She turned and stepped onto the bottom stair, less than a metre from the front door. "What's up Lu?"

"Is Mark here? Can I come down and say hello?"

"Why aren't you asleep?"

"I had a bad dream." He leant his face against one of the wooden bars so that his cheek squished forwards and closed his eyes, clearly fighting sleep in an effort to join the grownups and see what all the fuss was about.

"Go back to bed. I'll come up and tuck you in again in ten minutes, okay?" He nodded without opening his eyes, and pulled himself up on the creaky wooden railings before padding back to their room.

"What did she say when you asked her?" She didn't offer him a drink, and they sat opposite each other in the dark kitchen. One ear listened out for noises from her first born, while the other focused on the conversation about the child still inside her. "Was she judgemental?"

"No, to be honest she wasn't. Not at all. She agreed pretty quickly, I was surprised by how quickly. Almost like she had been waiting for me to ask, although she seemed a bit clueless about how it all worked."

"Must be nice, being clueless." Her bitterness at the situation permeated her words, darting around, searching for a host, and latching onto Alice as the most obvious target. "I bet she's so proud of herself, saving her *poor, good-for-nothing cleaner*. Again. Probably bored of her own perfect life."

"That's a bit harsh, Sam. She seemed to genuinely want to help."

"That's just it. I don't want her to have to help. I don't want to owe her. I don't like owing anyone." The words were spilling from her before she recognised them as thoughts. She wedged a fingernail in a small crack in the wooden table and traced along it, backwards and forwards. A small splinter snagged under her nail and she gave a sharp intake of breath.

"You were going to owe that bloke." He pointed out. "*Gregg* or whatever he's calling himself."

"That was different." She struggled to find the words to explain how it was different, other than being obviously worse. "That felt like… like a business *owing.* Like I was an adult making a decision to do something and knowing I'd need to pay for it. It wasn't a favour."

"Well, to be honest, a favour is what we need right now."

"I know." She softened. "I know." He had taken the hit - both the humiliation of asking Alice, and the subsequent heat of Sam's wrath - so that she could maintain a semblance of dignity. She reached across the table and took one of his hands, squeezing it. "Thank you, Mark. Thank you for asking her so that I didn't have to." She examined her other hand, where a small frame of blood was forming around the fingernail that she had caught on the uneven wood.

Without speaking, he took her finger and put it into his mouth.

"We're having a baby Mark." She whispered. Warmth billowed in her stomach, and she wondered if the baby felt it. The thought comforted her. It might not feel conventionally heroic in the way that risking her safety with the loan sharks might have done, but accepting this arrangement, despite her pride, was still a maternal sacrifice.

"A little brother or sister for Lucas." He said, her finger still in his mouth so that the words were slightly garbled. She laughed, and for the first time, she let herself believe, and all of a sudden she was crying again.

"Hello, stranger!"

Sam hosted Maya and Scoot for dinner the following evening, reinvigorated by the changes in their fortunes. She felt charged with hope. Here were these people, whom she had known for little more than six months, gathered in the tiny living room on the ground floor with its one window and its walls stencilled with mould. She'd missed them over the past few weeks, but only realised that now. Until Alice's gift, she'd had no capacity to miss anyone other than the baby that she'd missed pre-emptively, already grieving it in her mind even as it grew in her belly. But now, she felt energised, ready to re-join the world. It was with some sense of incredulity that she waved them into her living room, blinds firmly closed to hide the group from prying eyes in the street. New friends – best friends, she thought, waving at Maya as she came in with a precious crate of beer, - a partner who supported her, and all the while, growing inside her, now with prospects of a future: their child.

"Is this a piss up or a baby shower?" Mark asked, pointing at the beers.

"I can take them home with me if you prefer." Maya winked and dropped the crate onto the other sofa before throwing her arms outwards in triumph. "And I brought *you two*-", she pointed in a circular motion around Sam's face and stomach, "- these. From me and Scoot." She pulled a small pair of knitted white baby booties from her back pocket.

Sam stood up to greet them.

"Thanks guys." She hooked an arm around each of their necks, pulling them to her, before taking one of the tiny booties and examining it.

"As if any feet could ever be small enough to fit into these little things!" Maya dangled the other in front of her face, amused, before handing it over. The two women stepped past her to thump Mark on the back.

"Hey Mark, what do pregnant women and burnt cake have in common?"

"Hi Maya." He feigned a long-suffering sigh. "I don't know, what do pregnant women and burnt cake have in common?"

"You should have taken it out earlier!"

"Hey Maya?" Mark clicked and pointed at her, "What should pregnancy and a joke have in common?"

"Uh…?"

"Good delivery. Which yours was missing. Here," he offered her a pint glass. "Grab yourself one of these."

Scoot gave her girlfriend a commiseratory pat on the back, and fell back onto the sagging sofa with a satisfied sigh. "Pass me one too Mae. God I'm getting old."

"So are you gonna fill them in?" It was dark outside, and the crate of beer was almost empty; two indicators that at least an hour had passed. Scoot was sitting contentedly, eyes half-closed as she spoke, legs across Maya's lap.

"What do you mean?" Sam was tucked into the corner of the sofa on the other side of Scoot, her safe spot, protected on three sides.

"Shouldn't really, s'not procedure. But as it was your idea I guess we can give you the basics." Maya sounded tentative, as though she were worried how Sam might respond. Sam wasn't sure where she was going with all this, but waited for her to continue, the regular knit of the white yarn soft between her fingers as she toyed with the booties in her lap.

"Well, basically," she took a long breath, then began to speak quickly, "I just wanted to start by saying sorry."

"Sorry?" Sam felt unsettled at the unexplained apology, unsure what subsequent offence might be unveiled.

"Yeah. We didn't want you to think we had completely ignored your idea. I know it was well over a month ago that you told us, and –"

"My…" Sam had forgotten all about it, an insignificant episode archived in the back of a dusty filing cabinet. Her preoccupation with the pregnancy, and the loan sharks, and the drama with the points, had driven all thoughts of Alice's ridiculous scheme from her head. She dug out the memory now and examined it, and she almost laughed at the absurdity of it all. Like an adult looking back on their childhood fantasies, their games of make-believe, and shaking their head in fond bemusement. "Oh! Don't worry Maya." She gave an amused exhalation of air through her nose. "I haven't been losing sleep over it. I've had other things on my mind." *And it was a ridiculous idea anyway*, she wanted to add.

"No, I know, exactly. So I didn't want to bother you with it all. But let's just say… we didn't exactly forget about it."

"Honestly, I'm not bothered guys." She looked between the two women, keen to convince them that her feelings hadn't been hurt, that she couldn't care less about the silly idea, that she didn't need mollycoddling. "To be honest with you all, I'm actually relieved. It was a –"

"Will you just hear me out woman?" She was impatient and amused in equal measure. "Stop blabbering on and let me speak."

"Sorry, I was just saying that I really wasn't offended. If anything –"

Maya cut her off again. "Sam? We're doing it."

Maya, and Scoot's friend Bricks, she explained, had taken up the details of the planning - her knowledge of the PowerCut network, and his knowledge of British infrastructure far more extensive than Sam's. All of a sudden Sam felt as though she had tipped over a bucket of water in a moment of impulsivity and now wished she could scoop all of the water off the floor and back into the bucket, but it was running away, forming channels and gullies in the concrete, before draining away and being lost forever. Too late. Regret - panic - at the irreversibility of what she has set in motion. So instead, she pulled her knees in tighter to her chest, and said nothing. But Maya seemed to read her expression, and verbalised Sam's concerns better than she would have been able to herself.

"Don't worry, Sam: I get it. Stakes are raised now, and you don't want a part in this. To be honest, the less you know, the better. But I just wanted you to know that what you said to us was the *key*. There are all of these people, all over the country, who just fucking hate their lives and are ready to fuck some shit up!"

"Maya! Language in front of the baby!" Mark feigned sternness.

"Sorry Marky-boy." She gave Sam's stomach a sarcastic but tender pat and pulled out her phone. She opened some sort of presentation: a series of photographs, and below each one a small paragraph of text.

"We've managed to recruit someone at all of the key points needed for this to work. It starts here." She pointed to a photo of an old man with glasses and a grey moustache. "It just so happens, my old Chemistry teacher from school recently fell on hard times." She counted each blow on her fingers. "Got accused of being inappropriate with a student. Lost his job, and his wife gave him the boot. Tried to claim unemployment benefits but as we know they're basically not giving them out anymore. They just tell you to sign up to OffSet instead. So basically, sucks to be him right now. But his loss is our gain-"

"Ever the empath." Scoot patted her thigh affectionately.

"- because he just so happens to have a PhD in Chemical Engineering, and is going to help us out with the fuel part of it."

Maya continued, running through a list of various unfortunate people for whom life has become so difficult that they were willing to risk their jobs (and their freedom, or what was left of it) to stick it to the system. The knowledge that each person on the list - their current employment; without exception unpleasant, difficult, and essential to the basic functioning of society - was forced to subsidise their work with the sale of their carbon quota, settled like layers on top of Sam, each one light and barely noticeable, but with the result that by the end of the list she felt heavy and as though the light were slightly obscured. There was the man who worked the night shift to sign the paperwork for each tanker at the refinery, working on his feet twelve hours at a time, often in the rain, to verify that each tanker had been checked and processed. There were the two women who directed the tankers and other vehicles to the right lanes and refuelling stations, running between huge articulated vehicles and receiving thanks in the form of the incessant blaring of tanker-sized horns. Someone on the ground in quality assurance at London Heathrow and was in charge of collecting the fuel samples for testing when it arrived at the airport, inhaling potent fumes for ten hours a day and assuming a huge amount of responsibility for little pay, and someone else who did the same job at Manchester Airport.

"So you see? You were right about there being plenty of people out there who've been fucked over by the system, who are more than willing to stick it to the man."

For every safety net put in place by the aviation and oil industries, Maya had needed to find someone willing to go against their duty; to overlook, to falsify; even to intentionally sabotage. And Alice had been right: it was an easier task than it should have been. Still, the fledgling plan sounded far-fetched at best.

"So, back to the real reason we're here." Scoot cut in when Maya had finished flicking through the photographs. "Have you come up with a name?"

"We don't even know the baby's gender yet," said Mark.

"So?" Scoot demanded. "Gender is a social construct, and even if you're not on board with that, you've got to agree that *names* having genders definitely is. How can a sequence of letters have a gender?"

"Here we go, you've activated one of Scoot's favourite rants," said Maya.

"What about 'Scoot'", Sam asked, realising for the first time that this was unlikely to be the name on her birth certificate. "Is that a nickname? Where does it come from?"

Scoot shrugged. "Been called it as long as I can remember. My uncle says it's because my cousin always used to say *'"it's cute"* when he saw me as a baby. *S'cute, s'cute,* eventually became *Scoot,* and it stuck."

"I can't believe I never knew that!" Maya punched Scoot on the arm.

"Oh yeah! That's right. I'd forgotten all about that!" Scoot laughed, then paused, then laughed more deeply, as though remembering additional snippets of the deception, embellishing the private joke playing out in her head.

"Feel free to let us in on the joke when you fancy it, won't you."

"Oh Maya stop stropping." Scoot slapped her thigh as she emerged from the bout of mirth that had singularly enveloped her. "So basically," she wiped her eyes, then snorted again at the perturbed look on Maya's face, before continuing, "when we first met, I told Maya that I was called Scoot because I was the scooter champion in our local skate park when I was eight. I thought it sounded cooler than the real story." She turned to Maya and pinched her cheek like a small child, putting on a soppy voice. "I was trying to impress you."

She turned back to Sam, her eyes bright with the memory. "I know, I know, I'm a catch. I'm sure you're wondering why the hell *I* would ever have thought I needed to lie to impress someone. But that's what love does, innit?"

Chapter 24

Alice

Andrew, predictably, had not been impressed to emerge from his home office yesterday evening to discover that the car had been sold. She, on the other hand, had been on a complex high since Mark's visit. Satisfaction at finally feeling good about something she had done, at the knowledge that she was choosing the harder path. Guilt at the privileges it might take away from Tommy; relief at having made a decision. Emotions tumbled and reacted with one another inside her like chemicals. It was sometimes hard to differentiate excitement and anxiety, not enough conviction to temper the adrenaline, so that it boiled in her stomach. Hoping to remedy this, she had intentionally coincided with the coffee mothers this morning and instigated a post-drop-off cafe trip. She stood there now, listening to Rebecca telling them about a friend-of-a-friend whose hairdresser's daughter had just won the million carbon point jackpot on last Saturday's Euromillions carbon lottery. She was almost taken aback by the mundane familiarity of the cafe, the fact that nothing and no one here had changed, when she felt like a completely different person. Yet here it was, with its neat white tables and carefully-tended pot plants, and here was Rebecca, telling a banal anecdote, the listeners far enough removed from the subject of the story that it was almost folkloric, no one ever quite sure that it really happened.

"My turn to buy." Bel insisted in the queue for the till, as Alice had known that she would. And that was her 'in'. "Oh, thank God." She said, taking her cue. "I just remembered I wouldn't have had the points to get these. It's taking some getting used to."

"What's that sorry?" Bel had asked, out of politeness more than interest, as she scanned her app for the order. "Oh, just that I've given up my extra quota." She tried not to overdo the casualness in her voice: they would all be aware that it was a significant admission. And she didn't mention the baby. "I've decided to go *au naturale,* so to speak."

Bel looked at her properly; she had her attention now. She flapped a hand to get Rebecca's attention. "Did you hear that Rebs? Rebs!" She shook the woman's shoulder, drawing her attention from the display of gluten-free flapjacks behind the glass. "Alice has *given up* offsetting." Rebecca's features drew apart in surprise, as though making space for the news.

"Wow. If I could whistle I'd be giving you an impressed whistle right now woman. That is seriously worthy."

"Seriously!" Bel picked up the tray of coffees. "I salute you. There is just no way I could swing it."

Alice smiled with the pleasant unpleasantness of receiving a compliment and not knowing how to react. The balance of acidity in her stomach tipped to positive again and she felt happy in her decision once more. She realised, in this moment, that arrogance and insecurity often manifest themselves in the same way. At first, she had felt ashamed of her need to tell someone about what she was doing, because it felt like bragging. But with further introspection she realised it was quite the opposite; she was so uncertain in her new direction that she needed external validation, and she knew that this was the place to get it.

"I sold Andrew's car." She added, prodding the compliment piñata a little more; and sure enough, praise rained.

"Wow Alice. You mean business. I am seriously impressed." Bel carefully lifted a coffee from the tray and set it in front of her. "Here, you've earned it."

Alice took the coffee, satisfied, and redirected the conversation. She felt temporarily lighter. "So, when do you climb to base camp again, remind me?"

When she got home Andrew was waiting for her.

"We need to talk, Alice."

"If this is about the car, then I am sorry, and I know I should have discussed it with you. But it's -"

"It's not about the car."

That was when she noticed Sam peering around the archway that connected the living room to the kitchen, looking sheepish. *Shit.*

She didn't really know what to say. The car was one thing. She had felt secure enough in the moral high ground that she almost wanted him to challenge her about that, to dare to try and win that argument. But this was different. She had effectively given up all of their additional points without telling him, and then there was the added sensitivity of it funding someone else's pregnancy, at a time when having a second child themselves was an elephant in the room. The complexity of the betrayal was greying his face; his features seemed to have shrunk inwards, protecting themselves from her. "Sam, would you mind starting upstairs today please?"

Sam nodded, mouth slightly open as if a little shell-shocked by her blunder, looking between the two of them as she began to walk towards the door to the hallway, giving Andrew a wider berth than strictly necessary. As she towards Alice she mouthed at her, without turning her head so that Andrew would not be able to detect that she was speaking; "I'm so sorry. I thought he knew. I'm sorry." She was wincing as though she had tasted something very bitter, or as though she had just broken something very expensive. Alice gave a small shake of her head. *It's fine.*

When she had left the room, and they could hear her footsteps receding up the stairs - something conciliatory, even in the sound of them - she stepped towards Andrew and ran her hands down the outsides of his forearms, catching his fingertips at the bottom and giving his arms a gentle tug. "Hey."

He looked up, but not at her, rather out of the window at the bright white sky. She wondered if she had pushed him too far, or whether she had pushed just far enough. Enough to do damage that *needed* to be repaired, could not be ignored, so that they could unpick the dull knitwork of their relationship and use the unencumbered yarn to do something completely different. But still together. Unless she had gone too far.

"Andrew? Look at me."

A muscle in his jaw tensed, adding resolution to his averted gaze.

"Andrew. I really believe in this stuff."

"You should have told me." He inhaled deeply, and on the exhale he turned to look at her properly for the first time. "You *could* have told me. Why didn't you feel like you could tell me? Did you think I wouldn't want to help? Is that it?"

And it occurred to her then that she had never stopped to ask herself that question.

"No of course I knew you would, Andrew. That's why I didn't even need to ask you." It was an easy lie, because even though she hadn't specifically thought it at the time, she would have known it to be true if she'd stopped to think. "Of course you'd want to help her. Anyone would, we're talking about a baby for god's sake. Even the people who made the rule, it's just a point-raising scheme. They just want it to be paid so they get their stupid points. They don't care *how* it gets paid."

She wasn't sure what response she was expecting, but it was not the snort of derision that she received. "Alice, don't be so naive."

"What do you mean? You think they actually want to reduce the number of babies?"

"Not the *number* of babies, no."

"You're going to have to spell this out for me Andrew, stop being so bloody cryptic."

"Oh, like you spelled it out for me? I'd have taken *cryptic* over outright lies any day Al. At least I'd have stood a chance of understanding."

"I'm sorry Andrew. I'm so sorry. Listen, can we go for a walk? And talk about all of this."

"What, you don't want the cleaner to hear? You *bought her a baby*, but her hearing us argue is crossing the line?"

He's hurting, she told herself, hair follicles on her arms responding to the venom in his voice. *He's just hurting. You can fix this.*

220

They walked along the tree-lined road, stone pillars and great wrought-iron gates flanking the street. Two children chased one another with water pistols on a neatly-manicured front lawn. She watched Andrew watching them as they walked, and in that moment, she knew.

"You wanted another baby didn't you. For us."

His whole body flinched, so that it rippled through his stride as he walked.

"You knew that Alice." He said abruptly. "That was always the plan."

The realisation winded her. She had been so certain that her perception was the only truth, that she had not stopped to consider a different narrative.

"I know it was what we always talked about." She began the sentence without knowing how she would finish it.

"We can talk about it. Having another child, I mean. I get that my not telling you about this stuff with Sam hurt more because of that, but they are separate things. One isn't related to the other. And the reason I haven't brought up having another baby is just… well I thought things had changed. With us, I mean."

"They feel pretty fucking related, when you're going behind my back to help someone else have a baby, and we can't even talk about having another one ourselves. And *why* do you think things have changed? With us? Look at the kind of things you're keeping from me." He kicked a stone that Mr Mckenny at The Old Elm had placed along the edge of his front lawn to stop drivers damaging the verge. "Ouch. Fuck."

"Careful. Come here." She linked an arm through his and tried to guide him towards the middle of the road. His arm hung limply, not crooking in response. She wanted

221

to say that that wasn't fair, that things had gone wrong before that, before she'd ever kept anything from him. But something her mother had once said came back to her. *In an argument, you have to decide what 'winning' means to you. Is it defeating him? Or is it finding common ground together? That's the real victory.* She could defend herself, try to prove herself right, to beat him, but where would that get them? So instead she said "You're right. I shouldn't have kept things from you. And we should talk about this. When we're both feeling a bit calmer?"

His arm softened slightly at the elbow, an almost imperceptible concession.

"Thank you."

"I love you Andrew."

He squeezed her arm between his body and his own in response. She tilted her head so it rested on his shoulder, and they walked on like that for a while. Up past the coffee shop on the green, down the long sloping hill of the high street and into the park, neither of them needing to communicate the route that they had walked many times before. In the park they climbed the hill, steeply, breath matching their strides. They could see over the whole city, sweeping views of the Shard, the London Eye slowly turning to the left of it, and further East the abandoned buildings of Canary Wharf. She knew that if she didn't open up completely, now, then it would be worse, because an omission once you are specifically talking about something is no longer just an omission, but a lie.

"It's not just this stuff with Sam though," she began, and his arm stiffened again. And without taking her eyes off the view, tracing the bends of the Thames as it made its way through the hodge-podge of shiny sky-scrapers and greying council blocks that made up the city of London, she told him. She told him about the doubts she had been having and the guilt she had been feeling. About how she had been questioning the extravagances of lifestyle - *yes Andrew, extravagances, you can't deny that's what they were* - and about the unfairness of the system and that she felt it was their duty to speak up. And finally, she said, to test the waters more than anything, to see how he would react and how far she could push him, "I've actually been doing a few things for PowerCut. Nothing major!", she said quickly, looking at his expression. "Just bits and bobs. Some printing, posters for their campaigns. That kind of thing."

It was as though all of their previous tensions had been tectonic plates jostling gently together; frictional, causing vibrations, rippling the peace, but difficult to detect if you were not in the immediate vicinity. But now, the join between them, the place where they had always rubbed along together, getting by, had cracked right open. The fault line - when it finally appeared - was dramatic, and the subsequent earthquake extreme.

"What the FUCK Al?" A few flecks of spittle landed on her cheek as he rounded on her, lava flying. Pressure which had been building in his core for months - years, even - was bubbling to the surface. "What the fuck were you thinking? It's one thing helping someone out, someone you know. But the rest of it?" He couldn't quite bring himself to be specific, to name her crime and taste it in his mouth. "They're just not good people Alice!" Frustration and disbelief rasped at his vocal chords. "All their conspiracy theories, stirring things up, causing all this unrest." He paused, trying to recall more of their atrocities, "*Cutting off our power*!"

She let his anger wash over her, waiting for the initial eruption to pass.

"How could you do that to me? To *us*? To *Tommy*? How do you think he'd feel with his mother in prison for some kind of… some kind of *treason*?"

She focused on her breathing, in and out, in and out, trying to hold his eye contact without conveying defiance. She wondered how she would feel if the roles were reversed: if he had endangered their comfortable existence without her consent. Her silence drew out his rage, filling the space between them.

"I just don't understand it Al. I don't get it at all. Your life is perfect. We have everything. Literally everything you could ever want. Why would you…" The wave of molten rock was slowing, his features hardening, fury tempered by hurt.

"That's just it, Andrew." She said quietly. "That's just it. *We* have everything. "

Chapter 25

Pathetic fallacy… When she'd first heard the term, the night she'd finally kicked Caleb out of the house almost two years ago, and she and Lucas were staying with her mum while he packed his things during the worst storm she'd ever witnessed, she'd thought it sounded like another way of describing erectile dysfunction. But since being aware of the concept, she had often considered the appropriateness of the weather to the mood of a situation in which she found herself, in the way that learning the vocabulary to describe something intangible tends to make us notice its occurrence more readily: as is the case with '*schadenfreude*', '*déjà vu*', '*weaponised incompetence*', '*tautology*', '*victim-blaming*', '*meta*', and '*esprit de l'escalier*'.

And whilst the storm had transpired to be a false example of pathetic fallacy - because her separation from Caleb had turned out to be one of the most positive progressions of her adult life - when she woke up this bright, sunny Friday morning she knew that the elements had indeed conspired to reflect her mood and good-fortunes.

It was Lucas's 6th birthday, and her mother had bought them tickets to the Zoo. Whilst not many businesses had diversified geographically in response to the limitations Counters faced in terms of transportation - they were, after all, incontrovertibly the target audience with the smallest wallets - The London Zoo was an exception, and had recently opened a small branch south of the river, less than one mile from their house.

The baby had kicked for the first time yesterday, which had also marked twenty-five weeks of pregnancy. That was when they had finally made the decision to tell Lucas that he would be having a baby brother or sister. Enough time had passed that they were confident in the security of their family unit and the legal viability of the pregnancy, and had agreed that it was time to allow him to acclimatise to the idea. Skirting the biological explanations, they'd focused instead on Lucas's concerns around the practicalities as he felt the pattering kick of tiny feet through the wall of her uterus. *Will I have to share my yellow Lego?* He'd asked as soon as he'd got his head around the notion that he would soon have a sibling. *And why is it kicking you? Will the baby kick* me *when it comes out?*

When he'd asked if he would have to share his bed with the new baby, this had provided the perfect segue to her trump card.

"You won't have to share a bed." She had told him, excited to reveal the news. "In fact, Lucas, you'll have your very own room!"

They would be moving into Mark's apartment, which had two bedrooms. It was quicker than she would have chosen for them to live together, in an ideal world; but then so was conceiving a baby together after less than a year, and anyway it made sense financially. When she'd tucked Lucas in last night, in the small bed less than two metres from her own, she'd felt nostalgia, the sense of an era ending. But this new chapter was right for all of them, and Lucas's reaction to the prospect of a baby brother or sister had been more calm and positive than she could have hoped, once she had promised that the yellow Lego would remain firmly his.

Her initial unease at discovering that Maya had taken her suggestion for a plan seriously had faded, and she was back to attending the meetings as a bystander, happy to bob along as a supporting actress to the group without getting her hands dirty. She could enjoy some ongoing nugget of pride at her theoretical contribution - the notion that support for the group and its ventures could be leveraged by identifying the swathes of people most disadvantaged by the system - without risking complicity in anything concrete. The plan - if indeed it was still being discussed, or ever came to fruition, which she doubted - was no longer anything to do with her, and she was ecstatic about it.

To top it all off, yesterday, she'd had an interview for a new job as a teaching assistant in the secondary comprehensive just across the road from Lucas's primary school. It would be five days a week during term-time, with no need for childcare (as long as Lucas behaved himself and didn't get excluded again; and they seemed to be finally making some progress with his therapy). The steady income and regular hours would offer them some security for the first time since he'd been born, and once she'd passed her probationary period she could even give notice to OffSet. She could pay back the points to Alice, and then they could get their lives back. She'd woken up this morning and the sunlight streaming through her window, and the relief of Lucas's reaction to the baby news and the idea of moving house meant that the library of worry in her brain felt less hostile, as though the librarian had invested in a comfortable armchair and some soft mood-lighting. She had a *good feeling* about the interview, and she didn't have *good feelings* often. They'd said they would let her know before the weekend, and she'd woken up and checked her phone first thing. Nothing yet, but she was going to get the job, she just *knew it*.

She surveyed herself in the mirror now, a loose fitting dark green maternity dress emphasising her bump. Immy, the mother of Hannah, the little girl who lived a few doors down, had dropped a small bag of maternity clothes on her doorstep the previous week after spotting her rapidly swelling midriff. She had done so without knocking, preserving Sam's dignity in the face of charity, and Sam had thanked her with a note through the letterbox, the two of them since passing in the street without acknowledging the entire exchange.
Sam's cheeks had filled out, nourished by the rare diet of positive outcomes, as well as Mark's home cooking. She brushed her hair through, and tossed the hairbrush into one of the open boxes by her bed, into which the majority of their meagre possessions were now packed. A slant of sunlight fell across the room and, in its glare, she could almost be convinced that the grey hairs that had begun to appear in and amongst the brown were blonde. She checked her phone for a response from the interview: nothing yet.

"So, how did it go yesterday?" Her mother asked as they strolled past an open enclosure of peacocks, Mark lifting Lucas above the wooden handrail for a better view.

"Yeah, it was good. The hours seem great, and I'd get school holidays off, obviously, which would be great with Lu. I'm just relieved to have more regular work."

"*If* you get the job, you mean."

"Yeah, *thanks* mum."

She pulled out her phone and subtly checked for an update, heart pounding as she refreshed the portal. Still nothing.

"I'm just saying. It's important not to get ahead of yourself. And what did that woman say when you quit the cleaning job? Madam can't-mop-the-floor-for-herself."

Sam laughed and watched Mark and Lucas strutting across the path pretending to be peacocks.

"Alice. She was really good about it actually. I had my last shift last Friday. She's not so bad Mum, honestly."

She'd decided it was time. She needed something more regular, with more hours. But it was more than that: since receiving the loan she'd felt weird working there, like it was an ongoing act of charity. She needed a clean break; they all did. She'd realised when she'd left that she would miss Alice. It had been an awkward farewell; just a week after she'd inadvertently put her foot in it with Alice's husband about the loan for her pregnancy, which she'd suspected had finally caused them to have a proper, real-life argument, with shouting and everything. They'd even left the house in order to properly get into it with one another; Sam had wanted to ask her about it the following week, to apologise again for her indiscretion. But her resignation had marked a withdrawal from their friendship, an exit from the tentative no man's land in which they'd been experimentally co-existing, and a firm return to their respective trenches. As they'd said their goodbyes, Alice had promised to drop around some of Tommy's old things for the baby, and she in turn had promised to visit Alice once the baby was born; both women alluding to staying in touch without explicitly acknowledging that they *wanted* to do so, for anything other than practicality or common courtesy. She'd felt ashamed of the realisation that she considered Alice a friend, that her absence would leave a hole. She imagined the look on Maya's face if she'd told her that she had actually grown quite fond of her quixotic but well-intentioned employer, and this had been enough to prevent her reaching out. She pulled her phone out of her pocket and checked for an update for what must have been the twelfth time that morning.

"Sounds like it'll be tough though, the job." Her mum probed, drawing her out of her introspection.

"What do you mean?"

"You know, all them kids, and you trying to support the worst of them, the ones that don't give a damn about any of it."

"You do realise Lucas is the kind of kid that a teaching assistant would work with, right mum?"

"Well, yeah, I suppose." Her mum looked uncomfortable and waved to get Mark's attention to follow signs to the giraffe enclosure. "But that's different."

"Why is it different, mum? Don't you think there are people out there who'd look at Lucas and say *'oh, I bet he doesn't give a damn'*? When all the kid wants is to fit in for once in his life?" She could feel her dress sticking to her back as her agitation compounded the heat of the sun.

"Jesus Sam, keep your hair on. I was just making conversation."

"Let's just go and look at the giraffes and change the subject shall we?"

Part of her irritation was the knowledge that she herself would have made similar comments before being a mother to Lucas. It is much easier to have empathy for our own struggles than for something hypothetical, and she couldn't blame her mother for not having experienced the same learning curve as she had with Lucas's additional needs. She wondered, then, whether she would have joined PowerCut if she were well-off, if her situation had never forced her to sign up to OffSet, to resent the system and want - no, *need* - change. It followed that she should consider Alice's superficial contributions to PowerCut perhaps *more* admirable than her own involvement, for the fact that it was driven by selflessness, not personal necessity. The moral integrity of two people can only reasonably be compared in identical circumstances; when they have enjoyed (or missed out on) the same privileges, been exposed to the same media narrative, been surrounded by the same peers: all of the elements that constitute a lived experience. Can a husband of a century ago be judged for expecting his wife to be submissive? Perhaps; but not in the same way that you might condemn someone with a similar attitude today. And how many white people living in the 21st century, who now rightfully decry slavery, can confidently state that they would not have been happy to benefit from it, were they born in 1800? How many Europeans would in fact not have turned a blind eye to the Nazi regime, how many would really have risked their lives to save Jews from the Holocaust? Are the

231

people that denounce these historical atrocities inherently *better people*, or are they simply a product of their social context?

But Sam decided to focus on the giraffes, rather than these questions to which she wasn't sure she wanted the answers. Lucas was sitting on Mark's shoulders and trying to feed one of the giraffes a handful of grass, but the animals were responding with snooty apathy, heads roving like the booms of cameras on a film set. Lucas was not perturbed, waving his grassy fistful above his head with unrelenting vigour.

"Thanks for bringing us all here mum." She said, reaching for her hand.

"Smile, Lucas!" Sam ruffled his hair. "You'll look all grumpy in the picture." They were posing for a photograph by the exit to the zoo, having visited every enclosure in the zoo, and the penguins three times.

"That's just my normal face though! I've had the same face all day."

"Yes but in photos people always smile."

"Even though they weren't smiling before?"

"Yes."

"And then just stop again afterwards?"

"Yes."

"So they're just pretending? Who are they pretending to?"

"It's not pretending, it's just what you do for photos."

"Kid's got a point." Mark said. "It is kind of weird that if you don't put on a massive grin in a photo people think you were having a terrible time, but no one expects you to be smiling twenty-four seven normally."

232

"Oh don't start Mark! Lucas, stop asking questions and say *cheese*." Her mum cut in, impatient.

"Oh, God, now you'll have thrown him mum." Sam said, laughing, as Lucas started to formulate a response.

She dragged a thumb down the screen to refresh the portal again as they filed out through the ornate gates of the zoo and onto the street, Mark and her mum trying to explain the concept of *saying cheese* to a child for whom abstract social concepts were about as accessible as hieroglyphics. Usually, Sam hated photographs too; the expectation that the people in it should be grinning unnaturally, the instant slackening of the muscles in your face once the moment has been captured, creating (or highlighting) the feeling that the happiness was artificial and the drudgery real. But today, after the flash, the smiles remained. One new message has arrived on the portal.

"I got it!" She jumped up and down - not just figuratively, but took two or three leaps off the floor, waving her arms above her head. Then heaved Lucas off the floor and spun him around, before slumping against Mark, breathless with exertion and excitement. *I got it.*

Chapter 26

Alice

Wind buffeted them as they walked along the winding path dotted with cautious dog walkers, fresh-faced families, and relaxed couples strolling arm-in-arm, admiring the view. When you walk near a steep edge, the distance away from it that you need in order to feel safe is directly proportional to the height of the drop. You are no more likely to lose your balance and fall off a five hundred metre cliff than you are a two-foot wall, but greater consequence demands greater precaution, and Alice felt irrational waves of vertigo pummelling her even twelve metres from the cliff edge, the gravity of hundreds of metres of rock face tugging them towards the cresting waves below.

"Tommy! Hold my hand. Walk on this side of me."

"Why are you scared mum?" He began to run in zigzags towards and away from the edge, taunting her with the fearlessness of a child. Andrew was laughing at him, and at her, but with affection.

She was glad they'd come on this trip. In the wake of the eruption between them, the cloud had been quick to clear and the air was lighter. Neither of them had wanted a repeat; a somewhat selfish motive to behave selflessly, but one that mitigated the issues nonetheless. Andrew had complained a little about needing to take the train to Dover in the absence of a car, but she had accepted it without retaliation. And now, here they were. Staying in a small B&B next to a fish and chip shop, the quintessential British aromas of malt vinegar and old frying oil tinting their towels and pillowcases. It had been a long time since they'd been away, just the three of them. Alice had felt daunted at the prospect of such extended periods of unbroken time in each other's company, but she knew they needed it. As the ash of the argument had settled, Alice had reflected on their marriage, and the very real possibility that they might lose it. And in the moment that the death of their relationship felt imminent, images of it flashed through her mind. The day they had met - in the pub, of course; the setting for much of the first two years of their relationship. Not the pub right behind their college, which was a soulless, modern building that had been converted into a Wetherspoons in their first year. No, this pub was all wooden beams and sticky bar tops, a chalkboard as you came in that advertised the roast of the day and their 'special' - which was the same every day, steak and kidney pie. It had been called *Ye Olde…* something or other. The kind of place American tourists will flock to as though it were some sort of cultural icon which, she reflected, it probably was. She'd come there with Sophie because it was snowing outside and the pub had a real fireplace, and they'd convinced themselves that this would be a more conducive location to work than the chilly sterility of the college library. Andrew and a small group of friends had had the same erroneous thought process, and the two groups were soon embroiled in a heated game of *Risk*. "And I let her have Australia, and the rest is history." He liked to conclude the story of how they met to anyone who asked. And she would respond, with equal predictability and the required degree of mock-outrage:

let me? LET ME? But he'd been right about one thing; the rest really had been history. More scenes from this history presented themselves to her in a disjointed series; graduation, Andrew challenging her to see who could throw their hat higher for the photo, his getting stuck on the stone wing of the statue of an angel in the courtyard they were in. Laughing. Their first holiday abroad, in Portugal, worrying about the smell of garlic on her breath, and their honeymoon safari in India, seeing the tigers and suffering raging food poisoning. But laughing, always laughing. There had been no laughter recently, and she wasn't sure when it had stopped. But this trip was not only, finally, an admission of a problem, but a statement of intent to climb out of the rut in which they'd found themselves. A chance for redemption.

"Tommy, stop messing around. Come away from the edge, come on. Hold my hand." Andrew caught one of Tom's soft little hands and she grabbed the other and they swung him up into the air between them, the piece that connected them. He giggled and squealed, and Maisie barked, protective and excitable.

Back at the bed and breakfast they showered and made a cup of tea. Tommy started clamouring for ketchup and chips and fish (always in that order of priority). Andrew went to the shop downstairs and came back with three paper-wrapper packages, damp with steam and rustly with salt. They sat on the bed crossed legged and ate the food - fish for Tom and Alice, scampi for Andrew - and played a game of cards. Alice couldn't remember the last time they'd sat like this; no screens, no fancy restaurant; not even a table. Just comfort food and each other's company. A warm stodgy mass of potato sat in her stomach, and it felt like it grounded her.

After they'd put Tom to bed in the interconnecting room, they sat on the small Juliette balcony with a bottle of white wine and two hotel mugs.
"Cheers." Andrew clinked his mug against his. She drank.
"I guess we're going to need to start cutting back on even stuff like this," she said, indicating the bag of wrappers from the chippy which was hanging on the outside handle of the balcony door to keep the smell out of the room. She hadn't wanted to bring it up - knew that anything to do with OffSet was dangerous territory - but at the same time she felt she owed it to him to acknowledge the sacrifices they would be making.
"This wine is disgusting." He observed, without acknowledging what she'd said.
"I think it's the cup." She held up the mug to examine it, a brown circle of coffee-stain now visible above the level of the wine.
"Yeah, that can't help."
"Can you believe the crap we used to drink at uni?" She asked, smiling. She thought of the time he had made her a glass of vodka mixed with milk. *We don't have any other mixer in*, he'd said apologetically. He sipped his drink in silence. She wondered which memories he was re-visiting, hoped he wasn't thinking about work.
"I am sorry, you know…" she said, just as he said;
"remember that drink you made me that one time before the Christmas party in second year?", smacking his lips.
"Vodka with milk?"
And she said:
"That was you! You made that for me! "

And he said:
"I forgive you."
And she said:
"For the drink that I never made you?"
And he said:
"No, for the other stuff."
And she said:
"Oh."
And he said:
"I'm sorry too."
And they drank the wine from the coffee-stained mugs and basked in the cloy of oil drifting up towards them from the chippy, and the happy clatter of people on the street below them.

Chapter 27

Sam

TV-Pete was calling out to passers-by on the street through his open window as she and Lucas passed his house carrying two paper bags filled with a small selection of second-hand baby grows and soft cotton hats and socks on Thursday morning. He sounded like some strange, modern-day Pied Piper, rounding up the neighbours with promises of illicit screen time.
"Sam! Get in here." He called to her, eager to expand his audience. She imagined his excitement if he found out that she was behind it, even in such a small way. The thought thrilled her. "Someone's messed with a load of planes! You've got to come and see this."
They'd gone and done it. It shocked her more than she'd expected it would, as if a video game had suddenly come to life.

She felt that if she joined the others crowded around the screen in that little front room, they would just *know* she was involved. In the same way that the guilty child in a school assembly hall is certain that the headteacher's eyes are boring into their head and watching a playback of them throwing the rubber, or stealing the pastry from the canteen, or carving a penis into the surface of a desk, so too was she certain that her involvement would radiate from her skull and be detected by all around. It was not that she was ashamed of their actions; quite the contrary, and she knew that no one on this street would disagree with what they had done; would, in fact, be in awe of boring old Sam, the nobody from number 10, having played a part in something so big and exciting. But she couldn't risk them knowing. Aeroplanes were expensive, and the people who would even now be having their travel plans disrupted and flights cancelled were the kind of people who would want people's heads to roll for this. She couldn't risk her name being linked to this stuff. Millions of pounds of criminal damage; billions, maybe. She wasn't sur how much a plane cost. Probably a lot. And then multiplied by how many would be wrecked before they realised what was going on. She pictured pilots all over the country turning the key, or pressing the big red button, or whatever it was they did to start the plane, and nothing happening. She couldn't believe it had worked. Her heart pulsed against the inside of her ribcage, and she shook her head at her neighbour. "Sorry Peter, I've got to get on." She held up the shopping bags in evidence, then shuffled them into the crook of one elbow so she could get her key out of her pocket.

"Sam this is big news, you've got to see it. Four planes have come down already."

She stopped, key pressed between thumb and forefinger, her nails and fingertips white with pressure.

"What do you mean, *come down*?"

"Engine failure." He was triumphant at having got her attention. "Some others managed to land safely but apparently these ones were too far from an airport, or out over the sea."

They're saying it's some kind of terror attack. There are two more in the air with the engines failed that are probably coming down too. They reckon there could be around two and a half thousand dead."

240

It felt as though gravity had increased ten-fold, drowning her, pulling at her organs, and the skin on her face and the bags in her hands. Her fingers slackened, and the bags fell to the floor. A small white hat tumbled out onto the dirty paving stone.

"Oh careful, you dropped something." A swell of noise from the people in the room with him caught his attention and he turned back to the screen for a moment, before turning back to look at her. "Looks like another one has just crashed. Are you…" He looked at her again. Are you alright Sam? Your shopping's still on the floor. It'll get ruined."

Fighting her urge to scream, to run, she folded her arms across her stomach and pinched at the skin, hard, so that the physical pain would focus her enough to give her some control of her limbs. She had to know, needed to see it for herself. She left the shopping where it was and grabbed Lucas's hand, ignoring his confused protests over the shopping, and stumbled through TV-Pete's open door. Here, she leant against one of the walls in his tiny front room where she could clearly see the disaster unfolding on the small screen in front of them, and pulled Lucas against her side so that his head rested on her hip. The point of contact felt like an oxygen mask to her. Aerial images showed a burning wreckage in what looked like a densely wooded area, wings still supported by treetops. The picture cut to a wreckage at sea, suitcases and lifejackets bobbing. *British Airways flight BA2362 to New York crash landed in the ocean at 11.15am today after its engines failed more than two hours into its Trans-Atlantic journey. 332 passengers are still believed to be trapped inside* the scrolling text read. The image cut to a reporter speaking.

"Rescue efforts are currently hampered due to the nature of the sabotage remaining unknown. Helicopters are unable to take off until the issues affecting the commercial aircraft have been established and any further risks can be ruled out. Coast Guard boats are making their way to the aircraft which have crashed at sea, but this is slow progress with stormy conditions affecting the size and speed of the vessel which can make this rescue attempt safely. Meanwhile, an EasyJet flight to Lisbon from Manchester Airport is currently attempting to find a safe place to land in the North-West coast of France after its engines failed more than twelve minutes ago. The aircraft's current gliding altitude is now at less than 40% of the recommended cruising altitude and the plane is losing height rapidly. Hopes are that it will…"

It wasn't meant to be like this. The sound of the reporter became muffled, as though she herself were underwater. She felt as though a black cloud was billowing in her chest, leaking into her vision and reaching into her legs, robbing them of their strength.

"Ouch mum. You're hurting me."

She realised that she was leaning on Lucas's head like a crutch, and he wriggled from under her so that she stumbled, reaching for the back of the sofa for support. People were looking at her in concern, attention temporarily diverted from the chaos on the television. She needed them to stop looking at her, because in that moment she had become what she had done, and to others we can be nothing more than the sum of our words and actions. Suddenly, Mark was there, his arm under hers, holding her up.

"She's pregnant." He was explaining to those around them, brushing off their questions. "She gets dizzy sometimes with it. I'll look after her. Come on Lucas, take your mum's other hand, help me with her." Grateful for their direction, she closed her eyes, blocking out the images on the television, the curious faces of her neighbours.

As they emerged onto the street she vomited onto the pavement.

"Mark." She was sobbing, hysterical. She knew Lucas would be terrified by the state she was in, but she couldn't stop it. "Mark. Take Lucas." She took two great breaths, and it was as though the air were passing through a rusty vent, juddering. "Take Lucas upstairs please. Put a film on for him, with headphones. I'll sort the points, just do it."

Lucas looked like he wanted to object but knew better. He ran ahead of Mark, up the stairs and into their room. She pictured him diving into her bed and pulling the covers over his head. She wanted to join him.

When Mark came down, she was sitting at the kitchen table. He poured her a glass of water from the tap, and set it down in front of her. She considered swiping it off the table, the pieces shattering against the wall, maybe releasing some of the dense acidic ball of fear in her chest.

"I killed them Mark." Her voice was a strained whisper, self-loathing crushing them in her throat.

"All those people. They're dead because of me."

243

"Sam, don't say that. You can't say that. It was just an idea - not even your idea, it was Alice's idea. So many people were involved, this was not your fault."

"This wasn't my idea. This wasn't her idea. Not like this. This wasn't the plan." Images of twisted metal and flames burned her retinas. *Had the last two planes managed to land?* "How could this happen?" She said at last. "How did it go wrong?"

He didn't speak. She waited, waited for him to explain the problem with the science, the miscalculation from Maya's old chemistry teacher. Or maybe even for him to say that this was nothing to do with them - a freak accident. But she knew that couldn't be true. She waited. She was comforted by his presence, the knowledge that he was still here for her, even after her irreversible mistake. He was always there when she needed him most, always there for her. He had arrived so quickly, in time to catch her before she fell, almost as if he had known what would happen. *Please, don't let him have been involved in this.*

"Why are you…" she cleared her throat, bile and claggy saliva stretching across her throat. "What are you doing here, Mark?"

"I'm here to look after you. What do you mean why am I - I knew you'd be upset, by the news, by what happened. I came to support you."

"But how did you get here so quickly?"

She jerked her hand free from his.

"What do you mean, I -"

"You knew, didn't you."

It wasn't a question then. In that moment, it was obvious. He must have known, before the first plane came down.

"You used me!"

244

"No Sam!

"You did! You used me. You took my plan, all the clever parts of it. But you changed the cleverest part at all - the part that meant we could deliver the message with no one getting hurt. Remember that part?"

"Sam will you listen!" He begged her. "I only knew this morning. I swear to you." Then, more quietly. "Maya only told me this morning. And by then it was too late, everything was already done." His voice was pleading - whether desperate to convince her, or himself, she couldn't tell.

"It wasn't too late to stop this happening though." She spat. "Before any planes took off. We could have done something."

"You know that's not true Sam. There was no way of stopping them. What the hell could I have done?" He reached for her hand but she moved it backwards off the table, out of his reach.

"Why."

"Why what?"

"Why would she do this?" New realisations of betrayal floated around her like debris. "That was never the plan. *Non-violent.* I thought she had worked out how to do that, I thought she was on board with all of that. What happened? Why would she do this to them? To *me*?"

"Billy." He said quietly. Sam took a moment to place the name.

"Maya's brother? The one who's missing? What about him?"

"His body turned up, behind a recycling bin in the alleyway behind the O2 Academy in Brixton."

"What?" She had already disregarded the mention of Maya's youngest brother as insignificant, irrelevant in the scale of what had happened that morning, but the revelation crashed into her like an invisible wave. But she could not feel pity for her friend, or disgust at the news. Only anger.

"What, so she decided to just fuck with the plan, to kill people? The people on those planes weren't the ones who killed her brother."

"They were to Maya. You know how she thinks. They're all the same to her. All part of the same system."

"Don't justify what she's done! I can't believe I'm hearing this, Mark."

"I'm not! I'm not trying to justify it. I'm just explaining how she thinks. Why she did it."

"Tell me what happened."

"She told me this morning that she got an anonymous message, a few weeks back. Someone had seen the stuff she'd posted with pictures of her brother. She told me that's when she decided to go for it, with the plan. And it turns out that tampering with the planes to mess them up after take-off was even easier than what you'd suggested. You just needed to get water in there, apparently, with the fuel. And then when it gets up high the water freezes and blocks it, and, well…" he trailed off, his sentence finished already by the horrific footage that she'd seen on the news. She imagined Maya receiving the news. She did not picture her friend displaying any emotion at the news but instead the Maya in her mind seemed to glow red, eyes unblinking, possessed, as she planned her revenge. As she sought out the old teacher and questioned him, and upon learning how easy it would be, the caricature of vengeance in her imagination gave a small smile. Sam couldn't forgive her for it, couldn't accept that she had been made an unwitting accessory to mass murder - to terrorism.

"I'm going to be sick again." She said, half-rising from the table, elbows locked to support her weight.

"Please Sam. Try and relax. This isn't good for the baby."

"For the baby?" Her voice was laced with hysteria. "It's a bit late to think about the baby isn't it. His parents are terrorists."

Mark flinched and she was glad. She wanted to hurt him, wanted him to feel as though his head, his world, had been cleaved apart.

"There is no way they can link it back to us, Sam. No way."

"You think that's all I care about? Getting caught?" Although the two ideas were difficult to separate. It was hard to establish what was genuine guilt and what was fear of retribution.

"Well if you mean we're terrorists because we caused this, we didn't. We didn't know she would do this. We couldn't have known."

"I should never have got involved in any of this. What was I thinking? What the *fuck* was I thinking?" She slammed a hand on the already-cracked wood between them.

"Sometimes we set something in motion and then it becomes bigger than us. This was out of your control. And it wasn't even your idea anyway, you just passed it on. It was Alice's idea and -"

"Oh god. Oh god, oh god, oh god." She repeated. "Alice."

Chapter 28

Alice

It was just before noon on Thursday when she got the call. She was in the garden with Tommy, fulfilling her permanent assignment as goalkeeper. She'd never been sure of her stance on *letting kids win,* but the moral dilemma was somewhat redundant when it came to defending the goal, because losing was not a choice. She'd pulled a muscle in her groin whilst lunging to try and save a shot, and Tommy was running victory laps around her while she rubbed at her inner thigh. The phone began to ring inside the house; she heard it from the garden. She hobbled inside, and as she reached the open patio doors the ringing stopped. Tommy called her back to play. *No one is calling you anymore. You don't need to go inside.* The phone started ringing again. She swore under her breath, but really she was glad for an excuse to bail on the football. She had grass stains on the knees of her jeans and the back of her neck was damp with sweat. Her freshly-washed hair would be matting at her nape, as it always did. This time she answered the phone on the second ring.

It was Jack. It was odd for him to call. He never called - that was Sophie's domain. He just showed up when he was told, providing symmetry with Andrew; husband of the best friend. *He's probably calling about his laptop charger*, she thought, picking a piece of grass out of the corner of her eye and running the back of her hand across her upper lip to wipe away the sweat, excessive given her poor performance. He'd forgotten to take it when they last came for dinner.

"Jack? Is that you? We've got your charger, you left it plugged in behind the sofa. You can pick it up whenever, or Andrew can drop it off on Monday morning on his way to a meeting if that's easier. It depends if you need it before then."

She expected him to give a non-committal response, something he and Andrew were both guilty of, and she and Sophie often complained about; indifferent to the extent that they could never make a decision. *Just pick an option. It's really not hard.* Instead, she heard heavy, broken breathing. Something was wrong.

"News. The news. Have you… have you seen?" His words were barely coherent.

"Jack? What's wrong?"

No response.

"Jack! Talk to me. You're scaring me. Put Sophie on the phone."

She ran through to the living room, bare feet leaving misted outlines on the marble tiles of the kitchen.

"Jack, what the fuck. Tell me what's wrong."

She couldn't find the remote for the TV. Tommy was always taking it out of the room; to use as a cricket bat to hit an imaginary ball, to see if Maisie could balance it on her head, or, she was sure, just to inconvenience her, leaving it by the front door, or on the stairs, or on her bedside table for no reason at all other than that this is where he was when he realised he was still holding it. She pinned the phone between her ear and shoulder to free up her hands, frantic, and began to rummage down the back of the sofa cushions whilst trying to draw some sense out of Jack.

"Hang on Jack. Home: turn on TV."

Colour and light expanded in a perfect rectangle in front of her with a mundane normality that belied the unexplained distress pouring through the telephone and permeating the room.

"What am I looking for Jack?" She asked, but before he'd had time to reply, she had picked up the gist of the breaking news before her. Footage of multiple plane crashes - fire and water and death - filled her comfortable living room. She had never seen a disaster of this size happen in the UK, was taken aback by the scale of it all, but she refused to understand its relevance to Jack's call. Sophie would explain it to her. Maybe their apartment had been damaged again. The three of them would have to move in with her and Andrew again. They would lie on their backs again on the spare bed and talk about how terrible it all was, how lucky they were, how frightening this had been, and then they would stop and talk about what they were having for dinner. Maybe she would do sushi this time. *Yes, she would definitely do sushi. Sophie's favourite.*

"Jack, let me speak to Soph."

He didn't answer her, she wasn't even sure he'd heard. 'Jack…" Her words started to vibrate unsteadily as adrenaline fed through them. "Where's Sophie?"

"She's…" He stopped again.

Dread billowed in her heart then and was pumped around her body with each contraction. She imagined it like black ink, darkest in her ventricles but seeping through the red in her veins, spreading further and darker with each heartbeat, heavy and cold.

250

"Jack!" She raised her voice in agitation, half-shouting, "put Sophie on the phone. For fucksake! Let me speak to her right now!" The sound of him sobbing pummelled her and now she matched it, and she knew in that moment that her demands were childish, her denial futile, but she had to hear him say it.

"Jack!" She shouted into the phone, no space to consider his grief, so all-encompassing was her own.

"Not just Sophie." He said finally. "Both of them. Sienna. My babies. My babies…" A primaeval moaning from the other end of the phone, the sound of someone who has realised that everything they were ever afraid of has happened, that nothing can fix it. She heard screaming, too, abject terror. It was only when she had to pause to take a breath that she realised the screaming was coming from her. She threw the phone away from her as though it had scalded her, and leant over the sofa, pressing her face into the white cushions. She screamed again, despair and grief pouring hot into the fabric. She held her face there, not raising it to allow air into her lungs, the mounting carbon dioxide dulling her slightly. When she eventually lifted her head, strings of saliva stretched from her mouth to the material and then snapped, falling onto her chin, her eyes closed and mouth still open in silent horror as she pulled one of the pillows to her chest and sank to the floor.

She pulled herself together enough to put a kids' show on the television and call Tommy in from the garden, locking the patio doors behind him. She told him she wasn't feeling well and was going to lie down. He accepted this without questioning it, already absorbed in the adventures of invincible anthropomorphised cartoon rodents on the screen.

Upstairs, she pulled the curtains in their bedroom and lay down on the bed fully-clothed. It had taken all her strength to get herself to the sanctuary of her room and now she lost the last remnants of control. Shock waves crashed over her, and she let them batter her, welcoming the violence of the pain. Her consciousness drifted away as she lay there - almost as if she had fallen asleep, as if such a thing would ever be possible again. But the next thing she was aware of was the sound of talking from downstairs. Her eyelids felt thick and heavy, and her head was throbbing with the effort and aftershock of her grief. She sat up, her head heavy on her neck, aching her shoulders.

Downstairs, Andrew was on the telephone. He put a hand over the receiver when she came into the kitchen, and mouthed: *Jack's brother.* His features were pinched, and he looked older than she remembered. She nodded an acknowledgment, and sat on one of the leather stools by the counter. She leaned forwards and rested her cheek on the cool marble, letting Andrew's half of the conversation wash over her without processing the words.

Tommy came in and asked what was for dinner. Andrew held up a hand to her as she began to stand up, indicating that he would deal with it. Still on the phone, he moved to the fridge and took out eggs, sliced ham, and a block of cheddar. Alice kept her cheek on the counter, grateful for his composure, for the sound of the fork clipping against the edge of the bowl as he beat eggs for the omelette. Her mind began to drift to thoughts of Sophie. The time when they had got into their housemate's room in halls during freshers' week at University and wrapped every single one of his possessions in cling film. That time in their second year when they'd gone to try out for *Pointless* and Sophie had spent a whole month revising general knowledge, only to get on the tube in the wrong direction and end up at Cockfosters instead of Uxbridge, missing the whole audition. Sophie on holiday in Barcelona two years ago, falling asleep in the shower fully clothed after a night out, sitting on the plughole and blocking the drain so that the bathroom flooded and set off the fire alarm. Sophie, using blue tack to cheat in the egg and spoon race at Sienna's school and buying one of the other four year olds' silence with a KitKat when they'd spotted her. Falling off the treadmill when she'd tried to show Alice that she could run backwards. Trying to smuggle two bottles of wine into the Rugby Sevens in the sleeves of her coat, tripping over a step and smashing them both, sleeves dark purple, pungent, sopping; mostly being annoyed that she now had to pay bar prices for alcohol. Her funny, competitive, clumsy, generous, brutally honest Sophie. Her best friend.

"It's ready Tommo." Andrew's voice calling their son for dinner brought her back to the room. He was off the phone now. "I've grated some extra cheese on the side for you to add."

"Thanks daddy."

"So?" It was all she could manage.

Andrew raised his eyebrows as if to say *what are we telling Tom?*

She gave a small shake of her head: *Nothing. Not yet.*

"Milo didn't have any more information really." Milo was Jack's older brother. "He just said that the police came round to Jack and… to Jack's place, with a family support unit. But they already knew, because that flight… well, you know."

Alice nodded.

"Can I have ketchup?" Tommy asked.

"*Please*." She said automatically.

"*Please*?"

She peeled herself from the stool and went to the fridge to get it for him.

"So has anyone, err, claimed it yet?"

It was difficult to discuss what had happened with Tom in the room without him realising that something bad had happened. And he was getting to the age where he was constantly on the alert for adults withholding information or talking in code, determined not to let them pull the wool over his eyes. And sure enough, their cryptic tone had piqued his interest in a way that they never could when they were actually trying to communicate with him.

"What you talking about?" He demanded, small flecks of egg falling into his lap.

"Do you need a bib Tommo?" Andrew pointed at his t-shirt, and when he looked down, flicked his nose.

"Gotcha." Tom giggled and spooned another mouthful of omelette into his mouth.

"I'm going to go and have a shower." Alice said, unable to be part of such a light-hearted scene. "I'll see you upstairs Andrew?"

"Sure, or why don't I run you a bath?" This, his ultimate gesture of care. But the thought of stewing in the silence of a bath made her skin crawl.

"No, honestly, I'll just have a shower." He looked hurt. She wondered if he was thinking about Jack, never able to run a bath for Sophie again. "Thanks though." She walked back across the kitchen and gave him a kiss on the mouth.

"Eurghhhh. Gross!" Tommy shrieked, and threw a strand of cheese at them. Andrew picked it off his arm and ate it, then opened his mouth wide to indicate that Tom should try and throw the next piece directly into it. Alice went upstairs.

After her shower, she sat on the bed wrapped in her dressing gown, and turned on the TV. Thinking about what had happened made her feel physically sick, but at the same time she *had* to know what had happened

"*...it appears to have been an attack planned by PowerCut, the anti-OffSet rebel group, who managed to infiltrate the fuel delivery supply chain to four major airports and add a substance to the fuel which caused the engines to fail between forty and sixty minutes after take-off. Usually, commercial aircraft are able to glide without engine power for around twenty minutes, but due to the time elapsed from take-off some planes were unable to find a suitable landing strip in the time, resulting in….*"

And then it hit her. It was *The Idea.* Except it was *not* the idea, not the idea at all, not how the idea was meant to go. Like the notes of a familiar tune, that you're sure you've heard before, but butchered by some cover band, a once loved song now ruined.

She felt like a character in a video game who had been sauntering through a familiar world of colourful trees and small obstacles to climb over or duck under when, all of a sudden, she'd attempted a jump that she'd done a hundred times before but now the gap was inexplicably double the width and she was plummeting, plummeting down off the screen into nothingness.

She was still lying in her wet robe when Andrew came upstairs.

"I brought you a hot chocolate." He said as he came into the room. When she made no move to sit up and take it, he put it carefully on the bedside table and lay down next to her, like Sophie would have done. "How are you holding up?"

"I've made the duvet wet. Sorry."

"Don't be silly." He sat up and reached into her bedside table for the hairdryer. "Can I dry your hair?"

She'd asked him to do this so many times, but he'd always brushed her off, said he didn't know how, didn't have time. But now he was offering, and she didn't deserve it, wasn't worthy of such an act of love.

She thought of his face in the kitchen when she'd turned down the bath. She thought of two other hairdryers, the ones in the bedrooms of Sophie and Sienna, in her mind's eye already gathering dust. Would Jack throw them away? *No, he mustn't. He mustn't throw away any of it.*

So she let Andrew guide her head into his lap. She wasn't able to sit up yet, but he spread her wet hair over his thighs and began to gently run the hot air over it, teasing out the knots with his fingertips.

Chapter 29

Sam

The sound of hammering on the door explodes around its edges like dust. For one wild moment, Sam thinks it is Caleb, her neural pathways connecting overly aggressive thumping on the door with the sight of her enraged ex-boyfriend on the doorstep. But he doesn't even know where she lives now, and she smiles inwardly at the secure anonymity of living with Mark.

"I'll get it." She calls through to him in the kitchen. He is putting the finishing touches to his signature lasagne, layering aubergine and mushrooms and cashew cream between rigid sheets of pasta. *I promise, you won't even notice that it's not made with meat,* he'd assured her the first time he'd made it, closing the oven door and wafting away her scepticism. Even Lucas likes most of it, if you ignore the small graveyard of mushrooms that he deposits on the side of his plate. She can hear him in the kitchen with Mark now, and pictures him carefully placing the yellow rectangles of pasta in neat rows, years of Lego and a fascination for all things yellow being put to good use. She pushes herself to her feet, the arm of the sofa like a crutch against which she braces, unwieldy with the weight of her growing stomach, the taut flesh of it chafing gently against the slack cotton of her t-shirt. Another hammering on the door.

"Coming!" She calls, and it does not even occur to her to feel irritated at their impatience, so cushioned are her emotions by the tableau of domestic bliss which is unfolding out of sight in the kitchen, and right here in her imagination.

She moves slowly towards the door leading to the hallway, stepping over scattered books and Lucas's chalkboard, on which he has tried to write the ingredients for Mark's vegetarian lasagne recipe. 'L-a-z-a-n-y-a', he has written in sweet yellow letters, underlined. *Fair enough*, she thinks. And underneath it: '1. O-b-a-j-e-e-n'. She has to move a big bag which is blocking the door before she can open it. Inside it is a dismantled second-hand cot which Alice dropped around two weeks ago, the day before the planes. Caleb had taken Lucas's old one when he moved out, in a rush of spite. *I paid for it*, he'd said, yanking apart the joints and tossing it into a holdall along with a cheese grater, and a worn pair of red boots he'd bought her for Christmas two years earlier - the only items in the apartment that he could legitimately lay claim to -, *so I'm taking it*. She'd been glad of the space anyway.

She can see a soft-looking cream teddy in the bag, a sneaky extra from Alice. It occurs to her that Alice hasn't responded to her last message. She'd wondered briefly if Alice had connected what was happening in the news with the idea she'd given her, but she'd shrugged it off. It was a while ago that Alice had even suggested the idea, and anyway, it had been just that - an idea - and she had shut it down straight away. And the planes coming down *wasn't* the plan, so there was no reason for Alice to think that the two of them had played any part in it all.

She picks up the fluffy teddy and looks at it as she pulls down the latch and opens the door. Four Checker men stand in front of her, with a vehicle outside. They've left the engine running - she notes the irony.

Mark hears the commotion and comes to the door. The scene appears to play out in slow motion; Mark's anguish, Lucas's fear, and the soulless expressions of the Checker men. She is not sure what her own face looks like. It is tingling, and in her ears she can hear the sea. She still needs to take Lucas to the sea. She suddenly becomes aware that Mark is shouting. Volume rushes back in like air to a vacuum, and the noise around her is overwhelming.
"Stop. Mark. Stop. Please." She begs him. It is all she can do to stop herself falling to her knees.

She is handcuffed before they put her in the back of the car, engine still running. She does not notice that they do not read her rights - nor do they tell her what she is being arrested for. Of course, she already knows - she is implicated in what transpired to become an act of terror. Her chained hands rest on the swell of her stomach. She is six months pregnant. At her last scan, after verifying that she had sufficient carbon points for the pregnancy to go ahead, the doctor had told her that the foetus now has eyelids, and fingerprints. She wants to make a joke to Mark about the police taking the foetus's fingerprints as well as hers when they get to the station, but he hasn't been allowed to come with her in the car, and anyway she can't breathe properly. She leans her head against the window. There is a dead insect squashed against the outside of it. From this close up it appears in double, blurred by proximity, but if she focuses on it properly the two images slide on top of one another and become one clear insect, a small yellow secretion smudged between its two-dimensional splayed legs. Focusing this hard gives her a headache, so she allows the image to separate once more. *What will happen to her? Who will look after Lucas? Mark, she wants Mark to take him, because Mark will take this baby after it is born, and this baby will need its big brother nearby. Her mum won't like it, will probably give her a hard time. Not harder than she will already be having though. Maybe her mum won't want anything to do with her now. Will she even visit? Does she want her to? What about Lucas? Prison is no place for a child. or a baby. Lucas. The baby. Lucas.* She closes her eyes.

The car is slowing, the handbrake is on. She opens her eyes. They are not at a Checker station. Instead they have pulled into the side entrance of a medical clinic. They are taking her for a medical check-up before she can be locked away. The thought is comforting: she still has rights, even as a Counter, as a criminal. The peeling white walls of the car park seem to lean inwards when she is pulled out of the car, pressing on all sides. It is sunny, and she squints at the light in her eyes, but she doesn't want to close them, wants to savour this moment with the open sky above her, so she forces them to stay open, even as the glare dances on her retinas and her tear ducts protest.

Inside the clinic, they lead her into a small room. They weigh her, and ask her to lie down so that they can examine the baby. She is grateful for this, grateful that they care. A man comes in and explains that he is going to anaesthetise her. *What? What do you mean?*

Standard procedure, he explains. *For a termination at this late stage of the pregnancy. It's for your own good.*

Termination. The word perforates her diaphragm so that it cannot draw breath into her lungs, flaps uselessly inside her rib cage. Dark spots crowd her vision.
*What do you mean, termination? S*he wants to ask. *Take me to the station and arrest me, but this has nothing to do with my pregnancy.*
She reaches for her pocket, searching for her phone. Two of the Checkers grab her arms and pin them above her head.
"My phone! I'm just trying to find my phone. To show you. I have the points, I've got enough, let me show you!"
She writhes from her hips, trying to free her arms but the men are too strong. A third Checker steps forwards and uses her thumbprint to unlock her phone, pulling up the app. He shows it to the doctor, who nods his acknowledgement.
And then it hits her. Alice. She couldn't report her for her true crime - her involvement in the aircraft sabotage - without implicating herself. And so, instead, she has lashed out another way. An image comes to her of the other woman seeing the news; angry, betrayed at the violence and malice that have been injected into her precious idea, making it something it was not. Exactly how she, Sam, had felt after seeing her words devilised before her eyes.

The men holding her arms are passed restraints which they strap around her wrists, binding her to the trolley. She was still holding the teddy but it tumbles to the floor in the tussle, and its loss feels symbolic. She kicks her legs, thrashing, overturning a metal tray filled with silver instruments. Her ankles are also bound. She is prostrate on the firm blue padding of the hospital bed, cannot even clasp her own hands together.

As the needle approaches, she is alone; her, the anaesthetist, the doctor, and the four men in green. Mark has no way of getting to her. She pictures him now, where they left him in the doorway by the jumbled bag of cot pieces, not knowing that their baby is about to be cut from within her and tossed aside. She lets out a long, low moan which curls upwards at the end into a frenzied shriek, screaming, drumming her arms and legs against the leashes that allow no more than five centimetres of movement. She wants him here so badly it causes her physical pain. She imagines that her desperation is strong enough to pull him through time and space and conjure him by her side. He doesn't appear. *Of course he doesn't appear.*

When she wakes there is a dull ache in her abdomen. She is still tied down, unable to investigate what is going on *down there,* but a rustling when she adjusts her pelvis tells her she is wearing an adult nappy. A sharper pain radiates through the ache when she moves. She imagines the soft lining of her womb protesting against the violence that has been inflicted upon it, lamenting the abduction of its helpless cargo. She thinks of their yearly pumpkin carving at Halloween, of scraping the seeded flesh from the inside of the bulbous fruit with a tooth-edged spoon, tossing the stringy pith into the compost. Tears creep from the outside corners of her eyes and down into her ears, tickling, but she cannot wipe them away. Tears run down the back of her throat and make her cough, trapped on her back. She is glad of the physical pain, she deserves it, deserves to suffer. She has failed to protect her child. She wishes she hadn't woken up, that they had injected her with enough to let her sleep forever. The teddy is on the floor under the table, and there are small droplets of her blood congealing in the soft white fur of his ears.

She is discharged from the clinic later that day with a prescription for antibiotics and a carbon debt for the procedure. She is told she and Mark will appear in court in two weeks' time for theft of carbon points and the unlawful continuation of pregnancy beyond twenty weeks. She learns that Alice has gone to the authorities and reported that her cleaner's boyfriend coerced her into transferring a large number of points onto her cleaner's account. The motive is obvious, and the evidence two-fold. Checkers show them damning video footage of Mark at Alice's house, clearly handling her phone in the minutes leading up to the transfer, recorded on the state-of-the-art home system. And then there is the second piece of evidence, this one unspoken but equally damning: Sam and Mark are Counters, Alice is not. Maya brings flowers, but Sam asks Mark not to allow her in.

On Monday, she goes back to her job as a teaching assistant. She is still bleeding and suffering frequent cramping, but she can't afford not to be paid. Her abdomen remains swollen, and her colleagues assume that she is still pregnant. Someone has arranged a whip around for donations, and they present her with a mobile,

the type that hangs over a cot and dangles stars and the
moon for the baby to watch as they fall asleep, little legs
kicking in awe. It will take a few weeks for her uterus to
acknowledge the loss, for her abdomen to contract to its
pre-natal shape. She has time to decide what to tell
people. When she gets home that evening, Lucas has
drawn a picture on his chalkboard. A stick person, limbs
and torso all fleshless straight lines save for the huge
circle of a stomach. Inside it stands a miniature stick-
human with a smiley face and arms flung outwards like a
starfish. Mark tries to grab the chalkboard from him and
turn it away before she can see it, as though what has
happened might have momentarily slipped her mind and
he doesn't want her to be reminded, as if it ever could.
But she shakes her head with a small smile and reaches
for the chalkboard, pulling Lucas onto her lap with her
other arm.

When she finds the chalkboard later that evening it has
been broken in half but she can still make out the angry
red cross that has been scored across the sketch of her
pregnant stomach. She collects up the two broken pieces
and puts them in a drawer in the kitchen. She doesn't
know this yet, can't imagine ever having the strength; but
in a month's time, or maybe two, when she is ready, they
will join the wall of images of people lost to the system,
and she will look at the fractured picture of her fractured
family, and she will never give up the fight.

Epilogue

22nd October 2042 - BBC News

Major changes are expected in the wake of the devastating 4th October terror attack that caused the death of over 200 people, widely accredited to a militant wing of the campaign group *PowerCut.* The government has announced a set of stringent new laws, with the Prime Minister keen to take a tough stance on national security and to demonstrate, both at home and abroad, that the UK is serious about meeting its climate commitments. The new measures have been backed by many as necessary steps to counter what is seen as a growing and dangerous subversive faction in British society.

Temporary curfew declaration
1.1 Until further notice, all UK residents with Counter status will be required to remain at their registered address between the hours of 21.00 and 6.00 unless they have obtained prior permission to attend an alternate location for work or medical purposes.

1.2 UK residents with Counter status may not gather in private residences in groups of more than three.

These temporary laws are made in accordance with the Counter-Terrorism Act of 2040, and the Environmental Protection Act of 2039.

Amendment to reproduction laws

2.1 In order to carry a pregnancy to term, the pregnant person must be able to demonstrate that the required carbon fee has been accumulated from their own allowance or has been purchased through the official OffSet channel. Unexplained deposits will no longer be accepted.

Amendments to immigration law

3.1 From 1st November, a more open border policy will apply. Refugees from listed nations will be permitted to move to the United Kingdom, with the following conditions:

3.1.1 A one off carbon fee will apply in order to register an asylum claim.

3.1.2 All arrivals seeking to claim asylum will be fitted with an OffSet tracker.

3.1.3 Upon arrival, all immigrants will be added to the United Kingdom total population count, and as such their per-capita carbon quota will be absorbed by the UK government.

3.1.3 Until the asylum seeker's application is approved, they will receive a basic (reduced) carbon quota.

Acknowledgements

First and foremost, I need to thank my amazing, patient, endlessly positive husband Charlie. Without his willingness to read (and re-read) chunks of text, providing the constructive criticism I asked for - and then dealing with my inability to accept said criticism - I would have given up a long time ago.

Secondly, my mum. Our relationship has not always been the easiest, and my teenage years in particular were difficult for both of us. She works harder than anyone else I know, but she still found time to drop everything and read what I had written every time I asked. She believes in me an unwarranted amount and managed to strike the perfect balance between encouraging me and checking in on progress, and not overwhelming me (something of a new achievement for her).

And finally, to Bunny, my lovely little cat. She didn't help me whatsoever with writing my book, but I want her to be immortalised in these pages forever.

Printed in Great Britain
by Amazon

46098515R00158